SAINT

TARA LEE
DL GALLIE

TRIGGER WARNING

This book deals with assault and abuse. These scenes are not graphic but they do allude to what did occur.
If these scenarios are triggering, we suggest proceeding with caution.

The Lords rule supreme. They're cruel, reckless, and
crave the power their status brings.
Their world is corrupt—filled with lies and secrets.
They rule Crestwood Prep like their fathers before them,
but nothing lasts forever.
Secrets are about to spill free, lies uncovered.
The Lords aren't as invincible as they once thought.
Let The Games Begin.

This is our school, our kingdom.
My brothers and I rule, we are The Lords.
Secrets never stay hidden so I shout mine from the rooftop.
That was until her—Rowan Ashford.
We kept ours close, but now, everyone knows what we were hiding.
With everything revealed, we thought it was over.
Some secrets run deep, but we have each other, we'll be fine. Right?

ROWAN

PROLOGUE

GOING from the highest of highs to the lowest of lows is pretty much how my life runs. One minute I'm up. The next I'm down and the one after that, I'm down even farther.

Today, I was so freakin' excited because my bestest friend gave birth. A new baby has entered the world, and there is nothing more exciting than that, but I'm Rowan Ashford, and I went from the highest high to the lowest low because my biggest secret has been exposed.

Finally.

I knew this day would come, but I was also hoping, somehow, it would remain mine and Saint's forever. But as soon as I walked into that room, I knew. They all knew what my father had been doing to me. At first it was just verbal, but as soon as I grew tits and Mom died, well, you can guess what happened next. It's funny, I remember having a great childhood until it wasn't. My life went to shit not long after Mom died and now that I'm older, I'm beginning to wonder if she really did die of Creutzfeldt-Jakob or if she killed herself and made it look like it was from her illness because it was the only way to escape *him*.

Luckily for me, I found my escape in the form of Saint Vanderbelt. One of The Lords of Crestwood Prep, but not even his Lord status could save him from my monster. Together we suffered at his hands, but now, now it's all out, and I don't quite know how to proceed from here.

When it was our secret I felt safe, but now I'm more scared than ever before.

A shudder runs through my body at the thought of what's to come. An arm snakes around me and I immediately relax. "I've got you, my sweet Dove," Saint whispers into my ear, gently placing a kiss on my temple.

Just hearing his voice calms me.

He always calms me.

He's always rescuing me.

For years now, I've dreamed of the day we could both get away from here. From the monsters. From the secrets. From everything that is shit in this town and now that it's here, I'm just numb.

Rolling over to face him, I raise my hand and cup his cheek. "You're always rescuing me, Saint."

"And I always will," he replies. "You're it for me, Rowan Ashford. I'm not going anywhere."

My eyes well with tears. "How … how can you be with me when *he's* my father? When he …" Emotions take over, and I break down in his arms. Saint pulls me in closer and holds me tight.

"*HE* has no bearing on what we have. When I'm with you, *he* doesn't exist. It's just you and me, Dove."

"How can you just forget?" I blubber into his chest.

"Because when I'm with you, everything else ceases to exist. My world starts with you, and it ends with you. The rest is just filler."

"Saint." I nuzzle farther into his chest and hold on for dear life. I hold tightly on to the man who is my everything.

Lifting my head, I stare up at him. Reaching up, I trace my finger down his cheek and along his jawline. Running the pad of my thumb over his lips, he gently nips at it, causing a giggle to spill free and that's why I know I'll be okay.

With Saint, he makes it all better.

With Saint, *he* doesn't exist.

With Saint, I know I'll be okay.

Shuffling myself upward so I'm half lying on him, I lean down to cover his mouth with mine and kiss him. His tongue licks along my seam and slips into my mouth. Mine pushes into his and our tongues start an erotic dance together.

"Please," I whisper into our kiss.

"Please what?" he asks.

"Make love to me, Saint. Erase his touch. Make me forget."

"Anything for you, my sweet Dove. Anything."

He pushes me to my back and kisses down my neck. With nimble fingers, he removes my clothes piece by piece. He showers me with love and adoration and like always, he makes me forget that Matthew Ashford exists.

He makes me forget my father is a monster.

He makes me feel alive and safe ... he just makes me feel.

ROWAN

… Age fifteen

WALKING across the lot with Dad on my first day at Crestwood Prep is nerve-wracking. It's always scary being the new kid, but being the new kid of a teacher is scarier, especially at an elite prep school like this one. I've heard stories about this place and to say I'm apprehensive is the understatement of the century.

"Stop fiddling," Dad growls at me as we reach the stairs to the administration building.

Craning my neck, I look up at the Gothic-style structure before me. It looms high above with its medieval aesthetic and ivy-covered walls, characterized by arches, vaulted ceilings, and small stained-glass windows. Then I shudder when I see them—gargoyles.

There are freakin' gargoyles manning the building. Those little critters give me the heebie-jeebies. How anyone in history thought they were cute, and anyone would want them watching over their estate is crazy.

The hairs on the back of my neck prickle and the ones on my arms stand on end. Glancing over my shoulder, I look around and that's when I see them. Four boys are walking along the path Dad and I just took. They all have athletic shorts on and are covered in sweat. The dark-haired guy at the back has no shirt on and from my spot here at the bottom of the stairs, I can tell that he's the jock type and with time—and countless hours in the gym—he's going to grow muscles on muscles and it will only enhance his looks.

Even from where I'm standing, I can tell these four rule Crestwood Prep. There's an aura about them that screams, 'We are the kings. Bow down to us, ohh meek ones.'

I may only be fifteen, but I know how hierarchies in places like this work. These academies have a pecking order, and I bet those four are at the top and think their shit doesn't stink.

The guy at the back looks up, and when our gazes connect, something happens inside me. His intense stare burns through me, and I feel a pull toward him. You see shit like this happen in movies and television shows, I never expected it to happen to me.

Standing here, I watch him with the other three. It's like I'm in a vortex and have no control of my body. Powerless to stop myself from observing them, well him.

"Rowan," my dad snaps.

"Coming, Daddy," I reply, my feet rooted to the ground. My eyes still locked on the boy across the quad.

"Hurry up, otherwise we're going to be late. I cannot be late meeting Róisín on my first day. I need to make a good impression."

"Who's Róisín?"

"Your new Dean," Dad says as if I'm supposed to know this.

Dad has been cranky lately and seems to be taking whatever is wrong out on Mom and me. He yells constantly and tells Mom she's useless. I'm pretty sure the other night, I heard him hitting her after I went to bed, but the next morning at breakfast, it was a happy family as usual. Mom didn't seem to have any marks and she was her usual bubbly self.

My mom is my best friend. Being an only child, it's been the two of us most of the time, with Dad at work Monday to Friday and the occasional weekend spent at school. He loves being a teacher, and by all accounts, he's a great mathematics teacher. Being his daughter, they don't usually put me in his class and I'm thankful for that. Being the daughter of a teacher at the school you attend is hard enough as it is. I can only imagine how it would be if he was my math teacher too.

Hopefully, now we have moved here, things will return to normal. "Hurry up, my precious girl. We don't want to be late on our first day."

Nodding, I turn away from the mystery guys and quickly make my way up the stairs to where he's waiting for me. "Sorry, Daddy, I was just taking it all in. This place is huge." Stepping closer to him, I lean in and whisper, "But there are gargoyles."

Dad laughs, a full-on belly laugh. The sound echoes around us. "You and your fear of gargoyles. They're just cement statues. Nothing more. Nothing less."

"Yeah, that come to life after dark and fly around causing mischief and mayhem."

"When have you ever seen one come alive?"

"*Ghostbusters, Ghostbusters II,* and *The Wizard of OZ.*"

"They're movies, my precious girl, therefore they don't count."

"You mean to tell me the Stay Puft Marshmallow Man isn't going to materialize when I accidentally make a wish?"

"Ummm, no," he replies, offering me a smile.

"Well, there goes my lifetime supply of marshmallows for s'mores. What will we ever do now?"

"They have this thing called Walmart and you can get marshmallows there."

"You don't say. You'll have to take me to this Walmart place after school ... maybe we can try their marshmallows, and you could buy me a new outfit."

"You and your imagination are amazing, Precious Girl. Don't ever lose your innocence."

Too bad he didn't mean that because years later, my innocence is lost because of him.

SAINT

"WHO'S THAT?" Hendrix asks as we head back to the dorms after our morning run.

"Who's who?" I ask.

He head nods to the chick and stuffy dude walking along the path toward the administration building.

"That's the new mathematics teacher and his daughter," I tell them.

"How do you know that?"

"Was in admin last week when he was finalizing things with the Dean. Said some bullshit suck-up crap about being an honor to teach here, blah, blah, blah. Also said that his daughter was excited to attend such a prestigious school. To be honest, the asshole gives off creepy vibes."

"How so?"

"Can't put my finger on it, but my spidey senses tell me we will have to watch out for him."

Nodding his agreement, we make our way back to the dorms and then split up to go and get ready for the school day ahead. As luck would have it, I'm in the new dude's mathematics class.

"Morning all, I'm Mr. Ashford, and I'll be your new mathematics teacher. If we all work together we can make this class fun. So, let's get started on an owl's favorite type of math, owl-gebra."

Yep, I picked it, total douche.

He's trying to be our friend as well as our teacher and that never works well. Just ask Ms. Gaskill, our old math teacher. She was sooo friendly—and I use that term loosely—with one of the seniors that she ended up pregnant with his baby. Quite the scandal for such a prestigious school, but we've all seen *Gossip Girl*. That show is nothing compared to what actually goes on in the classrooms and behind closed doors here.

Lunchtime rolls around and it's burger day, my favorite day of the week. The chef here makes the best triple cheeseburger ever and each week, she makes one especially for me with extra bacon and cheese, because, well, I'm a Lord and I may have threatened her job—what can I say, I'm an asshole at times, but if you've had her burgers, you'd understand my threat.

"You'll die if you eat that all the time?" a soft voice says from behind me.

Turning around, I look at who dares to criticize my lunch choices and I'm pleasantly surprised when I see it's the new girl.

"We're all going to die at some point," I nonchalantly tell her. "May as well enjoy things while we can, and this triple cheeseburger with bacon and creamy mayo is totally worth an early death."

"Why triple and not quad?"

"Why creamy mayo and not ketchup?" I throw back at her.

"Touché," she replies, looking impressed.

"Saint," I tell her, offering her my hand.

"Rowan," she says, placing her hand in mine.

My hand dwarfs hers, but somehow, they fit together like two puzzle pieces. Staring at her, I lose myself in her vivid blue eyes. I have never seen blue eyes like this before.

"Join me for lunch," I say, shocking both of us with my request.

"Ohh, I, umm …"

"It's just lunch. It's not like I'm proposing marriage or anything. I am only fifteen."

"So, you aren't going to go all Romeo on me?"

"Huh?" I deadpan, confused as to what the Shakespeare character has to do with me and her.

"Never mind," she shakes her head, "but I would love to have lunch with you."

"Excellent," I say, sounding very much like Monty Burns in *The Simpsons*.

With two burgers—hers normal—and two servings of fries in hand, we walk over to the table where my brothers are joking around. We may be related and three of us shared a womb at the same time, but we are all different and unique in our own way. Thatcher is a manwhore, plain and simple. A picture of his smirking face would be in the dictionary next to the word. One day, he's going to meet 'the one' and she's going to bring him to his knees. Hendrix is, well, Hendrix. He'd give you the shirt off his back if you needed it and if you find yourself in a jam, he'll be there to help you through it. And lastly Reign, our baby bro is the quiet one. He sits on the sidelines and watches. He's super smart, like crazy smart. But we all have two things in common, big dicks and a protectiveness for those who we care and love.

"Rowan, these assholes are my brothers, Thatcher, Hendrix, and Reign."

"Hi," she timidly says with a wave and then takes the seat I pull out for her.

The three of them say their hellos and then return to the conversation they were having when we arrived.

"So, you're the new math teacher's daughter," I say, pulling out her seat for her. "That's gotta be rough?"

She shrugs at me. "Meh, it doesn't bother me to be honest. It's like we get to school and he becomes Mr. Ashford and I'm just another student."

"That's good. I'd hate it if my father taught here, but then Daddy Vanderbelt is a cunt." Her eyes widen at my use of the 'c' word. "Sorry, don't know what other word to use to describe him."

"There are many to choose from, Saint," she says and then proceeds to list a few for me. "Asshole, jerk, douchebag, miscreant, pissbutt, swine—"

"I'm sorry, excuse me but did you just say pissbutt?" She nods, and I can't help but laugh. A full-on belly laugh that garners the attention of all of those around us. "That's a good one, but seriously, all those words are too nice for Thornton Vanderbelt."

"Surely your dad isn't that bad?"

"Give yourself a few weeks here and you'll see that cunt is the best way to describe him."

"Ohh," she replies.

"Dig in," I tell her, nodding to her burger. Picking up mine, I take a bite and as soon as the meat and cheese and sauce flavors hit my tongue, I'm moaning in delight.

"Shall we leave you and your burger alone?" Rowan teases, nibbling on a fry.

"You'll moan like this too once you take your first bite. You will always remember your first Crestwood burger day, and I'm honored to be here with you."

"You're such a dork," she states, picking up her burger.

Placing mine down, I lean forward and watch her. She slowly moves the burger to her mouth, opens and wraps her lips around the soft bun, and bites into it. Sauce spurts out the end and lands on the table, but I'm focused on her face. She closes her eyes, and I can tell she's enjoying it. She's smiling while chewing and when she opens her eyes, our gaze connects, and like the first time I saw her with her dad, I feel a connection. It's weird, I don't know this chick from a bar of soap, but the overwhelming need to protect her envelops me.

"It's good, hey?" I say when she opens her eyes.

"Sooo good, it's—" But she's interrupted when her dad growls her name and marches over to us.

"Rowan Ashford, what are you doing?" he sneers, his

eyes locked on Rowan and I don't like the intensity in his gaze.

"Having lunch, Daddy. You need to have one of these burgers. It's better than the ones at Gizmo's."

"Let's go," he growls, ignoring his daughter and her praise of the burger.

"But—"

"No buts, move it." And before she can reply, he roughly grabs her by the wrist and all but drags her out of the cafeteria, shoving her in the back with his other hand when she doesn't walk fast enough.

All eyes are on the two of them, but no one intervenes when it's a teacher, or us, manhandling a student.

"What the fuck?" Thatcher hisses.

"What the fuck indeed," I repeat. Looking to my brothers, I lean in and whisper, "Told you we need to watch that fucker."

"You think he's beating on his daughter?" Reign asks, his tone low and menacing.

"Not sure, but I don't trust him one iota."

ROWAN

"YOU ARE NEVER to be seen with that boy again," Dad growls at me when the door to the cafeteria clicks closed behind us. "You hear me?"

"I was just having lunch, Daddy."

"Find new people to have lunch with," he snaps at me, spittle flying from his mouth. He squeezes my wrist tighter to get his point across, and I wince from the pain. The pressure makes me worried he will snap it in half. "Those Vanderbelts are nothing but trouble, and if you hang around with them, they'll drag you down too. I will not have my daughter consorting with hooligans like those boys."

I've seen Dad angry before, but this is a new level of angry, even for him, and I'm scared. He normally saves this behavior for home. Behind closed doors so for him to be like this in public, maybe I need to heed his warning about Saint and his brothers. So I nod. "Okay, fine, I won't have lunch with them again."

"Good. Thank you, I appreciate it. I worry about you, that's all. You're my precious girl." And Dr. Jekyll is back … or is it Mr. Hyde that's the nice guy? Either way, he's done a complete one-eighty. "You know, you can always come to my office and have lunch with me. Just the two of us."

"Thanks, but no thanks, Dad. It's already hard enough having a parent working here. I can't be hiding out and having lunch with you too."

"Fair enough," he says with a smile. All the anger from moments ago has disappeared. "Now you better get going. You don't want to be late for your next class."

Nodding, I smile at him, but I don't say anything because what I want is to go back into the cafeteria and finish my burger. Saint was right, it's the best burger I have ever had, but I don't want to enrage Dad again.

He kisses me on the cheek and heads off, leaving me alone. After he leaves, I glance at the cafeteria doors, the temptation to go back is strong, but something is niggling at me to follow Dad's request. I don't want to get off on the wrong foot on my first day, so I turn around and head in the direction of my locker.

Unlocking the lock, I stare into it, thinking about that burger … and Saint, when someone taps me on the shoulder. I jump six feet in the air in fright and let out a squeal.

"Shit, sorry," a soft feminine voice says, and when I turn my head, I come face-to-face with a dark-haired beauty. "I didn't mean to scare you."

"It's fine," I tell her, shaking off her concern. "I was just …" Thinking about the mousey brown-haired guy with the mesmerizing blue eyes that remind me of the Caribbean Sea. "It doesn't matter what I was thinking about. What can I do for you?"

"Nothing in particular," she says with a smile. "I'm Quinn." She outstretches her hand, and the first thing I notice is the bright orange nail polish.

"Rowan," I reply, sliding my hand into hers.

"Welcome to Crestwood where The Lords rule."

"The Lords?" I question her.

"You'll find out soon enough but just so you know, Hendrix Vanderbelt is mine … even if we want to kill one another most of the time."

"Considering I have no clue who or what a Lord is, I'll remember that Hendrix is yours."

"Good." Now that she's staked her claim, she links her arm through mine and closes my locker before I can get out my books for my next class. She drags me back toward the cafeteria and I start to panic, but when she pushes the door open and we step inside, Saint and his brothers are no longer there.

"It's burger day," she says.

"I know, I just had one."

"Well, while I stuff my face, you can tell me all about you. You grab a table, and I'll get a burger. You want any fries?"

"Duh," I reply, "a girl always wants fries."

"You and I are going to get along just fine."

Quinn walks over to the food line, and I sit down at a table and wait.

This is the weirdest first day ever. Meeting a boy who after one brief conversation I'm enthralled with, and a girl who I think is my new BFF—which shocks many because Quinn is the 'Queen Bee' around here. She doesn't 'chat' with the new girls. I feel equally honored and scared to be her friend.

Quinn rejoins me and we easily fall into conversation. There are no awkward pauses but there are plenty of laughs, and over burgers and fries we cement our friendship. She gives me the 4-1-1 on everything Crestwood Prep, The Lords—which I discover Saint is one of—and she gushes over his brother, Hendrix. Seems the Vanderbelt brothers, aka The Lords rule this place. No wonder Daddy warned me off Saint, but surely they aren't that bad. Hell, they are only fifteen. You'd think one of the seniors would rule but then again, this is an elite academy and places like this have their own weird and wonderful hierarchy.

The rest of the day passes by quickly and before I know it, I'm heading to Dad's office for him to drive us home. On the trip home, I tell him about Quinn, and he seems happy that I've made a new friend who doesn't have the last name of Vanderbelt.

When we get home, I say hello to Mom and then head up to my room and get started on my homework. Most of my teachers didn't go easy on us and there's a heap to get through, and it's only the first day. *Welcome to Crestwood Prep*, I think as I open my textbook and start reading.

The next time I look up, it's dark outside, and I can hear the hum of the television downstairs and the smell of Mom's chicken cacciatore wafts up the stairs. Going by the smell, I should have enough time to grab a shower before dinner.

Quickly, I repack my school bag for the next day and then head to the bathroom. I wash my hair, shave my legs, and slip into my pajamas then I head downstairs to help Mom with the last bits for dinner. I'm almost to the kitchen when I hear Mom whimper, and then I hear my dad say, "You are a worthless woman who can't even cook. I wouldn't feed this shit to a dog." Then I hear glass shatter and what sounds like a face slap.

Peeking around the corner, I peer into the kitchen and my eyes widen. There are broken plates and glass everywhere. Mom's cheeks are red from a combination of tears and Dad's palm.

He slapped her again.

"Please," Mom begs him, "Rowan is home."

"Are you telling me what to do in my own home?" Dad shouts at her. I have never seen him this angry before. I've seen the remnants of his anger many times, but I've never seen it firsthand. Mom tries to hide it from me, but I'm not stupid, my dad is an abuser.

"No, not at all. Sh-h-she … she doesn't need to see this."

"Might do the little bitch good to see what happens when you don't listen. You know what I found our whore of a daughter doing today?" He doesn't give Mom a chance to answer. He steps over to her, lowers his head, glares into her fear-filled eyes and grips her chin between his thumb and forefinger. He's squeezing hard because from where I'm standing, I see Mom wince and his fingers are turning white from the force. "She was talking to one of those Vanderbelt cunts and having lunch with him. She'll be pregnant before we know it."

"Rowan is a good girl. She won't do that."

"She's a cunt like her mother. Now clean this shit up before your precious Rowan sees how much of a cunt her mother is." He storms over to the back door, opens it, and slams it behind him. I swear the whole house shakes from the force.

Mom slides down to the floor, lowers her head to her knees, and begins to cry. Hearing the car reverse out of the driveway, I know we will have a few hours before he comes crawling home, no doubt drunk.

I wonder what set him off? I think as I walk over to Mom.

She lifts her head when she hears me and breaks down further.

Dropping to my knees, I pull her into my arms and hug her. There's not much else I can do right now. Once Mom has collected herself, together we clean up the kitchen.

When we are done, you can't tell Dad lost it in here earlier. It looks like our kitchen again, sans chicken cacciatore as that tray was broken during Dad's outburst.

Silently, Mom and I eat dinner together. We managed to put together a gourmet feast for two consisting of grilled cheese and tomato soup.

The next morning at breakfast, Dad is his usual chipper self. Mom's hobbling around putting on a brave face, and I play the doting daughter role. We're living a lie, and apart from my mom, I was all alone … until I wasn't.

SAINT

THE LAST BELL has just rung, and I'm making my way to the library to get some work done on my upcoming history assignment. Unlike my brothers, I don't leave these things till the last minute. Turning the corner, I see Mr. Ashford chatting with another student. The student looks uneasy, and the urge to mess with the asshole is strong.

As I approach them, I can't help but snicker under my voice about 'Mr. Asshole' as I walk past him in the hallway, and I chuckle to myself when his gaze flicks to mine.

The fucker is giving off creep vibes by the bucket load. I can't put my finger on it, but there's something about this guy that irks me. It's still early days so there's plenty of time for me to suss this asshole out, but my gut is telling me something is off. "Can I help you, Mr. Vanderbelt?" he bellows. His voice echoes around the hallway. He and I both know who's in charge here. He's trying to sound like it's him, but we all know, it's not. He's nothing in the hierarchy of things here at Crestwood Prep, and I'm going to make it my mission to remind him so each and every-fuck-ing-day.

"Nah," I say with more snark than I should, "I'm all good … sir."

"Then get to class," he orders as if it will have any effect on me.

"School's over," I inform him, rolling my eyes as I continue past. Spinning around, I head back toward him. Stopping in front of him toe to toe, I lord my height over him, thanking the heavens for my tallness right now. "I'm not afraid of you, old man," I goad him.

His eyes bug out of his head and his jaw ticks. His fists clench at his sides and he breathes deeply like a rabid pit bull ready to strike. I can tell he wants to hit me, and I'd love nothing more than to taunt him into it, but I decide to take the high road, for now. And by the high road, I mean, I laugh right in his face. Still chuckling, I walk backward staring at him until I reach the corner. Then I turn around and smack right into Rowan.

My chin collides with her head, "Ow." She laughs, rubbing her head.

"Shit, sorry," I say, rubbing my chin.

"Totally my fault," she quickly says, lifting her bag over her shoulder.

"I mean, I wouldn't complain if I ran into you again." My words cause her to smile, and in that moment, I make it my mission to make her smile each and every day. "I mean, it's no problem bumping into a gorgeous girl like you." Her cheeks tint to a soft pink color, and I have never seen anything more gorgeous in all my fifteen years.

"Do you—"

"Rowan," Mr. Ashford yells behind us. At the sound of his voice, we both turn our heads and watch him storm down the hall toward us. Reaching us, he grabs her arm, forcefully dragging her away from me.

"Hey," I growl and chase after them. Like he did to her, I grab him and shove him away from her. "You don't need to manhandle her like that."

Turning his angry scowl at me, he stares me down, and if looks could kill, I'd be six feet under right now. "Don't tell me what to do with my daughter, Vanderbelt. Now, back off."

Something comes over me, and before I can stop it, I shove him hard. His body crashes into the wall of lockers. I'm not sure how I managed to move him, but the anger radiating from me right now matches his.

"Dee-tention," he growls before adding, "Now."

My eyes move to Rowan. She has a soft smile on her face and nods ever so slightly in a silent thanks.

"Move it, Mr. Vanderbelt," Mr. Ashford sneers, pointing his finger toward detention.

Seems he's as big of a cunt as my father. Not wanting to enrage him further when Rowan is still here, I nod and begin to walk away—not to detention by the way, he can get fucked. Then I hear him scold Rowan, "I told you to keep away from that boy, no good will come of knowing him. Stay away, Rowan."

Looking back over my shoulder, my blood once again boils when I see him grip her arm, a little too tightly if you ask me. He forces her down the hall. She struggles to keep up with his long strides, and I wish in this moment that I had knocked him out.

She looks over her shoulder at me, and even though her dad is all but dragging her, she smiles at me.

Lifting my hand, I wave back, earning myself another one of her gorgeous smiles.

As they exit the building, I stand here and begin to wonder what Rowan's story is. Why do I feel like this girl needs saving? And why do I feel like I'm the one to do it?

Her father can push me away and threaten me as much as he wants, but if she needs me, I'll be there because even at fifteen, I know a damsel in distress when I see one.

ROWAN

EVER SINCE WE moved to Crestwood, Dad's temperament has worsened. He's always had a bit of a temper, verbally snapping at me here and there, but lately, it's bordering on verbal abuse. My mom always steps in, and as a result, he'd hit her and not me. As if that wasn't enough, my whole world came crashing down the day I discovered that not only was he beating her, but he was also taking her against her will. My dad was raping my mother, and there was nothing she or I could do about it.

It's funny, I always thought my mom was clumsy, turns

out her bruises and scrapes were from *him*. Her supposed loving husband.

He's never hit me or done *that*, and I'm positive it's because of my mom. She takes the hits—literally. She protects me from the man who before God vowed to love and cherish her till death do them part.

The few times he's grabbed me roughly, Mom always steps in. Saving me from his clutches.

She's my savior.

She's my saint. But who's her savior and saint?

Most nights now, I lie in bed and listen to him hitting her. *How did I not know this was happening*? I'm a bright girl, I should have known.

Some days I wish I could return the favor and hit him. I wish I was strong enough to step in and save her like she saves me, but I'm a chicken and just lie here, listening.

I'm woken to the sound of the front door slamming shut. Glancing at the clock, I see it's well after midnight and it can only mean one thing, Dad's done something to Mom. Like always, I wait five minutes and then exit my room and go find Mom. It's the only way I can help because at the end of the day, I'm just a kid.

Their room is empty so she must be downstairs. Quietly, I make my way down the stairs and walk into the kitchen. An audible gasp escapes me when I see my mom. My eyes widen and they fill with tears at the scene before me. I'm pretty sure I stop breathing as my eyes roam over her bruised and battered body, he was extra vicious tonight. Her nightgown has been shredded and there's blood everywhere. Bruises mar her delicate skin. Dad has never been this violent before. I wonder what set him off tonight?

Like always, we don't utter a word as I clean her up

and tonight is no different. Well, it's different but only due to the severity of her beating.

Helping Mom shower and change is an effort, but we get there, like we always do. When she's redressed, we head back down to the kitchen. I cleaned it up while she was in the shower.

Mom turns the kettle on and makes us each a cup of tea. With our mugs in hand, we sit at the table. An awkward silence falls over us until Mom reaches over and covers my hand with hers. "It's all going to be okay, Rowan. We're going to be okay."

"How can you say that, Mom? He's … he's a monster."

"He's my husband and your father."

"No, he's a monster who beats and rapes his wife."

Her eyes widen at my last point, but she shakes her head. "He's my husband," she murmurs, and a tear streaks down her cheek. "He's my husband," she repeats again, a little stronger this time. I hate seeing Mom like this. I wish I could do more, but I'm only a kid. She shivers so I jump up and grab the blanket that sits over the back of the sofa in the living room.

"We should leave, Mom," I say as I cover her with the blanket. She looks up at me with sad eyes. Silently, we stare at one another, and her once vibrant blue eyes fill with tears.

"Where would we go?" Her question shocks me, and all I can offer her is a shrug. Closing her eyes, she begins to sob. Looking back up at me, she offers me a sad smile. "I'm failing as a mother and a wife," she blubbers. "I keep letting everyone down."

"No, Mom, no. You aren't failing." Dropping to my knees, I take her hands in mine and squeeze. "You're the best mom and friend a girl could ever need. As long as I have you, we can go anywhere. We can—"

"Like fucking hell you're going anywhere," the deep angry voice of Dad echoes through the kitchen.

My eyes widen, as do Mom's.

The sound of his feet thumping on the floor booms as he storms over to us. Turning my head, I come face-to-face with a seething Dad. He's literally foaming at the mouth. Reaching out, he drags me up by my hair. I shriek from the force. The follicles rip and tear, leaving my scalp burning as he pulls me to my feet.

"You ungrateful little bitch," he sneers in my face. "We should have aborted you like I wanted." Those words hurt because up until this point, I thought I was wanted. "You're just as ungrateful as your whore of a mother."

"Leave her alone, Matthew," Mom voices from behind. Hearing Mom's voice, he throws me aside like the unwanted child I apparently am and arches over to her. "I told you never to lay a hand on her. Beat me. Fuck me. Do whatever to me, but you will leave Rowan alone." My eyes widen at Mom's words. For some reason, hearing it out loud makes it so much worse.

Dad breathes deeply, sounding like a bull ready to charge. "What did you say, woman?"

"I said," she pushes to her feet, "leave my fucking daughter alone." Mom turns her head toward me. "Rowan, go upstairs and get dressed. Go for a run and get out of here."

Furrowing my brows, I look out the window and see the sun is just peeking over the horizon. Huh, it's later? Earlier? Than I thought. Looking back at Mom, I just stare at her. Why is she pushing me away right now?

"Go for a run, Rowan," she forcefully commands.

"Mom," I plead, "I'm not leaving you here."

"I'll be fine, munchkin." Her tone leaves no room for argument, but I open my mouth to protest. "No buts, Rowan. Just go."

Mom looks so fierce right now, and all I can do is nod. Leaving the kitchen, I go up to my room and change into my running gear. Picking up my sneakers, I head back down to the kitchen. Mom and Dad are sitting at the table, chatting like nothing happened.

"Hey, baby," Mom says when I walk into the kitchen. She stands up and walks over to me. "I want you to go for a run. Clear your head so you can have an amazing day. Enjoy the sunrise."

"Go for your run, Rowan," she says again, a determination in her voice. "And when you get back, I'll have breakfast waiting for you."

I really don't want to leave her here alone with *him*, but I do as she asks, but before I go, I pull her in for a hug. I hold on tighter than I usually would. "I love you, Mom."

"Love you too, baby girl. Have a good run."

She pulls away from me and walks over to the stove, turning the element on, she starts cooking eggs and humming to herself.

"See you at school," Dad growls, not looking at me. He's focused on the newspaper in his hands.

Looking at him, I just nod and then walk out. Leaving my mom cooking my dad breakfast, as if he didn't beat the ever-loving shit out of her not five hours ago, I go for my run like my mom told me to.

I wish I was stronger.

I wish I could get us out of here.

I wish for my dad to die a horrible, painful death.

I wish for so many other things, too—world peace, to

travel the world, to be able to eat chocolate and never gain an ounce. But most of all, I wish I had a safe space to go to that's just for me.

Luckily wishes are free, but on this day, one of my wishes does come true.

SAINT

THERE'S nothing better than being out for a run just as the sun is rising. Well, actually there is. Having a pretty girl join you on said run is freakin' amazing.

This morning I was shocked when I rounded the corner and saw Rowan jogging toward me. Her hair is tied back off her face. She's wearing black figure-hugging athletic pants that show off her frame and a lemon-colored crop bra thingy that pushes her tits together. I let out a moan as I take her in, and it's obviously loud because she lifts her head and her gaze connects with mine.

When she sees me, her steps falter, and she stumbles

but manages to right herself before falling flat on her ass. Her perky, I want to take a bite of it ass.

Racing over to her, I pull out my earbuds. "You good?"

"Fine," she breathlessly pants. "What are you doing out early?"

"Running, you?"

"Same. I needed to clear my head."

"Same," I tell her. She drops her gaze to the ground, and I notice a sadness about her. "Wanna talk about it?"

She lifts her head and glances around, but it's just the two of us. Her mouth opens and closes but she doesn't utter a word. She looks hesitant and I don't like it, not one fucking bit.

"Come with me," I command, and before she can protest, I take her hand in mine and drag her along behind me. We walk into the dormitory wing, and I take a right. We walk down a corridor and come to a stop halfway down. Now it's my turn to look around and make sure we are alone.

"What are you doing?" she whispers.

"Do you trust me?"

She nods. "For some odd reason, I do. There's something about you that makes me feel safe."

Nodding, I smile at her and before I do something stupid like kiss her, I push on the wall and the secret door slides open.

"What the fuck?" she curses.

"There is so much you don't know about this place. Now, get in before someone comes along."

"Are you going to kill me?"

"There are so many things I want to do to you, but kill you is not one of them. Now, get in."

"So bossy," she teases.

"You ain't seen bossy yet, Ro."

She stares at me, and I lose myself in her gorgeous blue orbs. Voices down the hall interrupt the moment, and without a second thought, she steps into the wall and looks at me over her shoulder in a 'are you coming' kind of way. My brain kicks into gear and I follow her.

The door slides closed behind us, and I take her hand in mine again. Weaving my way through the walls, I lead her to what I call 'my spot.' It's not much, but when I need to get away and don't want to be disturbed, it suffices. Plus, my brothers don't know about this room, and it's just how I like it.

There's a mattress with a black sheet on the floor and a battery-operated lantern. This secret room is deep within the walls of Crestwood so I can have the light on in here and not be discovered.

"What is this place?" she asks, dropping onto the mattress.

"It's my secret hiding spot."

"Why do you need a secret hiding place?" She looks at me as if I'm crazy.

"Look, sometimes a guy just needs a time-out … and I think you might too."

"You have no idea," she says, tapping the mattress next to her.

Taking a spot beside her, I shuffle around and get comfy. The mattress is thin and uncomfortable, but what do you expect for a hidden room inside a school? From next to me, Rowan moves, and my mouth goes dry when she rests her head on my shoulder.

Dropping my gaze, I stare down at the girl that's made me feel so damn much in a short amount of time.

"You're staring," Rowan says, glancing up at me.

"You're beautiful, I can't help it," I tell her.

She lets out a soft sigh before wrapping her arms around one of mine, holding me in place like she's afraid I'll run off at any moment if she doesn't hold on tight.

"I like you, Saint. You make things fun," she murmurs into the silence that envelops us.

"I like you, Ro," I say, trying my best to sound cool and not like a total fool.

"I hate being home," she says out loud. Her tone is broken, and I hate hearing her like that. She closes her eyes and sighs like the secret she just shared wasn't supposed to leave her lips.

"Me too, sometimes," I tell her. My father can be a lot and being a Vanderbelt comes with a price, one I wish I never had to bear, but I get by. Unlike Rowan, I have my brothers. They help me survive and right here, right now, I vow that I'll help her survive too.

"You'll always have me," I tell her, knowing she needs to hear it.

She smiles and sighs again. "You really are perfect, aren't you?" she whispers.

"Nah, not perfect, but I know you need a friend and I'm willing to be that friend for you, always," I say, looking down at her.

"You really are a saint, Saint Vanderbelt."

"Let's just keep that between you and me, Rowan Ashford. I do have a reputation to uphold."

She stares up at me, and I feel her gaze deep in my bones. "Your secret is safe with me … and thank you, thank you for finding me this place."

"I'd do anything for you, Rowan Ashford. Anything."

"You really mean that, don't you?" she questions as she

continues to stare up at me, her eyes holding so much pain.

Words elude me, so I just nod.

"Thanks for being my friend, Saint Vanderbelt."

"Anytime, Rowan Ashford. Anytime."

ROWAN

… a few weeks later

SAINT HAS BEEN my saving grace these last few weeks. Dad's becoming unhinged. I know Mom is doing everything she can to keep me safe, but at what cost to her?

I wish we could leave. I wish we could escape him, but he'd find us.

Luckily, I have Saint.

When I'm with him, I feel safe and I'm glad to have

him in my life, especially when we get the devastating news that Mom is sick. She was diagnosed with Creutzfeldt-Jakob disease, commonly referred to as CJD. It's a rare brain disorder that leads to dementia, or in Mom's case, death. She was given twelve months to live due to the advancement of the disease since she didn't seek treatment when the symptoms first started. She didn't want anyone to know that Dad was beating her but by the time she did see a doctor, it was too late. She died exactly six weeks after her diagnosis.

Suddenly, I was all alone … with a monster.

My mom was no longer around to save me, and I'm more alone than ever. I didn't just lose my mom, I lost my best friend. It was she and I against the world, and Dad.

Dad didn't take her diagnosis very well, and he became unbearable to live with in the six weeks leading up to her death. I thought my world in her last stages of life was horrible. I didn't think it could get any worse but I was wrong.

So

Fucking

Wrong.

Thankfully, I had my secret space at school. I can never thank Saint enough for sharing his spot with me. The refuge that place gave me was the reset I needed to cope, but it turns out CJD wasn't the only monster ravaging our house. After Mom died, I learned just how much of a monster he is.

My dad, Matthew 'I fucking hate him' Ashford is a bully … and a predator.

With Mom gone, I'm his new prey. I never knew what my mom saved me from.

I never knew the extent of his abuse, and in the weeks since her death, I've come to realize that my mom was protecting me from *him* in ways I never could have imagined.

Vivian Ashford, even in her last days on this Earth, protected me. She was a saint. She protected me like a parent should … I just didn't realize to what extent she was protecting me.

"Rowan," he shouts as the front door slams open, making the hole in the wall from the doorknob bigger. "Where are you?"

Taking a deep breath, I center myself and call out, "In the kitchen." I never know what mood he's going to be in when he gets home these days, and from the sound of his stomping feet down the hallway, he's not in a good one today and I fear that I'm in for a rough night, again.

"Evening, Daddy." I greet him with a smile when he enters the kitchen. "How was your day?" His tie is askew, his shirt is half untucked, and to be honest, he looks like shit.

"Where's dinner?" he sneers, ignoring my question about his day.

"It'll be ready in a few minutes."

"Why isn't it ready now?" he growls, stalking over to me.

"I … ummm, the-the oven isn't working—"

"Sounds like excuses to me. I give you a roof over your head. A bed to sleep in. Food to cook for me and this is how you repay me? You make me wait? You are just as useless as your bitch of a mother."

Roughly, he grips my arm and spins me to face him, but in the few short weeks since I've become his punching bag, I've learned to not tense up. Relaxing the muscles makes it hurt less. It still hurts but not as bad. If only I could turn my brain off and not feel at all.

"Huh, bitch. Why isn't my dinner ready? Are you whoring around? That's it, isn't it? You've become a whore. Maybe I should test you out, huh? Do you want Daddy's cock? You want me to fuck you and show you what a real man is like? You'd like that, I just know it and now that your mother isn't here, maybe I will. She always stopped me from taking what I wanted from you, but she's not here anymore. Maybe it's time I take what's rightfully mine. After all, I brought you into this world, therefore I can do with you as I please."

My eyes widen at his words but not at the 'whore' remark. He … he wants to have sex with me. I'm his daughter, that's … that's wrong.

I'm so lost in my head that I don't see his hand coming. He slaps me across the face. Hard. My head snaps to the side from the force. The sound of his palm colliding with my cheek echoes around the kitchen. He backhands me again, this time on the other cheek and it causes me to stumble. He grabs me by the upper arm and pulls me into him. He licks up my neck and breathes in deeply. He moans and mumbles something about smelling like her, and that's when I feel it. His dick is getting hard just from smelling me.

In this moment, it all makes sense, and things are clicking into place when it comes to my father. After Mom died, he made me start using her body wash. Her hair products, even her perfume. He told me it was to keep Mom's memory alive, but right now, I'm starting to think otherwise because my father is a sick and twisted individual.

Just like the shock of the slap, what happens next

shocks me even more, but I know one thing, Rowan Ashford died that day. In that kitchen, the girl I once was, is torn from me and life would never be the same again.

ROWAN

AFTER HE DID *that* to me, we ate dinner like nothing had happened. Dad chatted happily about his day, and I was lost in my head. I was shocked and numb, and I wanted to die. When Dad went to bed, I climbed into the shower and broke down. I turned the water on to the hottest I could stand and scrubbed my body until my skin was red raw.

Turning the water off, I grab my towel and dry off. I change into a cotton nightie, but as soon as I slipped under the cover and closed my eyes, I was accosted with visions of what happened earlier. Sleep eluded me. I just lay here and stared at the ceiling.

Broken and alone.

Time slowly ticks by and with each tick of the hand on the clock, life goes on as if those events never even happened, but it's a night that will stay with me forever. It was the night I lost my innocence. My virginity to the one person who was supposed to protect me, love me, and cherish me. Instead, he took from me and broke me.

The sun is going to rise soon, and I'm still awake when I suddenly get the urge to run. I can't stay here any longer, I need to get away. I need to clear my head and running seems like the best way to do that.

Jumping out of bed, I throw on some yoga pants, a hoodie, and joggers, and then I set off on my run. I run until I can't breathe anymore due to the tears cascading down my cheeks. Falling to my knees, I let the tears track down my cheeks and I sob. I haven't sobbed this hard since Mom's funeral and once again, I'm heartbroken.

How could he do that to me?

Why did he do that to me?

He's my dad. He's supposed to love me. He's not supposed to do that. My first time should have been magical. Memorable, I guess mine will be memorable, just not in a happy kind of way.

The sound of a twig snapping causes me to lift my head and my eyes widen when I see a hooded figure in the shadows. The moon is hiding behind a cloud shrouding the early morning in darkness. The sun is yet to rise and shine, and I should be scared of this hidden figure, but after last night, the only thing I'm scared of is my father.

"You can't hurt me," I shout at the lone figure.

"I don't want to hurt you," they reply. The voice is

familiar, but I'm not thinking clearly right now and I can't place it. They step out of the shadows just as the moon reappears and as if he was sent from above, the moonlight shines down on Saint Vanderbelt. He's the most attractive out of the Vanderbelt brothers, he's also the most broken.

Like me.

"Are you okay?" he asks, and I chuckle to myself because that's a loaded question right about now.

"That's a question I cannot answer," I honestly tell him, wiping at my cheeks. I don't want to seem weak and fragile before him, but it's hard to maintain the façade.

"It's just a question," he states, plopping down next to me. He pulls his legs up and crosses them at the heels. Holding on to his knees, he stares at me. I can feel his gaze deep in my soul and the longer we stare at one another, the more I start to feel whole again. "Well, answer me this, what's a pretty girl like you doing out here at stupid a.m.?"

"What's a handsome boy like you doing out here at stupid a.m.?" I throw back at him.

"You think I'm handsome?"

"You know you are, Saint Vanderbelt."

"Well you, Rowan Ashford, you are the prettiest girl in Crestwood."

"You need your eyes checked."

"I have twenty/twenty vision, thank you very much. Now, answer me, what are you doing out here?"

"I ... I, I just wanted to sit in the dirt and cry." I go with that because I can never tell him what happened. I can never tell anyone what happened, not that anyone would believe me. My dad is the pillar of Crestwood Prep. No one would believe he would do that to his little girl or wife. Then it gets me thinking; *IS* he doing this to anyone else? You don't just decide one day to rape your daughter out of the blue. There must be others. I know he was raping Mom but is it rape when they're your spouse?

"What's got you thinking so hard over there?"

Shaking my head, I smile over at him. "Nothing, just thinking about life and death." *...and ways I can kill my father without it looking like murder. I can't go to jail, I don't look good in orange.*

"That's very philosophical of you this early in the morning."

"What can I say? I'm a ..."

"You're a what?"

"I'm a complicated girl."

"Aren't we all?"

"You're a complicated girl?" I throw back at him, biting my lip to hold back my smile. As I stare at him, I realize this is the first real smile since Mom died. I'm surprised my face remembers how to form one because there hasn't been a lot to smile about recently, and then it hits me. If I can smile once, I can smile again. *He* can't take my happiness from me.

"I'm a complicated boy." He pauses. "You know, complicated boys and girls go well together, maybe we should—"

"Not happening, Vanderbelt."

"Why not, Dove?"

Staring over at him, I blink a few times. "Why did you call me Dove?"

"Just did," he nonchalantly replies with a shrug.

"Bullshit, tell me. Because you aren't the kind of person to just do something on a whim."

He silently stares at me, and just when I think he's going to ignore me, he tells me. "I called you Dove because unlike me, you're innocent,"—*HA* I think, not so innocent anymore—"and gentle and tender."

"You don't know anything about me," I whisper.

"I know more than you think," he throws back at me. Shuffling closer, he drapes his arm around my shoulders and pulls me into him. It's just a hug, a one-armed hug at that, but it's oddly soothing.

Lifting my head, I stare up at him, reminding me of the first time he showed me his secret place. And like that day, something again is drawing us together. I wonder if it's Mom guiding him to me. It's almost as if she knew that in the future I'd need a saint in my life. I find myself smiling at that thought and it's a real genuine Rowan smile.

"I love when you smile," he whispers.

"I love you making me smile," I reply.

He lowers his head, and I think he's going to kiss me. I've never kissed a boy before and suddenly I'm nervous, but he doesn't kiss me. Well, he kisses the tip of my nose, and it's somehow perfect. If we kissed right now, it would have ruined the moment, but it's like he knew. Saint knew it wasn't time to kiss me.

Without a word, he stands up and leaves.

Sitting here, I watch him walk away, feeling calmer than when I first got here and I realize, I'm still smiling.

My mom was my saint when she was alive, and I know without a doubt she sent Saint to me to be my new saint. Just as he turns the corner and out of sight, I know that with Saint by my side, I will survive *him*.

Saint will be my savior ... if only I knew what was to come for *my* Saint.

SAINT

… a few months later

MR. ASHFORD GLARES at me when I throw the balloon filled with water at him. It smashes, soaking him. To piss him off further, I also throw the one filled with flour, making a goopy fucking mess on the floor and all over him.

You can't wipe the smile off my face when I see Fuck-face Ashford's face turn red with anger underneath the white gooey mess.

Raising my eyebrows at him in a 'what you gonna do

about it' kind of way, I wait for him to explode, but unfortunately, he reins in his temper. "Mr. Vanderbelt, please head to detention," he says, his tone level and calm.

"Nah, I think I'll stay here thanks, Teach." I laugh, fist-bumping my best friend Lennon. He chuckles, and it causes Mr. Ashford to lock his jaw, and *that*'s when his anger begins to build. He walks over and stops in front of me. We are toe to toe. "Now, Mr. Vanderbelt," he demands, his tone a little angrier than before and I can tell he's trying to rein it in.

Silently, we stare at one another. Everyone in the quad around us is frozen still, waiting and watching the standoff between us. Taking a deep breath, I smile with glee and pretend to wipe something off his cheek. "You had a little something there," I goad before I step around him, and with a swagger in my walk, I stride past him and up the stairs. Before I step into the administration building, I turn back around and stare down at him. "You really gotta remove that stick up your ass, old man." Saluting him, I step out through the doors and make my way to detention.

If this fucker thinks I'm going to back down he better prepare for war because nobody does war like the Vanderbelts, and this douche just moved to the top of my shit list. I don't have definitive proof of his crimes, but I know he's hurting Rowan. She's as sweet as pie and if he thinks I'm going to stay away all because he said so, then this fucker hasn't had the pleasure of meeting Saint Vanderbelt. I'm going to become his worst nightmare.

"Saint, this behavior has gotten out of hand," my father berates me later that day. We've been summoned for dinner and a bonus for me, I get a lecture too. Crossing my arms over my chest, I roll my eyes at his dramatics, and it pisses him off. "It's unacceptable," he continues. "You're a Vanderbelt. A Lord, you need to instill fear in those around you, not play childish games."

"I am and I do, besides, it's all just fun with Ashford." No way in hell will I confide in Dad. He'd fucking welcome Ashford with open arms. Assholes attract assholes, and those two together would be double the asshole.

"You will stop taunting Mr. Ashford and you *will* stay away from his daughter, Saint," my father tells me as he leans over his desk. "Do I make myself clear?"

"Whatever," I nonchalantly reply because neither of those two things will be happening, and I don't care what either of them say. I'm not going to stop talking to Rowan.

My father sighs and without another word, dismisses me with a wave of his hand. Leaving his office, I head up to my old bedroom, shaking my head. I can't believe Mr. Ashford tattled on me, really?

When I enter my room, I find Hendrix lying on my bed. "What are you doing in my room?"

"Trying to make friends, I see." He smirks.

"Out," I growl, opening my door wider. Hendrix stands, shoving me in the side with his elbow as he passes.

"Don't whack it too much." He laughs as he leaves.

Slamming my door behind him and ignoring his taunting, I plop down on my bed and thoughts of Rowan run through my mind.

Flopping to my back, I stare at the ceiling and smirk. If Ashford thinks running to my father will stop me from speaking to Rowan, or taunting him, he's in for a surprise because I'm about to show him just what a pissed-off Vanderbelt can do … but first, I need to survive dinner with our parents and my brothers.

"Oh. My. God, Saint," Rowan growls when she sees me the next day. "Did you really do that to my dad?"

"Yep," I reply, letting the 'p' pop. A smile widens on my face as I think of Ashford covered in that goopy mess.

"Well, did you at least take photos?" she asks, and her question confuses me.

"You wanted pics?"

"Duh," she sasses, "next time, I want photographic evidence."

"Next time, huh?"

"Yep, next time because come on, this is you, and you love taunting my dad."

"With good fucking reason," I growl. My gut is telling me that he's abusing her, but she won't tell me what goes on behind closed doors. In my heart of hearts, I know, but Ro is one of the strongest people I know so no matter what he throws at her, she will take it.

"Let's not talk about my dad anymore."

"What do you want to talk about then?"

"Weeeeeell, I ummm," she's acting all sheepish right now.

"You know you can tell me anything," I offer.

"I know, but I was thinking." She steps into me. Resting her palms on my chest she lifts to her tippy-toes. Her breath skates over my neck, and my cock twitches. "I want you to kiss me."

She pulls back and stares into my eyes. Mine drop to her lips, her plump, delectable lips. Her tongue darts out and slides across her bottom lip. Leaving a sheen to it in the morning sunlight.

Lowering my head, I hover millimeters away but at the last second, I lift up and press a quick kiss to her cheek.

"There, I kissed you," I tease.

She slaps me in the chest. "You know that's not the kiss I'm wanting."

"And what type of kiss were you after?"

"One like this." Before I know what's happening, she grips my cheeks in her palms and presses her lips to mine. I'm frozen, shocked that she took the chance and kissed me. I've wanted to kiss her for weeks now, but I wasn't sure she wanted me like I want her.

Taking a step back, she stares at me and there's a crestfallen look on her face, and then I realize that I didn't kiss her back. "Shit," I hiss when she takes another step backward. Her eyes fill with tears, and I feel like a complete and utter jerk.

Reaching out, I grip her wrist and pull her into me. She lets out an oomph when she collides with my chest, and before she can say anything, I cover her mouth with mine. She gasps, and I take the opportunity to slip my tongue into her mouth. Now she's frozen, but I'm not, and when I swirl my tongue around her mouth, she snaps into gear.

Sucking on my tongue, she pushes hers into my mouth and together our tongues dance an erotic dance.

Sliding my hands around her waist, I cup her ass as I continue to kiss her. In the middle of the quad, Rowan and I make out like our lives depend on it.

She's the one to break our connection. She's breathlessly panting and seeing her cheeks flushed has my cock twitching in my pants.

"Wow," she mumbles, "that was—"

"Perfect," I finish for her, and it was as first kisses go, that is one for the history books.

"I think we should do that again."

"You do, do you?" I tease.

"Mmmhmpf," she says, nodding.

"Well, let's kiss again."

Draping her arms over my shoulders, she presses her lips to me and unlike last time she did that, this time I kiss her back. Winding my arms around her waist, I walk us backward till her back hits the wall. She runs her fingers up the back of my neck and gently rakes her nails over my scalp. It has my body coming alive, and if we weren't out in the open, I'd peel her clothes off her body and worship her.

Rowan Ashford is a queen, she's my queen, and I will do whatever it takes to keep her safe because her kisses are life and after two, I'm addicted.

ROWAN

JUST AFTER MY SIXTEENTH BIRTHDAY, I feel like my life is over. My period is late and I'm starting to freak the fuck out, excuse my language. Three minutes is a long time when you're holding a little stick that you just peed on in your hands to see if your life is about to change in a massive way.

I'm praying to the gods.

To Mom.

To everyone in the universe that it will be negative. I'm too young to be a mom. And I really don't want to have a baby with my father, I don't want to be *that* person.

The alarm on my phone sounds and I jolt in fright, dropping the stick when I jump six feet into the air. Bending down, I pick it up and take a deep breath as I turn it over. I sigh in relief when I only see one line.

It's negative.

I'm not pregnant.

There's no bun in the oven.

Halle-fucking-lujah.

The sound of my father's footsteps on the stairs startles me, and again, I drop the test. Picking it up, I struggle to hide it and the box, my hands shaking. The door slams open and I know, I'm too late. This is going to end badly but thank the heavens I'm not pregnant. That would be so much worse than the beating I'm about to endure.

"What are you doing in here?" he growls. His eyes widen when he sees the box in my hand. He reaches out, roughly grabbing my arm. He slams me into the vanity, and I wince at the pain lancing through me.

"Daddy," I stutter. He lets go of my arm and his entire face turns beet red when he snatches the pregnancy test box from my hands. The stick falls to the carpet, negative sign upward. He squeezes it vehemently. The cardboard crunches and crumbles in his fist.

"Were you trying to hide this from me?" he shouts, spittle flying from his mouth and landing on my face.

"No-no." I swallow hard, taking a step back. In the blink of an eye, his hand flies out and lands across my cheek. The force knocks me to the floor. "Daddy, please," I cry, trying to move away from him but there's not much room in the bathroom.

He pulls his leg back and kicks me in the side. His boot lands hard against my ribs. An audible crack echoes in the room, and he smirks, he smirks at the fact he just broke a rib … and I pray that it pierces my lung and I die.

Reaching down, he grabs me by my hair and pulls me upright. The hair follicles tear and burn. I cry out as he barks, "You stupid little bitch."

Raising his fist again, he slams it into my face. I cry out in pain as he continues to slap and punch me. Over and over his fist slams into my face. He never hits me in the face. Obvious bruises and injuries cause questions, so the fact he's hitting me in the face shows how angry he is.

He throws me back to the floor and begins to kick me again. Repeatedly his boot lands in my abdomen. Curling into myself, I lie on the floor, bleeding and unable to breathe without it hurting.

He's never been this vicious before and just when I can't take anymore, he turns around and leaves me on the bathroom floor. He stomps back downstairs and out the front door, slamming it behind him.

Lying here, I stare up at the side of the tub. I'm numb. I can't even cry. Eventually, I try to push myself up, but everything hurts. Forcing myself to take small breaths, I move slowly because every single inhale hurts. I struggle to get off the floor and up into a sitting position.

Leaning against the vanity, tears slide down my face when I realize that no matter what I do, my father won't change. He's a monster, end of story. He beat me for something he would have caused, yet I'm to blame.

My father hasn't returned home so I know he's either sleeping at his office or staying out late on purpose, but I'm thankful for the reprieve. Stripping off my clothes, I carefully climb into the shower. The hot water feels amazing on my battered and broken body. Looking down at my skin, I begin to cry again. It's mottled with bruises.

I'm a kaleidoscope of purples, reds, and blacks and in the coming days, it will be littered with yellows and greens as the bruises begin to heal. The bruises always fade but not the memories. The mental scars, they will stay with me forever.

Climbing out of the shower, I gently dry myself, wincing and groaning when I press too hard against my body. Wrapping my towel around me, I head back to my bedroom. Dropping the towel, I reach into my drawer for some panties, but a noise at the window startles me, and when I spin around, I see Saint climbing through my window.

Dropping my panties, I gasp and watch as he straightens up. Silently we stare at one another, shock on both our faces. Me from him being in my bedroom and him at me and my body. My naked and beaten body.

"What the fuck, Rowan?" Saint growls as his gaze travels over me from head to toe before finally landing on my face. With wide eyes, he shakes his head and comes straight for me.

Unlike when Dad marched toward me, I'm not scared. I can't describe how I feel but just having him here is oddly comforting.

Stopping in front of me, he reaches out and takes my hands in his. His thumbs run back and forth along the backs of my hands. His gaze once again roams over my body, studying each and every bruise and mark.

Dropping one hand, he reaches up and cups my cheek, gently running the pad of his thumb over my cheekbone. His touch is soothing, but at the same time, it burns like the fires of hell.

"I'm going to fucking kill him," he sneers. His voice is full of venom. This is the first time Saint has seen me this bad. Actually, it's the first time anyone has seen my injuries, it also happens to be the first time in months that he's savagely beaten me. Normally it's just a slap here. A verbal 'you're fucking useless' there. A push when I breathe wrong, you know, the usual abuse a child suffers at the hands of a monster.

Before I can reply and tell him I'm fine—ish, he turns on his heel and walks out of my room, leaving me naked and alone. I miss his presence immediately, I can hear him rummaging around, and a few moments later, he returns with my brush in his hand. "Sit," he demands, pointing to the bed.

"Can I put some clothes on first?" He nods and bends down and grabs my panties. Holding them open, he helps me step into them. He slides my panties up my legs before grabbing my sweatpants. Again, he helps me pull them on and then assists me with my tank top. Once dressed, he points to the bed, nods, and whispers, "Sit."

Carefully, I lower myself down on the edge, wincing in pain with each movement. He climbs on behind me and begins to brush my hair. His gesture causes the floodgates to open, and I sit here sobbing as he brushes my hair.

"I need you to tell me everything, Ro, and don't even think about lying."

Nodding, I stare at the carpet and wring my hands in my lap. "It all started…" I tell him everything. What he did to Mom, and I end with what he's been doing to me since she died.

"I'm going to fucking kill him," he says, breaking the silence that befell us after I finished telling my story.

"Saint," I say his name as a plea.

"I mean it," he interrupts. He climbs off the bed, squats down in front of me, and takes my hands in his again.

"One day I'll kill that bastard." He drops one hand and wipes a tear from my cheek. Then he gently wraps his arms around me. I slide mine around his waist and silently sob into his shoulder.

If my father catches him here, it'll be game over for both of us, but being in Saint's arms has become my happy place, and right now, I need him. Need this. The selfish part of me is saying 'consequences be damned' so I hold on tighter.

"Saint," I whisper into his chest.

"Yeah," he mumbles.

Lifting my head from his chest, I look up at him. Reaching out, my fingers grip his shirt and I tug him down to me and place a kiss on his lips. He groans and starts kissing me back. Sliding my hand down his body, I squeeze his dick. I want him to make love to me. I want to feel pleasure. I want Saint to erase what my dad does to me. I want Saint to make me feel alive.

Breaking our kiss, he pulls back shaking his head. "Baby, you're hurt, I can't."

"Please," I plead with him.

Saint growls and just when I think he's going to push me away, his lips crash to mine. We fall to the mattress, his body cocooning mine and a painful moan slips out. Saint carefully maneuvers us around so I'm on top. He's always looking after me, and with the simplest of things, he makes me smile.

"Tell me what you want?" he says, lifting himself up to nudge his nose against mine.

Lifting my head, I stare down at him. "Please fuck me, Saint," I tell him. "I need to forget *him* and his touch."

He nods, and before he can change his mind, I lift my shirt over my head. I wince at the pain when I remove my shirt, but when Saint sits up and removes his shirt, all thoughts of pain and my beating disappear as I take in the man before me. Saint Vanderbelt is a masterpiece. Abs on abs and that illusive 'V' that makes girls go gaga. His fingers grip the back of my neck and he pulls me forward. Our lips brush together and we kiss. Wrapping his arms around my back, I wince, and he breaks the kiss.

"I don't want to hurt you," he murmurs, shaking his head.

"You won't," I tell him. "I need this. I need you."

He stares at me, and when I think he's going to deny me, he grips my cheeks and his lips collide with mine. Our tongues duel together, reminding me of our first and I begin to grind over him. He hardens under me, and his shaft hits me in that spot that has my body coming alive. I've never felt pleasure like this before and know that this is a moment I will remember and treasure forever.

"Fuck," he hisses between kisses, "Dove, you drive me wild."

"Feeling's mutual," I tell him.

He lifts me to my feet, and together we rid each other of our clothes. As soon as we're both naked, I push him down onto the bed and straddle him. His fingers grip my hips, and I grind myself over his cock again. Lifting myself up, Saint grips and strokes his cock twice before he guides it to my slit.

With our eyes locked on one another, I slide down his shaft. I'm soaked and he easily slips inside. I groan as he fills me, and a sense of unconditional love and pleasure rockets through me.

Saint's breaths are shallow as I move up and down his cock. He kisses me, thrusting his hips upward as I ride him.

Together we move in sync. We become one and lose ourselves in each other.

"Fuck, baby," he groans.

My body begins to convulse, I've never felt this sensation before. It's like I'm soaring, I never want it to disappear. Saint grips my ass, pushing deeper inside me. Pleasure overtakes the pain and for a moment, I forget about the beating and my fucked-up life.

"Oh, God," I moan as the pleasure wraps itself around me, squeezing tighter and tighter with each thrust. I've never felt so alive before, it's a hedonistic feeling and I can see why people love sex so much.

Breathless and panting uncontrollably, we move together as one.

Saint grunts and picks up speed. Using his hands under my ass, he moves me over him. My pussy tightens and then I explode, throwing my head back, I cry out like a banshee as I climax.

Saint growls and then hisses as he follows me over the edge, filling me with his seed.

Resting my forehead against his, we are both breathing heavily. Once I've caught my breath, Saint kisses me, and I feel whole for the first time all evening, but that feeling bursts when we both hear my father growl, "What the fuck."

I scramble off Saint's lap and turn around to find my father standing in the doorway to my room.

He's seething.

I've never seen him this angry before.

Stepping into my room, he shoves me aside and slams Saint up against the wall. His arm pressed against his neck.

Racing over, I try to pull Dad off Saint, but he shoves me, and I fall to the floor.

"Don't fucking touch her," Saint yells at Dad. He's struggling to get free, but when Dad gets angry like this, it's like he becomes the Hulk. His anger builds his strength, and right now, he's the angriest I've ever seen.

"She's my fucking daughter," my father screams at him. "I can touch her however the fuck I want but you, you on the other hand cannot touch what's mine, and I'll fucking kill you for touching what's mine."

SAINT

"SHE'S MY FUCKING DAUGHTER. I can touch her however the fuck I want but you, you on the other hand cannot touch what's mine, and I'll fucking kill you for touching what's mine." Those words light a fire deep inside, and I want to end this fucker. How dare he talk about Rowan like that.

"Not if I kill you first, you fucking scumbag, prick," I spit back at him.

"You fucking little punk. Think you can defile my daughter and get away with it?"

"Like you do? You're the sick fuck around here."

"You don't know shit, you little prick," he says, but I see the fear in his face.

Nodding my head to Rowan I snarl, "So the bruises on her body just appeared, huh?"

He turns his head to Rowan, and I notice she's pulled her comforter around her, covering her nakedness from us. "For all we know, you caused those bruises."

"Like fuck I would hurt her. I love her." Those three words spill from my mouth before I can stop them.

"Y-y-y-you … you l-l-love m-m-me?" Rowan stutters.

Looking over her dad's shoulder at her, I nod. "With every fiber of my being."

"I … I …"

"Ohhh, how sweet, but she's mine and mine alone. You come near my daughter again, and I will have you charged."

"Works both ways, asshole," I snap at him.

"And who will they believe? A respected teacher and member of the community who lost his wife? Or a degenerate Vanderbelt cunt? You have nothing on me, and if you want to keep my precious daughter safe, you will walk out of this house and forget that Rowan Ashford exists."

"Over my dead fucking—"

"Please, Saint," Rowan murmurs, "just go. I … I'll be fine."

"Fuck off you will, he's a monster. He's the fucking devil incarnate, and I am not leaving you alone with him."

She shakes her head, her eyes full of tears. "I don't need you to protect me, Saint." She closes her eyes and whispers four words that cut me deep. "I just need him."

"You don't mean that, Dove," I plead with her.

Stepping over to her, I take her hand and lace our fingers together. Lifting our joined hands, I place a kiss on her knuckles, and with a subdued tone add, "Come with me, please?"

She shakes her head again and a tear falls down her cheek. She lifts her gaze to mine, and I see hurt, fear, and worry in her eyes. "Please, Saint, just go."

"You heard her, get the fuck out of my house," Fuckface Ashford sneers, looking smug.

"I'll go but this isn't over." Shoving Fuckface Ashford off me, I turn toward my dove, but she steps away from me and pleads with her eyes for me to just go.

Stopping mid-step, I stare at her, taking her beauty in. I'd do anything for her so reluctantly, I do as she asks. Leaning into her, I press a kiss to her forehead and whisper, "I love you."

She smiles, but I notice she doesn't say it back. Turning on my heel, I leave my heart with her and I walk away.

With each step I take, my heart breaks but I know one thing, I need to get her away from him.

"You right?" Thatcher asks when he sees me in the dorm hallway the next day.

"Just fucking peachy," I snarl, continuing onto my room. Opening the door, I slam it behind me but a few moments later, it opens and I see Thatch standing there.

"I said I'm fine," I snap at him.

"I call bullshit, you look like you want to murder someone." I eye him. "Did you meet with Dad?" Shaking my head, I walk over to the wall, pull my fist back but before I can slam it into the drywall, Thatcher covers my fist and grabs my arm.

"Not the way to deal with whatever this is."

"How the fuck would you know?" I shout.

"Well, tell me and I can help you fix it without damaging your hand or the wall."

"I can't tell you, I promised I would never tell and I always keep my word." As much as I want to tell Thatcher everything, this isn't my secret to share. Killing Ashford would solve all our problems, but I'm not a murderer and if I did it, what would happen to Rowan? She has no family left here and the thought of not seeing her beautiful face each day is not something I want to think about. "I want to be alone," I tell him.

"I'll go, but you need to promise me you won't do anything stupid."

"Promise, I'm not Hendrix."

That comment causes him to chuckle.

He pulls me in for a one-armed bro hug and slaps my back. "You know where to find me if you want to talk."

Nodding, I watch my brother walk out. The door clicks closed behind him and I let out a frustrated sigh. Walking over, I flip the lock and slide down to the floor. Stretching my legs out, I tilt my head back and think of how I can help Rowan … and then it hits me, I know what to do but do I have the balls to do it?

ROWAN

AFTER SAINT RELUCTANTLY LEFT, Dad surprised me and also left. Without so much as uttering a word, he kissed me on the head and walked out. He closed the door to my room behind him with a gentle click and that was it.

No punishment.

Nothing.

Nothing verbal. Nothing physical and nothing sexual.

He just left and that is the scariest form of punishment ever. It means when my punishment does come, he'll have had time to stew on it. Therefore, when it comes, I'll be in for it.

For a long while, I just sit here. Staring at the closed door. Watching for him to return. Waiting for something but nothing happened.

Dropping the comforter from around my shoulders, I pull on my jammies and carefully climb into bed, but I don't dare fall asleep. I fear that as soon as I close my eyes, *he'll* come into my room and exact my punishment.

The sound of the front door slamming startles me awake and when I look around my room, I realize the sun is shining. I fell asleep in the wee hours of the morning and I slept soundly. I didn't hear a thing, until now.

Lying here, I close my eyes and listen, is he coming or going? By the silence from outside my door, I think he left. Letting out the breath I didn't realize I was holding, I sit up, wincing at the pull in my ribs. Lifting my tank, I look down at my body and my eyes widen. I'm covered in bruises and with each breath I take, I remember my ribs. I need to go to the hospital, but I wouldn't dare go. They'd ask questions and answering them would be harder than trying to breathe right now.

Climbing out of bed, I shuffle into the bathroom and use the toilet. Flushing, I walk to the sink and when I see my reflection, my mouth drops open and my eyes well with tears. My left eye is swollen shut and is a deep shade of purple.

Wiping at the tears, I pull my blond hair up into a ponytail and make my way downstairs and into the kitchen.

Grabbing some painkillers, I swallow them and then I pop a pod into the coffee machine. Resting my hands on the counter, I wait for the black nectar known as coffee to brew and wonder what I'm going to do. I can't go to school with my face looking like this, but if I miss school,

Dad will no doubt lose his shit. I'm screwed no matter what choice I make.

I'm so lost in my head, I don't even hear him return. It's only when he touches my shoulder and says, "Morning, my precious girl, did you sleep well?" That I realize he's here.

Looking over my shoulder at him, I take him in. Seems we are playing happy family this morning and forgetting he beat the shit out of me last night.

"I did, Daddy. And you?"

"Like the dead. Make your old man a coffee?"

"Yes, Daddy."

"You're such a good daughter," he says, pulling out a chair at the table by the window that overlooks the back-yard and pool.

Ignoring his remark, I turn the coffee that was for me into his, not wanting to make him wait. While I add the creamer and sugar to his, I pop another pod in for me.

Picking up his mug, I walk over to him and place it down in front of him. He smiles up at me and then frowns. "Your face, you can't go out looking like that. You will stay home. I'll tell the school that you're sick. Actually, no, I'll tell them you fell down the stairs and need to rest."

"Yes, Daddy," I repeat again then I ask the one question I know has the possibility to enrage him again. "I think I need the hospital. I think I broke a rib or two."

"No, no hospitals. We can't have any documentation of your clumsiness."

Nodding, I walk back over to the coffee machine and finish making my coffee. Picking up my mug, I wrap my hands around it and head over to join Dad.

Before Mom died, every morning the three of us would have a morning drink and breakfast together: Mom and Dad would have coffee and I'd have hot chocolate with marshmallows—on special occasions. Now that I'm older, I've upgraded to coffee, but I still sneak a marshmallow here and there 'cause hello, sugar. After that first sip of the black nectar last year, I was addicted, just like Mom was. I tell myself that being addicted to coffee is better than being addicted to crack so I don't feel bad about the amount I drink. Plus, each time I have one, I think of her.

"I love it when you smile like that," Dad says, snapping me away from the memory of coffee with Mom.

"Just thinking about Mom and our morning drinks together," I tell him. Looking up at him, I add, "I miss her."

"Me too, Precious Girl, me too." He pauses and takes a sip. "But we have each other now, we don't need her."

A shudder runs through me at his words.

"A girl always needs her mom." As soon as the words leave my lips, I know I made a mistake, but I quickly tack on, "I can't talk to you about girl stuff, that's just weird." Playfully, I giggle. "Do you really want to hear about periods and cramps and—"

"I get it. I get it. You don't need to paint me a picture. I still think of you as my little girl. You'll always be my little girl." Pushing his seat back, he taps his thigh. "Come sit on Daddy's lap."

Sitting here frozen, I stare at him and before I can stop myself, I start shaking my head. Dad grinds his teeth and his cheeks start to turn red with anger.

"I'm too heavy, I'll break your leg. Plus," I look at the clock on the wall, "you need to get going otherwise you'll be late."

He looks at the clock and his eyes widen. "Is that the

time?" It's a rhetorical question so I just nod. "I'll make you a to-go coffee while you finish getting ready."

"You are a great daughter, Rowan. I'm so lucky to have you."

He stands up and before he leaves the kitchen, he walks over to me and presses his lips to my head. Closing my eyes, I sigh deeply, wincing at the pain in my chest and shuddering at his touch. He feels my flinch. Lifting my gaze, I look up at him. "Breathing hurts my ribs."

He nods and without a word walks out of the kitchen, leaving me with my coffee and my sore ribs and body.

Holding my mug, I stare into it, but a tapping on the window causes my head to snap up. I smile when I see Saint on the other side, but then I quickly look over my shoulder to make sure Dad didn't hear it.

Standing up, I walk over to the back door and pop my head outside. "Are you crazy, my dad's still here."

"I had to make sure you're okay."

"I'm fine but if he finds you here, you won't be as lucky as last night. He'll kill you."

"He doesn't scare me." Lifting his hand, he traces over the bruise on my face. "Are you okay?"

Nodding, I smile, "I'm fine but you need to go."

"I'll see you in English," he says, but I shake my head.

"I won't be there." I point to my face. "Can't tarnish the good Ashford name."

Saint scoffs loudly and my eyes widen. Dad surely heard that. "Shhhh," I hiss, "he'll hear you."

"Fuckface Ashford doesn't scare me." A chuckle escapes me at that nickname. "I love hearing you laugh and hearing that gives me comfort, but I need to do this before I go to school."

Stepping closer to me, he slides his hand around my

neck and guides my face to his. Pressing his lips to mine, he kisses me deeply. His tongue licks along my seam and pushes into my mouth. Mine slips into his and they start an erotic dance together, sliding in and out of each other's mouths.

The sound of Dad's feet on the stairs pulls us apart. "Gotta go." Before I can say anything he's gone.

"Why's the door open?" Dad asks, entering the kitchen.

"I wanted some fresh air," I lie.

Dad nods and looks around. "Where's my coffee?"

Shit, his coffee. "Sorry, I was lost thinking of Mom. Let me quickly do it now."

Walking over to the machine, I quickly go about making his coffee and to soften the blow, I make him a pastrami and cheese sandwich too, just how he likes it. Handing both to him, he smiles. Bending down, he kisses me on the cheek and heads off to school. Before he exits the kitchen, he looks back at me. "Don't let anyone in."

"I won't," I tell him and when I hear the lock on the front door click, I sigh in relief. I have the next seven hours to myself, but all I want is to be with Saint. Last night he managed to make everything better, he always makes everything better … and little did I know, he was about to make the biggest sacrifice for me ever.

SAINT

WHEN I WOKE THIS MORNING, the need to see
Rowan was strong. I needed to make sure she was okay
because last night was a roller coaster for her. Her father is
a monster, even more so than mine, and Thornton Vanderbelt is a cunt. His smarmy smiling face is next to the word
in the dictionary. That's how much of a cunt he is.

Hiding in the bushes, I watch her with Fuckface
Ashford in the kitchen together. The two of them sit there
having coffee like nothing happened last night. How he
can be a two-faced cunt like that is mind-boggling. I knew
he'd been abusive toward Rowan, but I didn't realize the

extent of it. I thought it was just a verbal lashing here, a slap there, but her body, fuck, that wasn't a lashing, that was a severe beating. But my dove is still standing, she is the strongest person I have ever met and after seeing her just now, I know that I have to do what I have to do to save her.

Kissing her goodbye, I rearrange my semi-hard dick and race to school. I want to be there waiting for Fuckface Ashford because I have a proposition for him and I'm ninety-nine-percent sure that he'll take up my offer. Narcissists like him are easy to manipulate.

When I arrive back at school, I make my way straight to his office. I've beat him here because no doubt he'll stop at the diner in town to get himself and the Dean a coffee. Those two are quite chummy but not super chummy since his office looks out into the teachers' parking lot. Fucker isn't even good enough to get an office that looks to the garden or the bluff. It's like she knows he's a cunt and she shoved him in the naughty corner.

Picking the lock, I let myself in and relock the door behind me.

Twenty minutes after I arrive, his shit-brown Honda pulls into the lot and my heart rate picks up as I watch him climb out and grab his stuff. When he begins walking across the lot, I mumble, "Showtime."

Dropping into his chair, I spin it around so my back is to the door and wait for him to arrive. The sound of his key sliding into the lock echoes around the quiet of his office. When the door opens, I spin around to face him and with no expression on my face, I growl, "We need to talk."

SAINT

THE SHOCKED LOOK on his face when he sees me is priceless.

"How the fuck did you get in here?" He snickers, closing the door behind him.

Pointing behind him, I state the obvious, "Door."

My one-word answer pisses him off and it's hard not to smile. Me being here has rattled him and before he can say anything, I get right to it. "I have a proposition for you and the only answer is yes."

"And what makes you think I would ever listen to you? You just raped my daughter."

"This coming from the fucker who's been raping and beating *his* daughter since his wife died."

"You don't know anything, you little asshole."

"I know you're a cunt and you don't deserve your daughter. She's the only reason I'm here because I would never give you the time of day if it wasn't for her. Now. Sit the fuck down and listen."

Shocking me, he drops into the chair across from me. "You were saying?"

"From this day forward, you will not touch Rowan. Physically. Emotionally or … sexually. If you get the urge, you call me. You beat me. You don't fucking touch her ever again."

"I'm not a faggot," he sneers.

"Never said you were."

"But—"

"But nothing. You will never fuck or lay a hand on your daughter again. You get an urge, you find me. You will pleasure yourself or find someone your own age to fuck.

The room is silent as he processes my words.

"Let me get this straight," he says, breaking the silence. From the look on his face, I have no fucking clue what he's going to say or even if he will agree to my wild proposal. I know it's crazy, but Rowan doesn't deserve this. She is the kindest person I have ever met and if I can save her from her father, it's the least I can do. "You want to whore yourself to me to save my bitch of a daughter?"

"She's not a bitch," I snap, "And I'm not whoring myself, I'm your personal punching bag. I'm sacrificing myself for her. Do we have a deal?"

"Do I get a preview of what you're proposing? How do I know you aren't going to fuck me over?"

"I'm waiting," he hisses.

Standing up, I remove my shirt and turn around. His breathing deepens and then he strikes. His fist collides with my side and I grunt, letting him think he's hurting me but in reality, my mom hits harder than he does. It takes everything I have not to laugh right now.

By the time he finishes, he's huffing and puffing and I'll admit, my body hurts but for Rowan, I can and will do this.

He drops into the chair and looks up at me. A smug smirk on his face, he outstretches his hand. "We have a deal."

Nodding, I shake his hand and then I bend down and pull my shirt over my head. He sits there, thinking he's won, and I'll let him think that. "Ohh, and one more thing."

"What?" he growls.

"Rowan will be moving into the dorms with a room near Quinn."

"Like fuck she's moving out."

"Then when I walk out of here, I head toward Dean Doyle's office and you are fucked when I tell her everything … and show her the evidence of my beating just now."

"Are you threatening me?" He stands up and stops in front of me. I can feel his breath on my face. He's breathing as if he's just run a marathon but I see it in his eyes. He's scared right now because he knows I hold all the cards. Check and mate, you son of a bitch.

"If it means Rowan is no longer under your roof then yes, yes I'm threatening you."

We stare at one another.

Silence envelops us.

The tension in the air is thick.

"I'm waiting, asshole," I sneer when the silence becomes insufferable, "do we have a deal?"

"Yes, but I want Rowan to come to dinner once a week. Alone."

"Once a month," I counter.

I'm not a fan of this condition, but I need to get her out of that house and what's a few hours once a month? When it comes to this monster, a lot, but against my better judgment, I'll give him this.

With a nod of his head, he reluctantly agrees to a monthly dinner.

"But you lay a hand on her, and our deal is moot. I will end you once and for all."

"Look at you using big words." He's trying to taunt me but it's not working because I'm getting what I want. I'm getting Rowan away from her piece of shit father. Rowan and her safety are all that matters to me, hence my deal with the devil.

ROWAN

SPINNING IN A CIRCLE, I take in my new room at Crestwood Prep. Yes, my room at Crestwood Prep. Glancing around again, my smile widens as I think about making this place mine. Dropping down onto my bed, I take it all in again, not quite believing I'm here. I think I'm going to like my new room.

In

My

New

Room.

Jumping up again, I spin like Julie Andrews in *The*

Sound of Music, once again smiling like a carnival clown. A noise escapes me and my eyes widen at the sound. It's not a giggle and it's not a sigh. It's more like a 'I'm free of the monster' type noise. I cannot remember the last time I felt free and excited like this. I'm happier than ever right now and I don't think I'll be losing the smile on my face anytime soon. I've been grinning ever since Saint came to the house and helped me pack.

I'm still in shock that Saint somehow convinced my father to let me move into the dorms here. As soon as he told me, I wasn't going to argue. I wasn't going to give Dad a chance to change his mind.

I was just so freakin' happy to be out of that house.

A soft knock interrupts my spinning and when I turn toward the door, I see Saint pop his head in. He smiles at me before stepping inside my room. "Settling in okay, Dove?" he asks and before I answer, I launch myself into his arms. He catches me with little effort and holds on to me tightly. Lifting me up, I wrap my legs around his waist and kiss him.

"Thank you," I whisper against his lips before kissing him again. "I feel like I've won the lottery, the freedom lottery and it's all because of you. My Saint."

Gazing back at me, Saint leans in and kisses me.

"But I have to ask, what did you agree to? I can't imagine Dad just letting me move out."

"I made a deal with him—"

"What deal? What did you do?" My mind is racing right now.

"For your freedom, he will beat me. He will never lay a hand on you again."

Blinking rapidly, I stare at him and process his words.

My head starts to shake. "No, Saint, I … I won't allow you to do this for me."

"It's done."

"Saint—"

"No, Rowan, listen,"

"Wow, you called me Rowan, it must be serious."

"Because this is serious. I cannot idly sit by and let him continue to rape and beat you."

"You are not letting my father fuck you."

"And I'm not. With you out of that house, he can't hurt you like that anymore. And when he needs to beat something, he can beat me."

"Saint." I shake my head, at a loss for words.

"I've made up my mind, Ro. I will do anything to protect you. I just wish I'd come up with this solution sooner."

"I should just go to the police."

"But then you risk them taking you away from here. Taking you away from me, but I can't live without you, Ro. I can't. You're my dove and if I have to take a beating to keep you safe, a beating I will take."

Wrapping my arms tighter around him, I snuggle into him. This is the ultimate show of love, and I will forever be grateful to Saint for this.

"Thank you," I whisper into his neck. Lifting my head, I stare at him. "How will I ever repay you?"

He waggles his eyebrows at me and his hands roam down my back until he's squeezing my butt cheeks. Giggling, I slap at his chest and wiggle in that 'let me down' kind of way.

"I need to finish setting up my room."

He loosens his grip and lets me slide down his body. My

nipples harden against my bra at the contact with his torso, and I know Saint feels them because he winks and leans into me. His heated breath fans over my neck and somehow my nipples harden further. "I'll sneak in later and you can thank me then." He bops me on the nose with his pointer finger.

"I'm sure you will," I reply, staring at him.

Crestwood has rules about after lights out and boys being on the girls' floor, but Saint is a Lord and The Lords are all too happy to break any rules set forth.

"Do you need anything?" Saint asks, taking my hand in his and entwining our fingers.

Taking a moment, I think and then shake my head. Then I grin when I realize, I don't need anything. Right now, I have everything I've ever wanted.

I have freedom.

For the first time since Mom died, I have freedom. I almost laugh out loud at the notion. For years, I felt like Rapunzel, locked away in her tower except instead of an evil mother, I have my evil father.

With one final kiss, Saint leaves me and heads off to class. I've been excused from classes today to settle in.

Ducking down to the cafeteria, I grab a coffee and head back to my room and begin decorating. I decorate my room with the few things I brought with me. The last item is a photo of Mom and me, which I place on my bedside table so it's the first thing I see in the morning and the last thing I see at night.

Staring at the picture, I smile. It's the last one we ever took together.

Picking it up, I drop to the edge of my mattress and run my finger over my face. The girl smiling back at me isn't the same girl I am today, that girl died when Mom did. Then she died all over again when *that* happened.

Pushing aside those memories, I focus and hold on to the good ones with Mom. It's those memories that push me to keep fighting.

And Saint.

He's a beacon of light when I'm sucked into the dark vortex that is my father. Placing the frame back down, I sigh. I want her back. I miss her so, so much but most of all, I want the young and carefree version of me back. Now that I'm free, it might be possible to get the girl I used to be back.

With Saint, Quinn, and Alani busy with class, I find myself flicking through social media to take away the boredom. It doesn't take long to set up when you don't have much.

A message from Saint flashes on my screen. Reading it over, I pout knowing I'll have to wait even longer now.

SAINT

Sorry, Dove, raincheck. Dad has summoned us to the house. I'll be there as soon as I can. I have a key, don't wait up **wink wink**

Of course he has a key, I think.

I shake my head because heaven forbid he would have to wait for me to unlock the door when he knocks.

ROWAN

Okay. I miss you, I'll see you later.

SAINT

Fuck, I miss you too, I'll be back as soon as I can.

Deciding to have a shower and wash off the day, I grab

my shower items and robe and head for the shared bathrooms—that's the only downside to being here, sharing the facilities with the other twenty girls on this floor.

Undressing, I'm about to step under the water when I realize I left my towel on the bench outside. I jump out quickly and grab it, hoping no one will come in and see the bruising on my naked body. I'm not ashamed of my body. I'm ashamed of the marks and bruises and questions they garner, so I make a note to be more prepared and careful when I have my next shower.

Stepping under the spray, I close my eyes and let the water wash over me. Lathering my hair, I shampoo it and just as I begin to rinse, I hear voices. Quickly, I add conditioner and wash my body, suddenly feeling awkward being naked in here.

Turning the water off, I grab my towel and dry my body. Reaching my hand out of the shower stall, I grab my robe and slip it on. Securely, I tie it around me and then I wrap my locks up in my bamboo hair turban—thank you Quinn for the best gift ever. Then I grab my things and head back to my room.

I'm not paying attention and I bump into someone who walks around the corner at the same time as me. They grip my arms to prevent me from falling and an audible gasp slips through my lips. I begin to panic but when a deep voice says, "Whoa, Ro, chill, it's just me." The panic ebbs when I recognize the voice, but it doesn't fall away completely until my gaze focuses and I see Lennon before me.

"Ohh, sorry, shit," I murmur, causing him to chuckle.

"All good, sorry for bumping into you." He rakes his gaze over my robe-clad body, I raise my eyebrows at him and he just shrugs. If Saint was here, he'd smack him up the side of the head for ogling me.

"Why are you on the girls' floor?" I ask, raising an eyebrow, Lennon just smirks then runs his hand across his jaw.

"I'd rather not say." He grins and I can only imagine what he's doing here, but I am curious as to *who* he visited.

"Well, enjoy." Stepping around him, I continue on to my room.

"Oh, I will," he calls out, and then I hear a hushed, "Hey, baby." I find myself shaking my head at Saint's best friend.

Unlocking my door, I throw all my items on the dresser and lock it behind me. Pulling on my jammies, I sit on my bed and pull my legs up, hugging them. Another smile, something I've done lots today, appears when I realize I won't be afraid to close my eyes tonight.

Waking the next morning, I stretch my arms above my head and then I feel a presence next to me. My heart rate speeds up at the thought of *him* being here in *my* space. Cautiously, I turn my head and when I see the person next to me, instantly I relax. Saint is in bed next to me, sound asleep. He must have come in late and I was sleeping so deeply, I didn't wake. That's something that hasn't happened in a very long time.

He's snoring softly beside me, and I giggle at the cute sound coming from him. He's too adorable when he sleeps.

Softly, I brush the hair away from his face. He makes a noise and then continues his snoring. Holding back a chuckle, I smile as he continues to snore beside me. Reaching over, I grab my phone off the side table but when

I swipe the screen, my smile drops when I see I have a message from my father waiting for me.

DAD

Dinner tonight, don't be late.

ROWAN

Yes, Daddy.

My stomach begins to twist in knots because I know these dinners will be his chance to get to me. To use me. To manipulate me like he always does. Saint assures me that it'll just be dinner, it was part of the agreement they made, but I know my dad, it will not be just dinner.

Saint stirs and pulls me into his side. "Morning, baby," he mumbles sleepily.

"Morning," I reply, snuggling into him. He pulls me into his body, rolls me to my back, and kisses me hungrily.

Groaning, he slides his hand down my thigh, lifts my leg, and reaches around to grab my ass cheek. His fingers dig into my flesh and I moan into the kiss. He shuffles on top of me, cocooning me. His hardening cock presses into my panty-covered pussy. I want him to tear my panties from my body and fuck me hard and fast, but we're at school and that's just weird, plus we'll be late for class.

"Saint, we'll be late for class," I mumble against his lips, but I make no move to push him off me when he grinds into me again.

"Don't care," he growls, echoing my thoughts.

Pushing himself up, he grabs my panties and pulls them down in one swift move. Just as quickly, he removes his pants and briefs and then he slams inside me.

We both moan at the intrusion and then he begins to

fuck me, hard and fast. Just like I wanted. Sooner than I'd like, I'm screaming his name.

"Saint. Oh, fuck, oh, God," I moan. "Saint," I hiss.

My entire body shakes uncontrollably and then with one final thrust, I'm coming. Saint groans and empties himself inside me.

Saint fucks like a machine and I'll never tire of being with him. I've never felt pleasure like this before.

Panting we lie still, savoring the moment. Saint lifts his body so he's not crushing me and stares down at me. "Well, that's one way to wake up."

We both laugh and then he climbs off me. I miss the feel of him immediately, but we need to get going.

Silently, I lie here completely sated and I watch him redress. Then he kisses me quickly and leaves to go and get ready for his day.

Pulling on my uniform, I think about all the sexy ways Saint and I can wake up in the morning, and I'm so glad he made that deal with my dad. Surely, if each day starts like this, it's going to be one hell of a day.

MATTHEW

… three months later

SIPPING my third glass of cognac, I growl when I think of recent events.

Róisín is busting my balls, worrying about things unnecessarily. Everything is running smoothly, no one is suspicious. This school is the perfect cover, no one suspects a thing. It's running so well, I'm even looking into something in Colorado.

Sitting at my desk, I sip my drink, and the anger I feel toward myself slowly ebbs away. I'm pissed off for letting that little punk talk me into letting Rowan move into the dorms because right now I need her. I need my precious girl.

I should have refused.

I should have beat his fucking ass for undermining me.

Then I could have whipped her ass for bringing that little cocksucker into this house.

Downing what's left in my glass, I drop my head back and stare at the ceiling. An image of my precious girl flashes before my eyes and I begin to calm down. Letting the image of her pouty lips come to the forefront of my mind, I let it take control.

Freeing my cock, I begin stroking my length. Thinking about my precious girl and how amazing she is. My strokes become frenzied and before I know it, I spill my seed all over my hand, murmuring her name as I draw it all out.

Then I become angry again because I came too quickly. Far too fucking quickly and it's left me completely unsatisfied.

I need more.

Picking up my phone, I shoot off a message.

MATTHEW

I need to see you, Mr. Vanderbelt.

I make sure not to allude to anything untoward that could come back and bite me in the ass. I wouldn't put it past the little punk to fuck me over, he is a Vanderbelt after all.

A few moments pass before my phone vibrates and when I see it's from him, excitement begins to build.

SAINT

Be there soon

Maybe this won't be so bad after all. I can play both sides now, therefore it's a win/win for me ... as long as the little bitch keeps her mouth closed and *he* keeps up his end of the deal.

Leaning back in my chair, I grin like the Cheshire Cat. This is turning out to be the best deal I've ever made. I am the king; everyone will bow down to me. Then I can finally get the respect I deserve.

SAINT

TONIGHT WITH FUCKFACE was different and I don't know how to process what happened. It's always confusing after I leave, but the events of tonight have left me in a daze.

Before I know it, I'm pulling into my spot at school. I don't even remember the drive from there to here.

Turning the engine off, I stare at the steering wheel and I think back on what just happened …

…As soon as I walk in, I know something is up. Call it a sixth sense and before the door even clicks closed, my thought is

confirmed. "I need more," Ashford commands from behind his desk.

"More, how?" I ask. As my questions passes my lips, he cups his miniscule dick and I know what he wants.

"I need a release."

Staring at the asshole, I swallow deeply and process his words. Can I really do this? "I'm not letting you fuck me."

"I don't want to fuck you, I'm not a faggot," he hisses, "I just need to come."

"What do you want then?"

"I need a visual. I need to ..." He doesn't finish his sentence and it's probably for the best.

"You don't fucking touch me," I tell him. "You lay one finger on me and I will fucking kill you." Without thinking about what I'm doing, I walk up to his desk and pull my dick out, showing him the goods. His eyes widen and the fucker licks his lips. He actually licks his lips.

"Well, show me what you can do?"

My eyes flick to the door behind me but who would be at Fuckface's house at this time of night?

Sensing my hesitation, he walks over to the door, closes it, and flips the lock. Turning around I track his movements, my eyes never leaving him. The air in the room heats. I hate what I'm about to do but I keep telling myself that it's for Rowan.

I'd do anything for my Dove, even this.

He stalks across the room and takes a seat in front of me. Shuffling in the chair to face me, I notice from his seated position, it puts his line of sight right at junk level.

His eyes are locked on my dick, and I notice his fist, clenching and unclenching in his lap. His dick is already hard, reconfirming to me he really is a sick fuck.

"Begin," he commands.

Closing my eyes, I wrap my hand around my dick and begin

to stroke. *My dick is soft and no matter how hard I stroke, it won't harden. I need to get hard; I need this to work. For Rowan. Closing my eyes, I think back to last night with Dove in my room.*

My dick slipping into her.

Her cunt sliding up and down my shaft.

Her perky tits bouncing as she rode me.

The sounds she makes when she comes.

That works and my dick hardens. Not wanting to look at him, I keep my eyes closed and continue to jerk myself to thoughts of Rowan and last night.

The sound of a zipper echoes in the room and my eyes fly open.

Fuckface Ashford has his dick out in his hand and he's jerking himself. His strokes are in sync with mine.

He really is a sick fuck, but I'm doing this for Rowan.

That's what I need to focus on. I keep reminding myself that I'd do anything for her, even pleasure myself for her father.

He comes before me, way too soon if you ask me, but what more would I expect?

"You didn't come," he states, putting his dick away.

"That wasn't a stipulation of our deal. You just said you needed a release. There was no mention of me coming."

"Well, that's not good for me. In the future, you will come too."

"Sure, whatever," I agree, tucking myself away.

My dick has never softened so quickly without coming, and I wonder if I will be able to come next time.

Without uttering another word, I exit his office feeling lower than I ever have before.

How did Rowan cope with this? He didn't physically touch me and I feel disgusted. She's the strongest person I know and to keep her safe, I will do this.

As the memory fades, I dive out of my car and run upstairs to my room. I only just make it to the toilet before I empty my stomach.

Dropping to the floor, I sit here completely dazed and then I see a cum stain on my pants. I thought I was prepared for the beatings and more, but I was wrong, so fucking wrong, but for my dove, I will do this.

The longer I stare at the stain, it starts to feel like it's burning me.

Jumping up, I rip at my clothes, tearing them from my body. Once naked, I turn the water to scaulding hot and enter the shower. I don't even wait for it to heat up before I stand under the spray and begin pumping body wash into my palm. Closing my eyes, I soap up and purge away the memories and everything else. I scrub and I scrub and I scrub, my body red raw.

After my shower, I climb into bed and hide under the covers.

When a knock comes, I hold my breath and wait for them to go away. I know it's my brothers, and it's confirmed when I hear them murmuring on the other side. I expect them to break it down since I've been avoiding them. I'm worried they will know what I've been up to. I'm worried that our triplet connection will come into action and all will be revealed.

This can never come out.

Ever.

I will do my best to hide this secret and take it to my grave. I'll force it down. I'll push it to the dark recesses of my mind so I won't think about it.

My brothers leave and once again, I'm alone. I know I need to see Rowan, I can't avoid her forever and I don't want to. I'm doing this for her, but will she look at me differently now? Will she be disgusted with me? She knows firsthand what goes on behind closed doors with her father.

Now that Rowan is here at school, I grab my phone and text her.

SAINT

Our place when you can.

Sneaking out of my room, I head to our secret spot. This is the one place my brothers won't find me but as soon as I hear footsteps, I flinch and tense up. When I see Rowan appear in the entrance, all the tension leaves my body.

She drops down and takes the spot right next to me. Silently she takes my hand and rests her head on my shoulder. We don't utter a word, but no words are needed. Her being here is all I need, and it reaffirms to me she isn't going to leave me alone to suffer by myself.

"Do you want to talk about it?" she asks, breaking the silence.

Shaking my head, I stare at the wall in front of me. "Nope, I just need you here."

Silence envelopes us again, until she breaks it again. "You know you can talk to me?"

"I know," I tell her but I don't want anyone to know what happens with Fuckface. She doesn't need to hear all of the depraved things her father did to me tonight, she's lived this before and I will never let her feel like this again.

"Saint, you're only in this mess because of me."

"And as I said when I first made the deal, I'm happy to do this because you are out of that house. I'll do anything for you, Dove." And after tonight, I really do mean anything.

Turning my head, I press a kiss to her hair. She lifts her gaze up to mine and when I see her blue eyes staring back at me, my heart breaks as I'm accosted with memories of what went down earlier. My eyes well with tears. How is she still this amazing person after all that she's been through?

She's far stronger than I am.

I'm ready to break and my agreement with Fuckface has only started a few months ago. She whispers, "I love you." Those three words make what I'm doing worth it. For her and her love, I will be strong.

I love her and she loves me, there is nothing I wouldn't do for her, nothing.

ROWAN

… Age seventeen

RESTING my head on Saint's shoulder, we sit here in silence, waiting until he's ready to open up. He never talks about what happens between him and my father. I've tried many times to get him to open up, but he always tells me I don't need to worry but telling someone not to worry only makes them worry more. I've told him on many occasions he doesn't need to do this, that I can just go home but he won't hear of it. *Stubborn asshole.*

So we just sit here in silence and I let him know that I'm here for him.

It's during these silent moments that I wish I was stronger. I wish I could make it all go away for us, but my fear of the unknown always wins out.

"Saint," I murmur. His gaze flicks to mine, the defeat in his eyes is so strong but I know he won't break, he never does. "I love you," I whisper, kissing his neck.

He turns his head staring down at me, lifting his hand he wraps his fingers around the strand of hair hanging by my face.

"And I'll always love you, Dove," he says, it's like he senses my unease that one day he will leave me because of my father.

His phone rings and I know it'll be one of his brothers.

Pulling it out, he looks at the screen and rejects Hendrix's call then shoves his phone back in his pocket.

"He'll keep ringing," I tell him.

He nods, knowing I'm right, and like I predicted, his phone vibrates again. Saint chuckles, shaking his head.

"He's worried about you." I catch my lip between my teeth. Saint follows with his eyes and for the first time today, I see something other than defeat flicker in his gaze. "So am I," I murmur, lifting my hand up to cup his cheek.

"I'm fine, Rowan," he says, tipping his head back to stare up at the ceiling.

My hand drops from his face and lands on his chest, his heart is racing. Sliding my hand down his chest, I thread my fingers through his. Lifting our joined hands to my lips, I press a kiss to his knuckles and then place them in my lap.

His gaze falls to mine, and I see that spark come back

to life in his eyes. He smirks down at me in that sexy way that melts my insides.

He lifts me into his lap so I'm straddling him. He leans forward and tilts his head, brushing his nose with mine.

"I fucking love you, Dove. So fucking much," he chokes out.

Tears fill my eyes hearing the pain in his voice. Wrapping my arms around the back of his neck, I bring him close to me and hold him. He buries his face in my tits and holds on to me with everything he has.

Hearing the hard swallow he takes guts me. I know he's holding back his emotions. He's always trying to be strong. For me. For everyone because that's who he is.

He's my savior.

My knight.

My Saint.

Like I told him, Hendrix keeps calling until he finally gives in and answers.

"Where the fuck are you?" I hear Hendrix bellow down the line at his brother when Saint finally answers.

"Right where I'm meant to be," he replies, winking at me as he says this.

Shaking my head, I try and hold back my smile, but I can't because when I'm with Saint, everything is right in the world.

He listens to Hendrix and nods. "Okay, fine," he hisses. "I'll be there shortly."

Hanging up, he looks to me. "I have to go."

Nodding, I know he's right. As much as it'd be nice to hide out here in our secret room forever, I know we can't.

Lifting myself up from his lap, I offer him my hand. He places his massive paw in mine and closes his fist around mine, enveloping it. He pulls himself up and I stumble due to his grip but like always, he's there to catch me.

Staring into his eyes, I want nothing more than to strip him of his clothes and make love to him, but he needs to go to his brother. I also really need to get some schoolwork done so I guess two birds, one stone.

He presses his lips to mine for a kiss that ends all kisses. I swear, each time is better than the last.

"You need to stop, otherwise, I'm going to throw you down on that mattress and fuck you."

"I'd be okay with that," I tell him, heat blooming in my gaze. "But you need to go to your brother. You know, I'm surprised after all these years your asshole brothers haven't found this place."

"Me too, but what's weirder is, how did we never run into Arlen and Reign when they went to their spot?"

"This school is a big place."

"You know what else is big?"

"Your ego?" I throw back at him.

"I was going to say cock, but I guess ego works too. But you know what else?"

"What?" I almost regret asking that.

"You love my big ego and cock."

"Cock, yes. Ego I can take or leave, but do *you* know what?"

"What?"

"I love you, all of you with my heart and soul."

"Back at ya, Dove. Now, let's go get this shit over with so I can fuck you before bed."

"You are such a sweet-talker," I tease, slapping his chest playfully.

"I know," he cheekily replies.

Placing a quick kiss on the tip of my nose, we exit our safe haven and split up. Him to see his brother's and me to the library to get some homework done.

Quinn joins me in the library and I'm trying my best to read over this book, but I can't focus.

"Are you okay?" Quinn asks when I throw my book onto the table and sigh.

Looking over at her, I nod and force a smile. I know she means well, but I'm not ready to share anything, and I feel like a bitch telling myself that because Quinn is my best friend. We tell each other everything, but this is one secret I will never tell.

Tapping my phone screen, it's still blank. Saint isn't done with Hendrix yet and I wish he was here. He's the one person I can be me, the real me, around. With everyone else they get a fake version. I wish I could talk to Quinn, but every time I go to say the words, 'my father is abusing me' my stomach knots and I become too afraid to say it out loud.

I hate *him* for putting me through this but most of all, I hate that it comes across like I'm protecting him and that I'm forcing Saint to keep my secret.

Our secret.

He's just as much a victim as I am and what makes it worse is that he's sacrificing himself for me. If I'm being completely honest, I think I'm keeping it quiet for my mom too. I don't want to tarnish the Ashford name. I can't do that to her memory, but how much longer can I do this? Maybe with graduation around the corner I can finally be free.

It's only a few more months. I can survive a few more months, right?

SAINT

… Age eighteen

"I CAN'T WAIT for the day my baby is growing inside of you," I whisper into Rowan's ear as we watch Quinn open all her presents and I stress the word all. My niece or nephew is one spoiled kid, and he/she isn't even here yet.

"Not for a long time yet," she tells me, leaning back into me. "I want to do so much before settling down."

"And where do I fit in all of this?" I ask, sliding my arms around her shoulders, resisting the urge to cup her tits since we are at a baby shower.

Looking over her shoulder, she gazes up into my eyes. "You'll be right by my side. Where you go, I go, Saint. You and I are a team and we stick together."

"Team Sowan or would that be Rowaint?"

"Sowaint?"

With her back to my front, I feel her giggle in my arms as we talk about couple names. I'm holding her tightly in my arms and with each chuckle, she relaxes farther into me. It's not often we show affection in public, but in this moment, I just want to hold her close.

It's moments like these I treasure.

It's moments like these when I don't think of *him* and what he's doing to me.

It's just Rowan, me, and our friends.

Do I have days where I regret making my offer to Fuck-face Ashford? Hell-fucking-yes I do, but then Rowan will glance my way and I remember why I made a deal with the devil.

"Where did you go?" she asks, spinning around in my arms.

"Nowhere," I reply, but she gives me that 'don't bull-shit' me look. "Really, I'm fine I just …"

"Got caught up in your head thinking about things that never should happen to anyone our age?"

"Yeah, that." I love how she can read me. How she accepts that sometimes I drift off and need a moment to myself.

Reaching up, she cups my cheek. "He's not here. Don't let him ruin this, now, let's eat some cake and then get out of here."

"What do you have in mind when we get out of here?"

"I was thinking we grab that bottle of chocolate syrup.

Then we head back to your room where I will lick said chocolate syrup off your abs, and then you're going to fuck me until I can't walk. Then we can have a loooong, hot, soapy shower together, followed by hot chocolate with marshmallows and then, you will walk me back to my room and you will kiss me goodnight."

"No sleepover tonight?"

"Not tonight."

"Why not?"

She lifts to her tippy-toes and whispers, "Because tomorrow morning, I'm going to sneak into your room and have you for breakfast ... and since it's still the weekend, I'll have you for breakfast and lunch and afternoon snack and dinner ... maybe even a midnight snack too."

"That's a lot of me to go around."

"Are you not up to the challenge, Vanderbelt?"

"Challenge-fucking-accepted, Ashford. You better bring you 'C' game?"

"I think you mean 'A' game?"

"I was referring to 'C' for cunt but we can always do 'A' for ass?"

"Yeah, no. My ass is a one-way passage and it's staying that way."

"Spoilsport."

"My ass, my choice."

"Hey, you don't have to protest. No means no. Me of all people get that." And I hate that I get the statement.

"Don't go there," she says. "Now, let's celebrate your niece and then we can celebrate."

"Niece?"

"Call it a hunch," she says and with that, we rejoin the party just as Hendrix declares it's time for presents.

"Holy shit," I murmur, "is that a giraffe?"

"Yep," Remy confirms matter-of-factly, smiling like a carnival clown. Only Remington Hearst would get a six-foot giraffe for a baby gift, and only Quinn Ellis would love it.

"Those two are nuts," Rowan says, shaking her head and laughing. The sound is music to my ears, and I can't help but smile and watch her.

"Yep, and my brothers are the crazy ones who love them."

"Sure fucking do," Thatcher agrees, coming to stand next to us.

"You knew about that?" I nod toward the giraffe.

"Yep," he replies, grinning just like Remy.

"You are just as nuts," I tell him.

"Yep." He lets the 'p' pop and I can't help but chuckle.

The rest of the shower flies by and before I know it, Rowan and I are in her room lying on her bed with our legs up, resting against the wall.

"Today was fun," she says, taking my hand in hers and bringing it to her lips.

"It was. I didn't know what to expect for a baby shower. Like I thought you'd need a baby to shower."

"Not you too." Rowan laughs. "Hendrix said the same thing to Rem when she broached the idea of a surprise shower."

"I'll have to tease him about that," I say, making a mental note to remember.

"And then I can tease you about it too." She digs her fingers into my side, tickling me.

Before she can tickle me any further, I roll on top of her. Half covering her body with mine. I stare down into her gorgeous blue eyes. "I can't wait to see your stomach swell as my baby grows inside you."

"As I said earlier today, not for a loooooong time." She reaches up and cups my cheek. "I don't want to have a baby while *he* is alive."

"We could always run away to Australia and live with the pygmies. Then you can be barefoot and pregnant without worry."

"You do know that they have real houses and wear shoes in Australia?"

"I do, yes, but how cool would it be to live among nature? To not need electricity or live by the confines of society."

"As much as that sounds amazing, this girl needs to have access to running water and a hot bath. I'd also like a flushing toilet and a house to protect me from the bugs—"

"I'll protect you," I declare, kissing the tip of her nose. "I'll be your knight in shining armor and protect you from evil."

"You already are, my studly Saint, and you already protect me from evil."

"And I will continue to do so until my last dying breath."

We stare at one another, the air around us beginning to crackle with desire. Want. Need, and everything in between.

"I need you," she whispers.

"You have me," I tell her.

"I know that, but I need you to make love to me, Saint.

Make me forget about all the evil in the world. Make me soar."

Pressing my lips to hers, I kiss her with everything I have.

My tongue slips into her mouth as I slide my hand down her side to her thigh. Slipping my hand under her dress, I skim my fingertips over her thigh and between her legs. Cupping her pussy, I press my palm against her clit, and she moans into my mouth. Running my finger between her folds, the material of her panties dampens and I cannot wait to slide inside her.

Fucking Rowan is like heaven on Earth, and I thank the heavens each time she lets me.

Nudging the material of her panties to the side, I circle her clit with the pad of my thumb. She makes the cutest sound in the back of her throat as she rocks against my hand. Pushing my finger in, her walls hug my digit. Back and forth I press my finger in and out. Thrusting deeper and deeper each time.

"Yes," she pants, and seeing her so carefree is the most beautiful thing in the entire world. "I'm coming," she mewls and then I feel it. Her walls stiffen and then she shudders, riding my hand as she comes.

"So gorgeous," I tell her.

The sound of my voice causes her eyes to open and she smiles up at me. "I need you," she whispers.

"You have me," I tell her. "Always and forever."

Lifting herself up, she straddles my legs and makes quick work of freeing my dick. She takes my shaft in her hand and pumps a few times. Leaning down, she swipes her tongue over the slit and I hiss. Opening her mouth, she hollows her cheeks and sucks. My dick slides to the back of her throat and I see stars as she bobs her head up and down. Sucking and licking me as if I'm a melting popsicle on a hot summer's day.

"Ride me, baby. Ride my dick." I somehow manage to string the words together and she does as I ask. My dick pops out of her mouth, and she shimmies out of her panties. Rising to her knees, she lines my dick up at her entrance and with her eyes locked on mine, she slides down until she's fully seated on me. Gripping my shoulders and without taking her eyes off me, she begins to ride me. Thrusting up to meet her downward thrusts, we fall into sync.

In and out.

Up and down.

Her pussy takes my cock and before long, both of us are moaning. Pleasure builds and builds, like a volcano, my blood simmers. I'm ready to explode.

Everything around me fades away and it's just my dove and me. The building could catch on fire, and I would be oblivious to the flames. Right now, my life begins and ends with Rowan. There is nothing I wouldn't do for this woman, she's it for me. She's the peanut butter to my jelly.

"I love you, Saint," she pants. "So fucking much."

"Me too, baby, me too. You are the air I breathe and without you, I'd suffocate."

"Well lucky for you, I'm not going anywhere."

She rests her forehead against mine. Our breaths mingle together as we rock back and forth. She presses her lips to mine and it lights the fuse. I pump my hips harder and faster and together, we explode.

Calling out each other's names, we ride our orgasms as they shatter through our systems.

Falling to the mattress, she snuggles into my side and

we wrap in each other's arms and blissfully fall asleep … if only we could have stayed in our blissful bubble for two for longer.

MATTHEW

SENDING a text to Saint demanding to see him, I anxiously wait for his reply and like always, I get his standard reply.

SAINT

Be there soon.

A smile appears on my face as I stare down at the reply. I knew he'd obey because he's as obsessed with my precious girl as I am, and he'll do anything for her.

Luckily for me, that includes being at my beck and call twenty-four seven.

While I wait, I pour myself another cognac and it's not long before there's a knock at my door.

Standing up, I place my drink on my desk and rub my cock. It always gets hard at the thought of beating him, it's almost as much of a high as when I take my precious girl. I wonder what the high would be like if I fucked him? Watching him is good but it's always better with someone else.

Before I can think on that, there's another knock.

With a pep in my step, I head down the hallway and answer it. Placing my hand on the knob, I turn it and open the door. Swinging it wide, I'm met with a glaring Saint, and him glaring at me is somehow more of a turn-on than if he was smiling.

"I'm here," he growls.

"A deal's a deal," I nonchalantly reply. I open the door wider and step aside to usher him into my home.

He swallows, takes a deep breath, and steps over the threshold. My dick twitches in my pants when I get a smell of him. It's masculine, it's raw. It's hypnotic.

Not waiting for me, he storms down the hallway and steps into my office … like the good boy he is.

Following behind him, I realize my palms are wet with sweat and my groin is pulsing, just like the first time I had my precious girl.

Entering the room, I give him a curt nod. "Strip," I demand and like the obedient boy he can be, he begins to remove his clothes.

One by one he pulls each item off until he's in nothing but his briefs.

I'm not gay, but even I'll admit the boy's body is something else.

"Take out your cock, boy," I order. My words shock us both, but before he can protest, I speak, "Our deal was you'd do anything to save her and right now, I want your cock out. I want you to pleasure yourself while I watch." He just stands there staring at me. Solid as a statue. My gaze roams over his exquisite body and I lick my lips, but anger builds when he just stands there, not doing as I ask. "I said take your cock out. Show me what you've got."

Dropping onto the edge of my desk, I patiently wait. I see the moment he's decided to do what I want and that's a high I never tire of. The power I lord—ha, lord—over him is hedonistic.

Intently, I watch him do as I ask. Him obeying is the highest of highs and I realize I'm turned on from the power and not from seeing him naked.

He pulls down his briefs and frees his cock. It's soft but impressive. "Get it hard," I demand, and when he lifts his hand and wraps it around his shaft, pleasure thrums through my body.

Sitting here, I lick my lips and watch as he begins to stroke himself.

"Faster," I demand, and wordlessly he follows my orders.

Leaning back on one arm, I watch him and give more orders.

"Faster."

"Slower."

"Squeeze the tip."

Seeing him comply gives me such a rush.

Leaning over, I grab my glass and take a sip. Saint watches my every move, and seeing the look on his face has me closing my eyes and soaking in the power. That's when I realize my own cock is hard. I'm so hard and high from the power I have over him that I need to pleasure myself.

This was never meant to be sexual with him, it was all just a power play but why not.

Waste not, want not.

Two birds, one stone.

Saint swallows and closes his eyes. He fists himself harder and faster but I'm not ready for this to end. "Uh-huh, not too fast," I warn him.

Pushing to my feet, he watches as I move toward him. His gaze falls to my hand, and I see him clench his teeth and hiss when I reach between us. Placing my hand over his, I help stroke him. Getting him right to the edge before I hold his hand at the tip, stopping him.

Smiling down at him, I lean in. "You're going to watch me come, Saint, then you're going to come too," I command.

His throat bobs and he audibly swallows as he looks straight ahead.

Pulling my cock free, I fist myself. Tugging back and forth, I'm so hard, the need to come is fucking strong. "I'm close," I murmur.

Nodding at his cock, I silently tell Saint to continue. With a shaking hand, he begins to stroke himself again.

Gripping his shoulder I hold onto him, my fingers digging into his skin as I come, shooting my load between us. Saint grunts and follows behind me coating his hand with his release.

Smiling, I pat his cheek. "Such a good boy, Saint."

Putting my dick away, I walk back to the desk and grab my drink. Taking a sip, I watch him put his cock away. He turns toward the door, ready to flee, but I shake my head and growl.

"Boy, I ain't done yet," I hiss at him and like the good boy he is, he drops back into the chair and awaits my next command.

SAINT

TONIGHT WAS A LIVING HELL.

A

Living

Hell.

He's never done that before with me and I don't know how I feel.

On autopilot, I drive back to school and before I know it, I'm pulling into my spot. Sitting in my car, I stare up at the cliffs, I can't face anyone right now. I need time to decompress, so when I get back I head to our secret place to hide out.

Dropping down to the mattress, I stare at the wall and play over the events of tonight. It feels like it was a changing point for Fuckface and me, I just hope I'm strong enough when he next summons me.

Then I think of Rowan and what she's been through all these years and push my pity party aside. If she can survive, so can I.

I'm woken a few hours later when a gentle touch traces down my cheek.

Opening my eyes, I see an angel hovering above me.

"Hey," she whispers.

"Hey," I reply back.

"You okay?" she asks.

I nod because I am, I'm okay … now.

"You wanna talk about it?"

Vehemently I shake my head. "Nope. I just want to hold you."

"That sounds perfect."

Wordlessly, she kicks off her shoes and lies down next to me. She snuggles into me, her back to my front. Breathing in deeply, her scent calms me, and I know that with her by my side, we can get through this.

Graduation is only a few months away and as soon as that diploma is in my hand, I'm whisking her away from this godforsaken place and we will never look back. It'll be Rowan and me against the world, and I can't fucking wait to see my dove soar.

ROWAN

LIFE since we got back from our New York trip has been crazy. None of us expected the trip to turn out how it did, but it was certainly eye-opening for all of us, Rian most of all. Looks like he may have found his twin, who he was separated from at birth. Turns out that Lauren, Hudson's sister, attends the same dance school, Stepz, as Risa, Rian's maybe twin sister. We are waiting on the blood test results to confirm it, but considering they look similar, I'm going to bet they are indeed siblings.

Personally, the trip was an emotional roller coaster for me. Saint was pissed at me because I didn't tell my father I was going away for the weekend, and he's worried that at my monthly dinner with him tomorrow night he's going to lose his shit and I'll be in trouble … but what's new when it comes to my relationship with my father?

He seriously is overreacting and him being all growly and protective like he was during the trip, pissed me off. Yes, it's sweet he's worried about me, but I'm a big girl, I can look after myself and due to his overprotectiveness, I didn't enjoy myself as much as I should have.

In fact, I spent the first few hours after we arrived, locked in the bathroom crying because of him and my dad …

… "What do you mean he doesn't know?" Saint hisses at me as I take my seat on the jet that's going to whisk us to New York for the weekend.

"Exactly that. He doesn't know we're going away because I didn't tell him."

"And you think that's wise?"

"Fuck him and fuck you," I snap. "I just want one weekend where I don't think of him and the pain he inflicts on us. I just want one weekend to be a normal eighteen-year-old who's going to New York with her friends to see another friend dance on stage. Then I want to go to a club and dance my little heart out. I think I fucking deserve a break."

I know I'm being unreasonable but I want to just be for once in my life. I shouldn't be taking this out on Saint, but I'm PMSing right now.

"I agree but—"

"Nope, no buts, now sit down and shut up about it, or you can fuck off to the back and sit with Rian."

He stands there, staring down at me. We enter a Mexican

stare-off, neither of us blinking and then he shocks me when he steps back into the aisle and strides down to the back and sits with Rian.

"Fuck you," I whisper-shout.

Leaning my head against the window, I stare out at the tarmac feeling like shit and no longer wanting to go to New York.

The plane touches down, and Saint hasn't uttered a word to me the whole flight. The air around us is tense and everyone seems to be on eggshells around us, and I hate that our tiff is affecting them too.

Standing up, I grab my coat and as I slip my arms into it, I feel him behind me. Being the gentleman he is, he helps me pull it on and rests his hands on my hips, gently squeezing.

Glancing back over my shoulder, I stare at him. "Are you going to apologize?"

"No," he exclaims, dropping his hands from my body.

Immediately, I mourn the loss of his touch, but at the same time, I'm glad because his attitude right now sucks donkey dick.

We may be fighting but I still love him.

With all the shit that's happened in my life, Saint grounds me, even when I'm angry with him.

In a sea of darkness, he's my beacon of light.

My savior.

My Saint.

"Because I think you've made a huge mistake not telling him." Like before takeoff, we stare at one another. "At least send him a text."

"No," I defiantly voice. "And until you apologize for being an overbearing pissbutt, I have nothing to say to you."

"You are being unreasonable, Ro. You know what he's like, and saying pissbutt is still calling me a cunt."

"I know," I growl at him through clenched teeth while also

trying to hide my smile, because pissbutt is a funny word. Even though it's a cleaner way of saying the 'C' word, it somehow makes it crasser. He's silently pleading at me with his eyes, but I don't want to ruin this trip. "Please drop it. I just want one weekend to feel normal."

"I get that, I do, but—"

"I don't want to hear it."

"For fuck's sake, Ro. Just listen."

He tries to reach out for me, but I shake him off, I'm trying to hold back tears right now. I know I'm being irrational, but I just wanted one weekend of freedom.

Wiping at the tear sliding down my cheek, I turn away from him and head toward the exit.

"Come on, baby. Please don't cry." Saint reaches out and takes my hand, gripping it tightly in his. I watch the anguish mar his face and not even Rian shouting, "Hello, New York," can put a smile on either of our faces. Even with the shit going on in his life right now, he's putting it all aside to just have fun. Hell, he invited himself on this trip and he doesn't even like dancing or big cities.

We all climb into the car waiting for us. Normally I'd take the seat next to Saint, but right now, I don't want to be near him so I choose to sit next to Quinn instead. She places her hand in mine, giving it a reassuring squeeze. Smiling over at her, I rest my head on her shoulder and dejectedly sigh.

Quinn is the ultimate bestie because she doesn't ask what's up, she just silently gives me her support and I love her for that.

I can feel his gaze on me the entire trip to the hotel, and when I look up, I start to feel bad but then he mouths "Text me" to me and I'm once again angry with the douchehole.

After weaving our way through New York traffic, we arrive at the hotel, and we all wait in the hotel lobby while Thatcher checks us in. He returns with room keys and hands them all out, and then I realize I'm rooming with Saint. Right now, he's the last person I want to be around and I stand my ground, not moving.

Again, we silently stare, well, I glare because I'm still being unreasonable. Everyone is watching us, and I hate being the center of attention.

"Please just come, Ro," Saint begs and sighs when I don't move. He runs his hand across his face and the need to cry again slams into me. Not wanting to melt down in the lobby, I turn away from him and storm off toward the elevators. Without having to turn around, I know he's behind me.

The elevator doors open just as we arrive and after the people exit, Saint and I step in. He swipes the key for our floor, and without uttering a word to each other, we make our way up to our room. The doors open and Saint slides his hand into mine and I slip my fingers through his. He and I walk to our room and with each step I take, I feel exhaustion kicking in.

Entering the room, he places our bags down and his phone pings with a text. When he scrunches his face up, I know it's from my dad.

"Don't tell him I'm in new York," I say.

"I'm not going to lie to him."

"I never asked you to."

"Yeah, you just did." He stares blankly at me.

"Please don't tell him where I am," I beg again.

"I don't like this."

"Well, I don't like a lot of things and, right now, you're one of them."

Before I say something that I'll regret, I march into the bathroom. Slamming the door behind me, I flip the lock, and slide down to the floor and cry.

Dad isn't even here and he's fucking with my life. Is this how it's going to be next year when I head off to college? Is he still *going to mess with my head? Is he still going to have this hold over me?*

"Why are you crying?" Saint asks, coming over to my bed and sitting next to me.

"'Cause you're still angry at me over New York?"

"I'm not angry, I'm just worried about dinner tomorrow night with your dad."

"You always worry about my monthly dinners with him."

"With good reason because on occasion, he hasn't kept his hands to himself, and you've gotten hurt."

And more I think to myself.

Saint can never know what sometimes happens at dinner because he will kill my father. Yes, I want to see him dead, a thousand times over, but I don't want his blood on Saint's hands. If anyone is to kill him, it's going to be me, but I'm not strong enough to do that because I'm a weak little girl. Just like my dad constantly reminds me.

"I can handle my dad. But you know what will make it all better?"

"What?"

Standing up, I step over to him and slide my arms around his neck and gaze into his blue eyes. "Knowing that you'll be here when I get back."

"You bet your sweet ass I will, and I'm not pissed at you. Get that thought out of your head right now, pretty lady."

"But you were pissed," I throw back at him.

"Yes, I was … and you were too, but somehow, we managed to have a great weekend."

"That we did," I tell him. "I especially like that thing I did with my tongue."

"And I reeeeeeeally liked that thing you did with your tongue, maybe you should refresh my memory about how good it was."

"That can be arranged, but first, you need—" Before I can finish my sentence, Saint tears his shirt off over his head, in that sexy one-handed way, and then drops his pants in one fell swoop. Leaving him in black boxer briefs and nothing else.

Stepping back from him, I trace my finger over his pecs. Pushing him backward, he falls onto the edge of the desk and I kiss him. Pulling me into his chest, he deepens our kiss and lifts me. Wrapping my legs around his waist, he walks over to the bed and sits on the edge with me in his lap.

Pressing on his shoulders, he falls to the mattress and with me still straddling him, he shuffles up the bed and rests his head on my pillow. Resting on my knees, I crawl up his body like a tiger stalking its prey. I reach that sexy as hell 'V' and I lick along the ridge of it and back down again before crossing over to the other side.

Saint reaches over to my nightstand and opens the top drawer. He digs out the syrup and flips the cap open. Squeezing the bottle, he covers his chest with the choco-latey goodness and I lick my lips.

Leaning forward, I run my finger through the syrup and smear it over each indent of his chest. "You have the sexiest chest," I tell him as I begin to lick each muscle clean.

"You have the sexiest mouth and body and mind. You are sexy personified, Rowan Ashford, and you are mine."

"I'm yours," I confirm, "and to show you how much

you mean to me, I'm going to suck your dick until you come down my throat. Then you're going to make love to me, and we are going to fall asleep in each other's arms and tomorrow, there will be no more anger. We will just be Rowan and Saint again. Deal?"

"Deal," he agrees and seals it with a wink.

"I'm not sorry for getting pissed, Saint. But I am sorry we didn't enjoy the trip like we should have."

"I'm not sorry for caring and worrying about you and I ,too, am sorry we didn't have as much fun as we should have. I'll take you back and we can enjoy New York together, just the two of us."

"Sounds like a plan."

He nods, and then says, "Now, less talking. More licking and fucking."

And that's what we do. We stop talking and we suck and fuck the night away but the next day at dinner, Saint was right.

Dad was pissed about New York, and I suffered the consequences of not being honest with him.

MATTHEW

I'M LOSING control and I don't like it. This isn't me, I'm levelheaded. I exercise control in all aspects of my life but right now, I'm angry.

So

fucking

angry.

The anger coursing through me was so ferocious I had to cancel dinner with Rowan and now I won't get an evening alone with my precious girl. That has soured my mood further, but I cannot be around her like this.

I've never felt anger like this before. I knew if we had

dinner together, I'd snap and lose it with her. As much as hurting them brings me joy and gives me a high like never before, I know that in this frame of mind, I'd take it too far. I could never live with myself if I hurt her like that, I never want to see my precious girl in pain because of me.

What's put me in this mood you ask? Well, her to be honest. She's pulling away from me. My precious girl is living her life and leaving me behind. She went to New York this weekend and didn't tell me. Her and my precious boy both went to New York with their friends and neither one of them told me.

I'm losing them. I can feel them pulling away from me and banding together.

I already lost my Vivian, I can't lose them too.

The only good thing to come from losing my wife was my precious girl. I finally got her in the way I'd always wanted. Then a few years later, my precious boy came along and completed me.

Between the two of them, I'm satisfied in a way I didn't realize I needed, and I will not lose them.

I won't survive another loss because I don't have a backup. Once they're gone, I will be all alone. I guess I could always put my hand in the proverbial cookie jar, but I never mix business and pleasure, I am a professional after all.

Needing a fix, I summon my precious boy. He can handle me no matter my mood, and right now, I need to let off some steam.

MATTHEW

My office. Now.

Sitting down in my chair, I wait and I wait.

Just when I give up all hope of my precious boy

coming, he saunters into my office, and just seeing him calms my inner beast and awakens another. "Close the door and remove your shirt," I command and like the good boy he is, he wordlessly does as I ask.

Taking off his shirt, he drapes it over a chair, and I watch as he drops to his knees and takes up his position at my feet.

"You are such a good boy," I tell him.

Running my hand over his shoulders, instant relief courses through me when my skin touches his. That relief intensifies as I dig my fingers into the muscles on his back. Picking up the metal ruler on my desk, I trace the edge of it over the ridges in his back then I pull my hand back and in quick succession, I hit him three times. His tanned skin turns pink, and the blood that was boiling in my veins turns to a gentle simmer. Repeatedly I strike his back and with each lick of the ruler on his skin, I become calmer.

The power I hold over him is like a hit of heroin.

Each lash filters through my system, relaxing me. It weaves its fingers into the deepest parts of me and explodes, giving me a high that's indescribable.

Once his back is red and raw, I wave him off. I got what I needed, and now I will be fine until I see my precious girl later this week.

"Do I need to be worried about that?" Róisín asks, walking into my office. She bends down and picks up the book I knocked off my desk when I was in the middle of my session with my precious boy. She places it down on my desk before taking a seat across from me, eyeing me suspiciously.

"No," I adamantly reply. "That..." I point to the door where my precious boy just left, "...and this"—I flick my finger between she and I—"are separate. Lines will not blur because as I've always said, he is off-limits."

"What about her?"

"She's off-limits too." She eyes me across my desk. This has always been a bone of contention with her. She wants those kids, but myself and Thornton never allowed her to touch a hair on their heads. That's the only thing he and I ever agreed upon. "What do you want, Róisín?"

"I want your head in the game. I want to get back on track."

"So, let's get back in the game? Those two may think they were in charge of this, but you and I both know, without your connections, this would never have run as smoothly as it did. Look what happened when you let *her* run the show? She ended up in jail. Thankfully, the bitch ended herself and our secrets were taken to the grave."

"Yes, let's go with that." She eyes me, and I begin to wonder if she's keeping secrets from me. Before I can probe her, she stands and eyes me across the table. "I'll set things in motion but, Matthew, do not disappoint me. You don't want to see me angry because when my Irish comes out to play, it makes Jeffrey Dahmer, look like a ... saint."

Without uttering another word, she exits my office.

Sitting here, I stare at the closed door and that feeling of unease washes over me again. Things are slowly unraveling before my eyes and I can't stop it. The scariest thing of all is, I don't know what's going to happen.

SAINT

"WE HAVE NEWS," Hendrix announces at the cafeteria a few days after we get back from New York. He's beaming. I don't think I've ever seen my brother smile so brightly.

"I'm going to be a dad," he proudly declares to the group. We all silently stare at him as if he has two heads.

"No shit," Rian scoffs, dropping his gaze to Quinn's bump. "That's old news."

"No, I'm actually the dad," he says again, emphasizing the word 'actually.' And if it's possible, his smile gets bigger.

"Huh?" Rian deadpans. "What do you mean?"

Looking around at everyone, we all have the same blank 'huh' look too.

"Well, Quinn thought someone else was the dad, but I stepped up, 'cause well, she's Quinn and I'm awesome like that." A scoff slips past my lips at my brother's cockiness, but then again, he's a Vanderbelt and we are pretty awesome—see cocky. "I couldn't leave her in the lurch, and so I stepped up, but when we were in New York the other week, she spoke with him."

"The dude who looked like you?" Hudson asks.

I find myself nodding along with Saint because that guy in New York was eerily similar to Hendrix. He's probably a long-lost love child of Dad's, it wouldn't surprise me. Dad keeps flipping us the bird from hell with all the shit we keep discovering, so I wouldn't be surprised. "Well, it turns out he's shooting blanks so that only left me, therefore, I'm officially the daddy, even though I was already the daddy."

Everyone just sits there, blinking at Quinn and him. Each of us processing what he just told us. Thatch is the first to move. He drops his fork, slams the table with his palm, and pushes himself up into a standing position. He walks over to them and pulls Quinn in for a hug. "Congrats, guys. So happy for you both," he says before embracing Hendrix. Then he whispers, "You are going to make an amazing dad, Hendrix."

"And you'll be an amazing uncle," he replies, but I need to put Thatch in his place so I loudly declare, "We *all* will make amazing uncles."

"Hell yeah, we will," Reign shouts before jumping up to embrace the new mom and dad-to-be.

I do the same and then it's the girls' turn. They all gush

over how amazing Hendrix is, and I swear I see his head and ego getting bigger and bigger, but at the same time, I know my brother. He didn't step up for the accolade of doing the right thing, he stepped up because he's a good guy. He's not a complete asshole most of the time, but that aside, I think it's because he and Quinn love each other deeply.

"This calls for a celebration," Thatch declares. He jumps up onto the table and announces to the cafeteria, "Party tonight in the cemetery. We are celebrating Hendrix being a dad and the upcoming arrival of my niece or nephew, Tootsie."

A chorus of cheers and applause echoes around the room.

Looks like we have a party to attend tonight.

ROWAN

QUINN HAS NOT BEEN herself since we got back from New York, and now I know why. *Why didn't she tell me?* I think as Remy, Alani, and I sit around the fire. Quinn's here too, but a moment ago she jumped up to pee, again.

When she returns, she drops down onto the log next to me and rests her head on my shoulder. "So, ummm, question?" I ask.

"Shoot," she says.

"Why did you keep the baby daddy stuff a secret from

me?" I grill Quinn over her keeping the paternity issue from me. Pot, kettle, I know, but I'm keeping my secret for her safety and everyone else's too. Who knows what my father would do if I ever told anyone. Actually, I know exactly what he'd do, he'd kill me.

"I know and I'm sorry." Her eyes well with tears, and now I feel like a bitch because I made a pregnant lady cry.

"Please don't cry because then I'll cry and it'll be a big snot fest."

"You are the only person I would ever want to snot fest with," she blubbers. "Just like you're the only girl I kissed —"

"You kissed me," Remy says, interrupting me.

"So, everyone here has kissed Rowan?" Alani says, her tone soft and kind of hurt.

Both Remy and Quinn nod. Alani looks at me with sad eyes. "What's wrong with me?"

"Nothing," I defend. "You and I have just never been in a position where it happened."

"Or you just find me repulsive." She crosses her arms and sits there scowling. She picks up her drink and takes a sip, and when she places the cup down next to her, I make my move.

Standing up, I walk around the fire over to where she sits. Leaning down, I grab her cheeks in my palms, and I press my lips to hers. My tongue pushes into her mouth and I kiss her with everything I have.

I've shocked her and she's not kissing me back. I'm about to pull away because this is awkward, when she covers my hands with hers and begins to kiss me back. Her tongue tangles with mine, slipping and sliding back and forth.

"What the fuck?" a deep voice bellows, and when I

pull back from kissing Alani, I look over my shoulder and see all the boys standing there, looks of shock all over their faces. Well, not Rian. His are wide and he's grinning like a carnival clown. What is it with guys when girls make out?

"Hey, guys," I nonchalantly say before I drop onto the log and sit next to a stunned Alani.

"Ummm, what was that?" Saint asks.

"Nothing," Alani and I both singsong at the same time. Giggling, we bump shoulders and then I pull her in for a sideways hug.

"So, you always just go around kissing other women?" Saint says, coming to sit next to me.

Lifting my head to look at him, I feel like teasing so I shrug and say, "Sometimes." His eyes widen in shock, and I can't help but giggle. Being a guy, I can only imagine what is running through his mind right now. "Everything all good?"

"Yeah, I'll fill you in later." He leans down and whispers, "That was hot, Dove. But I didn't know you liked girls like that."

"I don't," I tell him. "It was just a kiss between friends."

"So, you kiss all your girlfriends like that."

"I never said girlfriends," I throw back at him, and by the look that crosses his face, I let out a belly laugh. "Oh. My. God, down boy. I was just teasing, but if you must know, my first kiss was with Stacey MacDonald."

"She was my first kiss too," Hendrix says, earning himself a smack in the stomach from Quinn.

"What?" he hisses defensively. "I wasn't your first kiss either so don't get all pissy with me."

"He has a point, Quinn," I tell her. "None of our firsts were with the guys."

"Ummm, mine was," Quinn states.

"Bullshit," Hendrix shouts. "Really? Your first kiss was with me? We didn't hook up till we were what, like fourteen?"

"We aren't all manwhores like you Vanderbelts," she sasses back at him.

"Hey, don't bring us into this," Thatcher defends.

"When and who was your first kiss, babe?" Remy asks Thatch.

"Rhi Marina, age twelve," he says.

"Duuuude," Saint interrupts. "I kissed Rhi when I was ten."

"I wonder what she's up to these days?" Reign asks.

"I wonder if she's still hot?" Hendrix adds, and that comment earns him another smack in the stomach from Quinn, and we all chuckle but Hendrix is right, Rhi is hot.

Not wanting to be left out, Reign adds, "Lana Clarke, age eleven."

"Another hottie," Hendrix says, stepping back and out of hitting range from Quinn, but shocking him, Hudson slaps him up the side of the head.

"Thanks, Hudson," Quinn says with a smile.

Huddy Boy earns himself a glare from Hendrix and then we fall into a conversation of first times including, our first sexual encounter, first time drunk, and first time making it to third base. Obviously, I lie about my first time, but I don't think of *that* as my first. My first was the night that Saint snuck into my room, *that* is a memory that I fondly look back on. I'm glad Saint and I waited till that night. I'm pretty sure everyone thought we'd been doing it for months but sex isn't everything. Plus with what I was hiding, I wasn't ready to go there with anyone. Saint patiently waited for me to be ready and my first time with him was perfect … right up until we got busted.

As far as Lords' parties go, this one was tame. Maybe we are maturing and with the first Lord baby on the way, it's about time we tamed our wild ways … yeah, nah, that will never happen, we will be wild forever.

ROWAN

"HI, DAD," I say when he walks into the kitchen. On the night we have our monthly dinner, I'm required to cook. Dad canceled it last week at the last minute, so it's been a while since I've seen him. When I look up from stirring the spaghetti sauce, my eyes widen.

Dad's angry and I know what's about to happen.

"What's wrong?" I hesitantly ask.

"You went to New York and didn't tell me?" His voice is oddly calm, but his face is red, almost purple, and I see his fists are clenched by his side.

He closes in on me and before I have a chance to move,

his hand lands across my face. The sound of the slap vibrates through the kitchen. Tears stream down my face as he begins to slam things around.

I'm cornered between the counter and him. I have nowhere to run. He snickers and makes his move. He grasps on to my hair, pulling me forward and then pushing me down to the floor at his knees.

"You're a spiteful little bitch, disobeying me like that, Rowan," he hisses, spit flying from his mouth.

He backhands me again and the force knocks me to the floor. Curling into a protective ball, I whimper holding my hand to my face as he begins ranting and raving about Saint being a bad influence. Then he shouts that since being away from home I've become a brat.

"I'm sorry, Daddy," I whisper, trying my best not to agitate him further.

He moves toward me, and I flinch when he reaches out, stroking his thumb across my cheek. "I can't stay mad at you, my precious girl," he says, his tone now soft.

He stares down at me. I have no idea what's going to happen next, but never in a million years would I have guessed that we'd eat.

"Let's eat," he says. Standing up, he stretches his hand out for me to take. Slowly and hesitantly, I place my hand in his and he helps me up to my feet. Once again stroking my cheek.

"Yes, Daddy," I murmur, my face burns but I keep my mouth shut as we eat dinner. I make sure to ask Daddy about work and not mention Saint.

It's late by the time I get back to school so I head to my room instead of Saint's. I need a breather, but I know it won't take him long to come in search of me. He has a sixth sense when it comes to me.

I make sure to cover my face before Saint sees me. I only have a slight bruise, but it's one I don't plan on telling Saint about. I hate that he was right about my father getting angry about New York, and I know if I tell him, he'll only get angry about it. Then he'll go in search of my father, which will only cause more drama, and right now, I don't need or want drama.

Saint doesn't come to my room and I'm kind of relieved, but at the same time I miss him dearly. There have been very few nights I've fallen asleep alone. It isn't until lunchtime that I finally see him. Well, he sees me first, and while I'm in the lunch line, he throws his arm around me, licking a trail up my neck and nibbling on my earlobe.

"Hey, beautiful," he murmurs into my ear, and my body shivers at the timbre of his voice.

"Hey," I reply. Turning my head, I smile at him over my shoulder.

Saint stares down at me with complete adoration, and I have never felt more loved than I do right now. The way he makes me feel is indescribable. My heart beats faster and slower at the same time, and somehow, knowing he'd do anything for me, makes me feel treasured and safe. Even if some days I'm not.

When he looks at me like he is right now, like he would

burn the world down just to save me, that's when I know we are supposed to be.

Saint has always been it for me and I don't see a life without him in it. I know I'm only eighteen, but Saint Vanderbelt is my Prince Charming and nothing can tear us apart.

MATTHEW

"SHIT, SHIT, SHIT," I mumble to myself.

Lacing my fingers together, I place them on my head and press forward, hoping the pressure on my head will fix this. I need and want this new job in Colorado, but I'm close to losing it. They are going to give it to someone else unless I can sway this Davis guy's decision. I have until we meet next week to come up with a plan. I need to come up with an offering that will skyrocket me to the top of the list.

Dropping into my chair, I sigh and look to the ceiling. Sitting back up, I see the photo of Rowan on my shelf, and

I think back to the conversation with Davis while I stare at it ...

... "Who's that?" Davis asks, picking up the frame with a photo of Rowan.

"That's my daughter, Rowan. She's about to graduate from here."

"She's very beautiful," he says, licking his lips. He lifts his gaze back to mine and I see it. He likes her. He wants her.

"Yes, yes, she is. She'd do anything for me," I pause, "anything."

His eyes glimmer at that statement, and I realize that Rowan is my winning move.

"I'd love to meet her and your wife."

"My wife passed away a few years ago."

"I'm sorry for your loss," he replies, and I can tell he doesn't mean it. Most people don't when they offer their condolences. Yes, it's sad she died, but her death also brought Rowan and me closer. Silver lining and all that.

"Thank you. It's just Rowan and me now but we make it work."

"I bet you do," he says. He looks at me and I see it in his eyes. "I bet she'd do anything for her daddy."

"I bet she would too, and if not, I'm sure I can convince her. She'll do anything to please me."

"Maybe you need to bring her to dinner next week. Maybe ..." But he drifts off and doesn't finish that statement.

Davis and I wrap up the meeting and as he's leaving, he shakes my hand and stares intently at me. "I look forward to dinner with you and your daughter next week." He places emphasis on the word daughter, and I know exactly how he feels.

Rowan is special. She's my precious girl and she will do anything for me.

As the memory of earlier fades, the thought of seeing her with him has my dick rock hard.

Standing up, I walk over to the door and flick the lock. Grabbing the photo frame that started all of this, I sit back down, lower my fly, and take my dick out. I'm so worked up that I don't even need to call Saint into my office to help.

His proposition has come in handy but little does the asshole know, I still use my precious girl when I need. Her fear of me keeps her from blabbing, she's just as weak as her mother was.

Wrapping my hand around my shaft, I stare at my beautiful daughter and begin to stroke myself. I slide my hand up and down, squeezing tighter on the downward stroke. With my eyes locked on the photo of my daughter, I bring myself to climax.

Coming all over my hand, I mumble her name as I squeeze every last drop out of me.

Cleaning myself up, I put my dick away and grab my phone to text Rowan.

MATTHEW

Can we meet? I need your help. It's important.

Picking up my things, I head to my first class of the day. Disappointment hits me when she doesn't reply till after school that day.

PRECIOUS GIRL

Sure.

I knew she'd help me. She'll do anything for me. Saint may think he's her number one, but I will always be her first priority. I'm always her first and if I have it my way, I will be her last too. If I get this job, maybe the two of us can start over in Colorado. Leave that Vanderbelt asshole behind and it can go back to being just the two of us again.

As much as I've come to love my moments with him, nothing beats my daughter. She's perfect in every way. Just thinking about her has me hard all over again. Ohh how I wish she still lived at home, but I had to let her go.

Maybe I can get her to come for dinner tonight and that way we can have some fun before she goes back to school. With excitement in my veins, I text her my offer.

MATTHEW

Maybe dinner? Tonight? Just you and me.

PRECIOUS GIRL

Not tonight, I have plans with the girls.

I deflate at her reply, but smile when she makes a counter offer ... even if it's three days away but I guess, that will have to do.

PRECIOUS GIRL

Maybe coffee Saturday morning?

MATTHEW

Fine. Diner in town. 10am. Alone. Don't be late.

PRECIOUS GIRL

Yes, Daddy.

Her reply makes me smile, and I cannot wait for Saturday, but in the meantime, it looks like Saint Vanderbelt has a three-day one-on-one detention.

ROWAN

I'M WAITING outside the diner for Dad. He requested I meet him here alone, said it was important. There was something in the tone of his message that made me agree, and the only reason I did agree was because he suggested a public place. I refuse to be anywhere alone with him if I can help it. If I didn't have to attend our monthly dinners, I would never be alone with him. Hell, if Saint knew what happened at those dinners, he'd kill my father.

The hairs on the back of my neck prickle and when I look up, I see *him* walking toward me. Standing here, I watch my father approach and my heart begins to race the closer he gets.

He kisses me on the cheek when he reaches me, and I manage to hold back my shudder. He escorts me inside, his hand resting on my lower back. My skin burns at his touch, even through my dress.

We take a seat, and the waitress comes up and takes our coffee order.

We silently sit here, not speaking.

The waitress returns with our coffee, and needing to do something with my hands, I hold my mug tightly. "What do you need?" I ask when the silence becomes too much.

Lifting my mug, I sip my coffee—secretly wishing it was tequila.

"Rowan," he says my name with an edge of annoyance, and my hackles raise. "As I said, I need your help."

"Help, right. What do you need?" I ask again.

"I've been offered a position at a prestigious academy in Colorado, but of course, I'm up against a number of applicants. I need you to use your talents to get me the job."

"I'm sorry, what?" I question, confused as to what talents he's referring to, but before he can fill me in, the waitress returns to see if all is okay. Dad snaps that we're fine, his gaze never leaving mine.

"You heard me, Rowan. I need you to use your talents. I need you to whore yourself out to the man so I get the job."

My face heats with embarrassment and a mixture of so many other things. Hurt. Betrayal. Disbelief that my father would even suggest I do this for him.

"You want me to do what?" I hiss as a new feeling, anger, sizzles in my veins.

"Oh, don't act like you don't know how, Rowan. We both know you're perfectly capable of showing him a good time. You've proven that time and time again." He eyes me with that *knowing* look and a hint of a smirk.

Before I can stop them, tears coat my cheeks. "What did I ever do to you?" I softly ask him. After all these years, I ask the one question that has plagued me, but I should have known better, he just scoffs at me.

"Please, Rowan. Now is not the time to get emotional. You just need to do me a favor. It's nothing in the scheme of things."

Him asking this hurts more than any of the other abuse he's laved on me over the years. Shaking my head, I stand up, grab my purse, and begin to walk away.

The sound of my father's voice growling my name stops me in my tracks. Turning to face him, I regret coming when he says, "I'm not asking, I'm telling."

By the time I get back to Crestwood, my face is spotty and I'm a complete mess. I'm surprised I didn't have an accident on the drive back.

Pulling into a spot on campus, I begin to wonder when my father won't have a hold over me because even after everything, I feel more confused than ever. Maybe it's time to expose him. Put it all out there so it's behind me once and for all, but I'm not strong enough to face the truth. If it's just me, him, and Saint who knows, I can cope. The thought of my friends knowing makes me sick, so I push that thought aside.

Readjusting the rearview mirror, I fix my face as best I can, but you can still tell that I'm upset and have been crying. Climbing out, I pray I don't run into anyone, but this is me we're talking about, and I run into the one person who I didn't want to see me like this because when he finds out what just happened, I know he's going to react in a way that could possibly see him wearing orange for the next twenty-five years.

SAINT

I'M GOING to fucking kill Fuckface Ashford.

Trying to use Rowan, again, for his own benefit is the final straw. If it wasn't for the woman currently in my arms, I would have marched over to his house and killed him. Death is too easy for him, he needs to suffer like Rowan and I have. I just need to figure out a way to make that happen without either of us suffering. We've suffered enough.

Rowan cries in my arms while I hold her, I feel completely fucking useless right now. "I've got this, Dove. I'll fix it, I promise."

She sniffs and curls into my side. "But how?" she sobs. "It won't work, no matter what we do he's like Teflon and nothing sticks." Last year, Rowan and I made an anonymous accusation against him to the Dean, but nothing came of it because there was no proof. The whole school was put on alert and told there would be consequences for false accusations. Of course, Fuckface Ashford knew I had something to do with it, and the beating I took reminded me of the night I snuck into Rowan's room, and he beat her because of a negative pregnancy test. I will never forget that day for two reasons. One, it was when I discovered how sick and twisted Fuckface Ashford really was, and two, it was the day we made love for the first time and Rowan officially became mine.

"I *will* fix it," I promise her again, but for the life of me, I don't know how.

Maybe it's time I filled my brothers in. I could use their assistance with this but it's not just my secret, and I know Rowan, she doesn't want anyone to ever find out.

It's just after lunch and Rowan has finally cried herself to sleep. I'm pretty sure she exhausted herself. She's fast asleep and looks peaceful.

Carefully, I slip out of her room, and before I can make my escape unseen, I run into Remy and Alani. "Uh, oh," Remy singsongs, "why does it look like you're off to get in trouble?" She raises an eyebrow.

"I'm not," I protest, but we all know I'm full of shit. "Just do me a favor?" They nod. "Keep an eye on Rowan for me. She's asleep now, but I have something to do, and I don't want her to wake up alone."

"Is she okay?" Alani asks.

Nodding in response, I step around them and then turn

to face them and walk backward. "I'll be back as soon as I can."

Spinning around again, I make my way down the corridor. Remy calls out to me but I'm already halfway down the stairs and I'm on a mission. With a half-assed plan in my head, I keep going because if I stop, she'll ask too many questions. Then she'll tell Thatcher and I can't deal with him, or my brothers, right now.

Jumping into my car, I start the engine and I gun it out of the parking lot and make my way over to Rowan's house.

Banging my fist on the front door, I wait for Fuckface Ashford to answer. The door swings open and he looks at me, eyeing me like I'm a piece of dirt on his boot.

"Well, look who it is. To what do I owe the pleasure," he emphasizes that word and I shudder internally, "of a Vanderbelt being at my door?" His tone is sarcastic, and my hackles rise even further.

"You need to drop the idea of Rowan helping you with that job." He scoffs like the idea is atrocious.

"And why would I do that, Saint? You and I both know the girl has talents … unless you want to take her spot. But I don't think he swings that way, which is a shame because you too have talents, don't you, son?"

"Don't fucking call me son," I spit back at him.

Counting to ten, trying my best not to smash his face in, the longer I stand here, the more I realize my efforts here are futile. He doesn't care about Rowan, never has, why would he start now?

With that realization, I shake my head and sigh in defeat. Turning my back on him, I storm away before I do something that I'll regret. I tried to do this the easy way, I tried to handle it face-to-face but he's left me no choice.

Bringing up Google, I search for the college in Colorado's number. As the phone rings, I realize it's a Saturday but maybe luck will be on my side and someone will answer.

Just as I'm about to give up hope, someone answers.

"All State Prep, Colorado. How may I help you?"

"If you hire Matthew Ashford you'll regret it. Trust me, the man's a deviant sexual predator. You don't want him at your school."

"I'm sorry what?" they reply, confused and taken aback.

"Mr. Ashford is a liability, trust me, if you hire him you'll regret it. Forget you ever heard the name Matthew Ashford. He's a cu—"

"Sir," they interrupt, but having said all that I wanted to, I hang up.

Feeling proud of myself, I sit here knowing my call will have fucked things up for him. A smile appears on my face as I bring up Rowan's name to text her that I'm taking her out this afternoon, but before I can celebrate sabotaging his job prospects, my car door is ripped open, and I look up into the raging eyes of Fuckface Ashford.

Before I can process what's happening, he drags me out of my seat by my shirt and throws me to the driveway. I'm on the ground before I can catch my feet and his boot lands into my side.

Hard.

"You little fucker," he sneers. "I just heard your call, you little prick. We have plans and your call will have fucked us over."

Bending down, he smashes his fist into my face repeatedly. The sound of something cracking causes me to inhale deeply. Blood gushes down my face as he continues to beat me.

He rips me up using my shirt as leverage. He punches my face twice, square in the nose before throwing me to the pavement again. He lays his boot into my side and I'm sure he cracked a rib that time.

Groaning, I try to get up, but he kicks me down again and lays into my side. I hold my arm across my stomach as he continues to kick into my side before I land on my back staring up at the sky. Clenching my teeth, I try to breathe through the pain. My eyelids flutter and I close my eyes, seeing a white light, but my eyes fly open when he grabs my shirt and lifts me up until I'm millimeters from his face.

"If you ever mess with my affairs again, I'll make sure you and that bitch of a daughter of mine are finally taken care of."

With one last shove, he pushes me to the ground, and when his fist connects with my face one final time, my head snaps back, colliding with the driveway, and causing me to lose consciousness for a few seconds.

Gathering all my strength, I sit myself up. Dizziness washes over me as I try to stand. Using the ground, I roll onto all fours and push myself up. My face and body hurt like a motherfucker as I stagger over to my car.

Climbing in, I take a breath and my ribs scream at me in pain. "Fuuuuuck," I grunt out.

Adjusting the rearview mirror, I take a look at my face. Fucking hell, it looks like I went twenty rounds with Mike Tyson. My left eye is starting to swell shut. My nose might not be broken, but there's definitely something wrong.

Turning the key in the ignition, I start my car and get the fuck out of here. Not wanting to hang around in case Fuckface comes back for round two. My vision begins to dot and before I make it back to Crestwood Prep, I have to pull over. Turning the engine off, I lean forward, rest my forehead on the steering wheel, and let the darkness take over.

A tap on my window startles me and when I lift my head, I see a seething and worried Hendrix standing beside my car.

Sitting here, I stare at him and when I don't make a move, he opens the car door and leans on the frame glaring at me. "Care to explain why you look like you just went three rounds with the Hulk?"

"Not particularly," I say. Turning to get out, Hendrix steps back, and when I groan in pain, he helps me. Ripping my bloodied shirt over my head, I stand here, look at my abdomen, and shake my head. Hendrix reaches into my back seat and hands me a hoodie. Pulling it on, I lift the hood up, trying to hide my face as best I can.

Hendrix grips my arm. "Saint, man, what the fuck! Talk to me?"

"I've got it handled, okay?"

He stares at me incredulously and shakes his head. Without saying anything else, he walks back to his car and takes off like an extra from *The Fast and the Furious*.

Sighing, I lean against the side of my car. Dropping my head back, I stare up at the cloudless blue sky. Yes, I fixed the Rowan helping her dad situation, just like I told her I would, but at the same time, I think I made things worse for me but I'm okay with that.

I'll always fix things for her, even if it costs me something in return and today, I did just that. In all the years I've been protecting Rowan, he's never beaten me like this. Today I hurt his ego and he's going to want payback but at the end of the day, Rowan is safe and that's all that matters.

ROWAN

PLACING my head on Saint's shoulder, we sit in silence in our secret place. Lifting my head, I look up at his face and the anger I had pushed down thrums back to life.

I'm so angry at him for being so stupid.

"Don't, Rowan." He sighs, clearly sensing my anger.

"Don't you don't me, Saint Vanderbelt," I snap, my tone giving way to how pissed I am. "I can't believe you were stupid enough to confront him like that. You cost him the job. He's going to want retribution."

He points to his face and body, "Ret … retribution received."

Shaking my head, I sigh deeply and gently run my finger across his cheek. His jaw ticks and his gaze flicks to mine.

"There was no fucking way you were going to whore yourself out, Rowan. No fucking chance."

"I would have fixed it myself," I tell him. "You can't rescue me and save me from everything my father does."

"I can and I will."

"Saint," I beg but he presses his finger to my lips.

"I got it handled for you, okay? It's what I do, I fix things for you, Dove. Never forget that."

Placing his hand behind my neck, he pulls me forward and presses a soft kiss on my lips. He closes his eyes and rests his forehead against mine.

"I know you do, and I appreciate *everything* you do. I just don't want you to get hurt in the process."

"I'm fine, don't worry about me." He sighs and we fall silent. The silence is broken when his phone vibrates. Without looking at the screen, he hits the side button to ignore it. It begins to vibrate again. Turning it over, I see Hendrix's name and, once again, he declines the call. He does this again and again, but his brother is just as stubborn as him and he will keep calling until he answers.

"He'll keep ringing," I tell him.

"I know," he replies, just as it starts ringing again.

"For fuck's sake," I sneer. Snatching up his phone, I answer, "Hello?"

"Where are you?" he snaps down the line.

"I'm well, Hendrix, thanks for asking," I snippily reply and from next to me, Saint snickers.

"Sorry," he says, "can you bring my dickhead of a brother to his room ... please?"

Looking to Saint, he nods. "Can do, we'll be there soon."

Hanging up, I pocket his phone. "Guess we better go so you can face the music."

Saint nods and stands up, wincing as he straightens out. Offering me his hand, he helps me up but before we leave, he grips my cheeks in his palms. "Don't for one second think I won't do whatever it takes to keep you safe. I'll do anything Rowan, any-fucking-thing, understand?" My eyes well with tears and I nod. I know he means that because he's my Saint, my protector, but as I look at his bruised and swollen face, I wonder, who will protect him?

He places a kiss on the tip of my nose and then we sneak out from our hiding place, ready to face everyone.

"What the fuck?" An angry shout comes from in front of us.

Looking up, I see Thatcher marching toward us. He's practically dragging a fumbling Remy behind him, she can hardly keep up. When he reaches us, he drops her hand to grab Saint's face. Turning it side to side, he inspects it thoroughly before gripping Saint's chin between his thumb and forefinger, he growls, "What the fuck happened?"

"Nothing," Saint sneers before he rips his face free from Thatcher's hold.

"Bull-fucking-shit, asshole, your face looks like you went five rounds with Mike-fucking-Tyson," Thatcher snaps, anger is pouring out of him. I've never seen him this angry before.

"I got jumped, okay? I'm fine." Saint just lied to his brother … for me.

"Jumped, where?" Thatcher demands.

"Thatch, I'm fine. Don't worry about it, okay?" Saint pleads, he steps toward me and places his arm around my shoulder. "Rowan patched me up. Nothing is broken." Thatcher eyes him, not believing a word he says. "Dude, really, I'm fine. Really."

Thatcher sighs and shakes his head. He knows Saint won't talk unless he wants to and surprising the hell out of me, he drops it. "Fine, but take it fucking easy."

Without another word, he grabs Remy's hand and drags her behind him. She gives me a wave and a doubtful smile, and we watch as they head into Thatch's room.

When they are out of sight, we hurry toward Saint's room, but just before we open the door, Reign and Hendrix corner us. "For fuck's sake, Saint." Reign shakes his head and then does the same as Thatcher just did and grabs Saint's face, inspecting it. "Tell me what the fuck happened?" he growls.

"I'm fine," Saint says with a sigh. "Really, I am, I just got jumped," Saint snaps at his brother.

"Okay, chill ,man. We're just worried," Hendrix states, dropping his hand from Saint's face. While they were arguing, I grabbed his keys and unlock the door. The two of them follow me in. Reign gives me a worried look, one I'm sure I share, but we are worried for two different reasons. His is out of concern for his brother, whereas mine is for us and the need to keep our secrets secret. Maybe it's time for him to confide in his brothers? This secret is coming between them and I don't want to be the cause of that. Saint has already sacrificed so much for me, I won't have his relationship with his brothers on the line because of me.

"I'll look after him," I reassure Reign and that seems to appease him because he just nods and then storms out, slamming the door behind him.

Saint lies down on his bed, stretching his legs out, wincing as he does so. My dad really did a number on him and as someone who has been on the receiving end of a beating like this, I know how he feels.

Not wanting anyone to come barging in, I lock the door and lean against the wood. Then an idea hits me. "Be right back," I shout, and before he can say anything, I race to Rem's room and text her along the way.

She tells me where what I want is and tells me to have fun.

Finding what I came for, I grab it and head back to Saint's room. Nerves filter through my body when I step back into his room. Locking the door behind me, I ignore Saint and make my way into his bathroom. I can feel Saint's eyes on me and before I close the door, I see him staring at me curiously.

Within a few minutes, I've changed and I'm ready to go back out there. Staring at my reflection, I take a deep breath and then open the door and lean against the doorframe.

Saint's head is down and he's staring at his phone. Clearing my throat, I wait but when he doesn't look at me, I whisper his name. Finally, he looks up and his eyes pop open when he sees my sexy nurse outfit.

"Holy fuck, Dove." He adjusts himself as I make my way toward him.

Swaying my hips with each step I take, I stop by his

bed. Squishing my boobs together, I lean over him and seductively purr, "I'm your nurse."

"You are, are you? And what are you going to do?" He smirks up at me and all the fear I had before doing this vanishes. No longer is fear running through my veins, desire and wanton need for Saint is.

"I'm going to nurse you back to health," I tell him as I unzip his trousers.

"Yeah." He breathes deeply. He lifts his ass up so I can slide them down his legs. I haven't even touched him and his dick is already at half-mast. "What are you going to do?"

Taking his dick in my hand, I begin to pump. "I'm going to make you feel all better."

Before he can reply, I close my lips around the head of his cock and suck. Hollowing my cheeks, I take his shaft deep into my mouth, gagging a little.

Saint groans and hisses, "Fuck, baby."

Moving my tongue around the length of him I suck again, earning myself another grunt as he hits the back of my throat. His hands fist my hair as I pull back and slide my tongue along his cock. Licking back up to the tip, I open and suck again.

My head bobs up and down and his drops back, he closes his eyes as I take him deeper and deeper with each suck.

"Fuuuuuck," he growls, pumping his hips and fucking my face. I continue to blow him, using my tongue around the tip as I lick and suck him like a lollipop.

Saint grips my hair and curses, I feel his dick twitch in my mouth. "Fuck, fucking hell." He pants as warm cum spurts all over my tongue. I swallow every last drop down. His dick pops free of my mouth and I wipe at the corner, sucking my finger seductively as I stand back up.

"I think I'll need at least five more doses, Nurse, before I'm feeling better." He smiles up at me.

Placing one knee on the bed, I throw my leg over and I crawl up his body. "Is that so?" I question.

Nodding his head, I straddle his waist and lean down to kiss him. He grips my hips and then spins us, forcing me under him. He winces in pain at the sudden movements, but lust has overtaken him. He strips me of my nurse's outfit and gives me some medicine.

For the rest of the afternoon, we drive each other wild and administer several orgasms to each other before I blissfully fall asleep in his arms.

SAINT

... a few weeks later

MY BROTHERS and I are laughing while Mom just shakes her head, but she can't help the smile that creeps over her face. We may bullshit a lot and rule Crestwood Prep with an iron fist, but at the end of the day, we are mommy's boys. When she calls, we come running for dinner. She loves having us all together, and ever since Dad was murdered there has been a lot more laughter in this house. None of us dread coming to visit anymore, but most of all, Mom is happy again.

Thatcher is telling some cockamamie story about a dream he had. It's so in-depth and detailed that I'm calling bullshit. I'm so caught up in it I almost don't feel my phone vibrate in my pocket.

Lifting my ass cheek up a little, I dig into my pocket and slowly pull it out. I look down at the text and sigh.

FUCKFACE ASHFORD

Come over.

Now.

A groan slips free and Hendrix eyes me, giving me a funny look, but I pocket my phone and stand. "I need to go."

"Already?" Mom says with a sigh.

"Sorry, Mom, I'll make it up to you next week." Walking over to her, I kiss the top of her head before I turn and leave.

"Wait up?" Hendrix shouts just as I open the front door. He gives me a similar look to when I groaned earlier but this time, it's accompanied by a rub of his hand across his jaw.

"What the fuck is up with you?" he asks, placing his hand on the front door and closing it again.

Turning to look at him, he eyes me and I just shrug. He shakes his head but steps back, allowing me to leave. I'm halfway to my car when the door opens and he calls my name out again.

Waving at him over my shoulder, I don't turn around, I just climb into my car and grip the steering wheel. Clenching my teeth, I inhale deeply. Once I feel calm, I push the button and start the engine. Before I can pop it into gear and drive off another text comes through.

Pulling my phone out, I swipe the screen and when I see *his* name, the anger that just dissipated reappears with a vengeance.

FUCKFACE ASHFORD

Don't make me wait, Saint.

"Fucker," I growl and flip my phone off.

Dropping my car into gear, I spin the wheels and speed off, leaving Hendrix behind me with a concerned look on his face. Maybe once and for all, it's time I confide in my brothers. I could really use their brains, but I know my brothers, they will get angry and make the situation worse.

So for now, I'll keep my mouth shut and keep doing what I do. I'll protect Rowan from her slimeball father.

I'm doing this for Rowan, I repeat to myself over and over again. Those five words are always on repeat inside my head when I'm with *him.*

"You said you'd do anything to protect her, correct?" he asks me and today, it feels like he's in my head. If only he knew what I was really thinking.

Sliding his finger down my cheek, I nod because I can't speak around the lump in my throat.

Closing my eyes, I think of Rowan. I think of why I'm doing this. It's not often that he physically touches me— not wanting to be gay and all that—but when he does, it takes all my might not to flinch and punch the cunt in the face.

"Mmmmmhhhmm," he mewls, blowing his heated breath on my face.

He runs his hand over my arm and down my chest. Ever so gently, he brushes his fingers against my cock. Bile rises in my throat, but I don't flinch. I don't show emotion. I don't give him anything because that's what he wants.

Like a statue, I sit still and stare at the books on the shelf behind his desk.

"You're such a good boy, aren't you, Saint?" Fuckface Ashford murmurs, rubbing his hand over me again, harder this time. Dropping to his knees next to me, he stares at my flaccid dick. My cock doesn't flinch, but he keeps trying. When I still don't harden, he growls, "Take out your cock, Saint."

Swallowing, I let out a breath then slowly remove my cock. "Touch yourself," he demands, licking his lips. This time is so much worse because he's right there. When he's on the other side of the room, I can compartmentalize but not this time.

With the way he's gagging over my dick, you'd think he's gay. He says he's not into guys, but this is pretty gay if you ask me. Him wanting to see my cock. Thank fuck he never wants me to touch his pin dick because I don't know if I'd have the restraint to not rip it off and shove it down his throat.

Wrapping my hand around my cock I begin to stroke, moving up and down, thinking of anything but where I am right now.

My cock doesn't get hard, in fact, I swear it shrivels inside my body, trying its best to get away from Fuckface Ashford.

He places his hand over mine, helping to move it up and down. Closing my eyes, I think of Rowan. My dove.

My everything, and my dick begins to grow in our hands. Fuckface Ashford whispers, "Such a good boy, Saint. Such a good boy."

Hearing his zipper, I know he's pulling his own dick out. The sound of his grunts echoes around his office as he begins to stroke himself.

"Eyes open," he snaps.

Forcing my lids open, I stare ahead into space. Doing my best to focus on coming. Knowing if I don't, he'll beat me for disobeying him. His hand tightens around mine, and I make a noise in the back of my throat as an image of Rowan riding me flashes in my mind. It's the vision I need and a few seconds later, I grunt as I come all over our hands. Seeing my release sets him off and he follows. He continues to stroke me while he comes all over himself.

He lets go of my hand and runs his fingers across my cheek. "I think I'm going to enjoy breaking you, Saint."

Pulling his handkerchief from his pocket, he cleans himself up, then rises to his feet, readjusts his cock, and puts it away. I let out the breath that I was holding and take the opportunity to do the same but before I can stand up, he grabs my chin with his fingers. Leaning down, I can feel his heated breath on my neck and I shudder in disgust. "I so enjoy our time together, Saint." He lets me go and stands upright, staring down at me, he smirks. "Until next time, my sweet boy."

He walks out of his office, leaving me sitting here alone. I don't know how long I sit here but all of a sudden, I jump up and get the fuck out of there.

ROWAN

HE SHOULD BE BACK by now, dinner at his mom's never goes on this long. I pace back and forth in my room and I'm mid-step when it hits me, he's been summoned.

In the last few weeks, Dad seems unhinged, and if Saint knew what happens at dinner sometimes, he'd kill him. I wish I was strong enough to do it myself but I'm not.

Chewing on my nails, I stare at the door willing for Saint to step through when suddenly, the door flies open and Saint waltzes in. A look of unease is etched on his beautiful face and sadness washes over me.

Why does this have to happen to us?

As I stare at him, a vacant look in his eyes, I know I can't keep this secret. I have to tell him what's been going on so we can come up with a plan to end this.

Taking a deep breath, I blurt it out before I can change my mind, "Dad's still abusing me."

"He fucking what?" Saint screams, causing my entire body to twitch in fear. I've never heard him yell like this before, and I've seen him in Lord mode with freshmen who step out of line. He senses my unease and pauses. Dropping to his knees before me, he takes my hands in his and squeezes. "Shit, Dove, I'm sorry."

He shakes his head and stares up at me, smiling, but it doesn't reach his eyes. Closing his eyes, he takes a couple of deep breaths to calm himself. He opens them and I hate the look on his face, but most of all, I hate that I put it there. "Why didn't you tell me?"

Shrugging, I lower my head in embarrassment and stare at our clasped hands in my lap, but I do know why. It's because he's sacrificing himself for me and my safety, but my dad still abuses me anyway. He's a master manipulator and he knows how to control me better than anyone. I'm weak, just like Dad says.

"Rowan, look at me," he demands.

Lifting my gaze, I meet his and we silently stare at one another. "Are you telling me that he's still been touching you? That this entire fucking time, what I was trying to stop has still been happening even after we made a deal?"

My mouth opens and closes, but nothing comes out so I just nod. His face fills with anger and I whisper his name.

He growls and not in that sexy way I love, he growls in a pissed-off 'I want to kill someone' kind of way. "I'm going to fucking kill him," he sneers.

Pushing himself up to his feet, he turns and storms away from me. He opens the door but before he can step out, I jump off the bed and chase after him. Reaching out, I grip his arm and with a might I didn't know I possessed, I pull. Forcing his body to slam back into mine. The inertia sends me backward but before I fall to my ass, he reaches out and steadies me.

Pulling me into him, he grips my face in his hands and rests his forehead against mine. I can sense he's about to break down, so I pull us back into the room and close the door.

Silently and wordlessly, he follows and just as the door clicks closed, he drops to his knees and lets out a sob. Falling to mine before him, I pull him into my arms and hold onto him and he crumbles apart in my arms. All I can do is hold on to the man who sacrificed everything for me. I grip tightly on to the man who made a deal with the devil, only for the devil to screw him over.

In this moment, I don't know who I hate more; Dad for doing this to us or me for not being strong enough to fight him.

"I'm sorry," I whisper.

"I'm fucking sorry too, I failed you."

Shaking my head, I hold on to him tighter.

Lifting my arms, I wrap them around his neck and into his ear, with a subdued tone I tell him exactly how I feel. "You did not fail me, Saint Vanderbelt. You saved me. You save me each and every day. If I was still living in that house with that monster, I … I wouldn't be here in your arms now." My voice breaks. "You saved me."

Pulling me onto his lap, he holds me, and I keep whispering 'you saved me' over and over and over as tears streak down both our faces.

Saint lets out a huge breath, doing his best to regain his emotions.

"He still hurt you," he says, holding me to his chest. "He was supposed to stop."

Moving back, I reach up and cup his cheek. His eyes focus on mine briefly before his lips descend on mine. Curling his hand around the back of my neck, he pulls me into his chest and shows me with his lips and tongue how much he loves and cares for me. His tongue tangles with mine and what started as a soft and sensual kiss turns hurried and frenzied.

"Me and you, Dove," he murmurs against my lips. "Me and you."

"Me and you," I repeat. Then I utter the words that up until this point, I have never been strong enough to voice, "It's time to go to the police."

He stares at me and nods, then with a strength that amazes me, he lifts me up and carries me to the bed. Gently laying me down, he cocoons my body and starts to kiss me again. We kiss until I'm moaning under him. Our hands gently caress one another. With each swipe of his hand, he removes *his* touch. With each lick of his tongue, he brings me back to life. Being with him makes me forget all the bad things.

Saint makes me feel.

"Make love to me, please," I plead.

Lifting off me, he stares down at me and under his heated gaze I feel loved, cherished, and safe. And I know that he and I will survive this because we have each other.

"Anything for you, Dove. Anything."

Pushing himself up to his knees, he removes his shirt in that sexy one hand behind the neck way and drops it to the floor. "Take off your dress," he commands, and the tone of his voice has my body buzzing.

Doing as he asks, I remove my dress, awkwardly because it's hard to do so when a half-naked Adonis like Saint is between my thighs. Lying back down in my bra and panties, I stare up at him. Without uttering a word, his fingers grip my thighs and spread them apart. He stares down at my panty-covered pussy and then he tears them from my body, the cotton disintegrates between his fingers as he pulls the material from me. He leans forward and latches on to my nipple through my bra. Gently biting down, it causes a shockwave to spear from my chest to my clit. Kissing up my chest, he nibbles along my jaw before taking my lips again.

With his lips locked on mine, he pulls his pants down and frees his cock. With a flick of his hips, he slowly pushes inside me. His nostrils flare as he joins us together. My pussy hugs his dick and it's exquisite.

Reaching up, he cups my face as he fills me completely. "Mine," he hisses through clenched teeth when he's fully seated inside me.

He begins to move back and forth. He thrusts in and out and it's perfect in every way. He grabs my waist and gently grips my skin, his finger digging in as he increases his movements.

I let out a soft moan as pleasure builds in my system.

Saint drags in a deep breath, hitting deeper and deeper each time. Our bodies become one as we rock back and forth.

"Please," I whimper.

We move together as one as Saint makes love to me.

"Fuck," he groans. "You feel so good, Dove." As if he can read my body, he hisses, "Let go, Dove. Let go."

And let go I do.

My body tenses and I give myself over to my release.

Moments later, Saint follows. We each groan into our kiss as we ride out the ecstasy of our releases.

Saint dips his head, brushing his nose against mine. "I fucking love you, Dove."

Kissing me one last time, he rolls off me and positions himself next to me. Resting his head in the crook of my neck, we lie together, just feeling.

Saint trails his fingertips across my belly. Back and forth he traces circles over my skin.

Turning his head, he kisses my neck, sighing, and before he says it, I know what he's going to say. "It's time, baby. We need to."

Meeting his gaze, I nod.

My father deserves to be in prison and the time has come for me, for us, to make that happen.

Saint hands me his phone. Sitting up and with shaking hands, I dial 911. As it rings, I take a deep breath, preparing myself but as soon as the operator speaks, I hang up.

Throwing the phone between us, tears well in my eyes and I drop my gaze to my lap.

Saint grabs my hand and squeezes in that Saint way. "Hey," he says, forcing me to look at him.

"I … I can't," I cry.

My lip trembles as tears begin to cover my cheeks.

"Shhhh, I got you. I've always got you." Saint kisses my head as he holds me to his chest. Once again rescuing me.

SAINT

ROWAN CRIED herself to sleep last night. Prior to that, she kept apologizing for being weak. For not being enough and no matter how much I reassured her that she's strong and amazing and everything to me, nothing calmed her down.

Slipping out of her room, I head back to mine. After all the revelations the previous night, I need some alone time.

Entering my room, I flop down onto the bed and stare up at the ceiling, silently fuming. I can't fucking believe he's been touching her this entire fucking time. I'm going to kill him and take pleasure in destroying him.

Pushing myself up, I walk over to the wall and slam my fist into it. It punctures right through the drywall. Blood coats my hand as I pull it back through, I grimace at the slight sting but welcome the pain.

Turning around, I slide down the wall and I break apart. For the first time since making the deal that still screwed her over, I feel fucking helpless. Hanging my head in my hands, I let everything out. I blow out a breath when I realize I failed, I failed Rowan, I thought I was protecting her, but in reality she was never safe, not from him.

My deal was supposed to save her but it didn't. He still did those things to her. *Fucking cunt.*

After wrapping my hand, I hide out in my room and drink a third of a bottle of tequila. Hoping it will help ease the pain of my failure. FYI, it doesn't. All it did was give me a tequila headache and a dry mouth. And in the light of the new day, my tequila stomach is trying to force its way out.

Feeling groggy and exhausted, I push myself up and climb into the shower. Once I'm dressed, I leave my room because I'm not a coward who hides. I've had my pity moment, now it's time to face my failures.

Managing not to vomit, I slowly walk toward my first class.

Everyone is steering clear of me this morning. I'm guessing I look like shit and when I catch my reflection in the glass on the trophy case, I realize why, I look like a swamp monster.

"Fucking hell, man. You okay?" Lennon asks, bumping my shoulder.

Shoving him aside, he slams into the wall from the force of my shove. A grunt escapes him and he grumbles about me being a 'fucker' but I ignore him and continue walking the halls toward my class.

Rowan stops up ahead and she spots me. She lifts her hand in a small wave. Lifting my lip in a half smile, I stride right past her, causing her to frown.

Without even turning back, I know she's following me. She has to run to keep up. Eventually, she calls out, "Saint," and her soft fingers wrap around my elbow, forcing me to stop.

I'm still angry and I don't turn to face her.

She steps around me and stares at me. In the middle of the hall, we stand here, silently staring at one another while everyone hurries past us. I stand here and gaze at the one woman who's owned my heart for as long as I can remember.

"Are you okay?" she asks.

"Just peachy," I slur and squint when I hear my voice, guess I'm still a little drunk.

"Saint, talk to me," Rowan whispers.

"He promised me if I …" I swallow and drop my gaze from hers for a moment but, Rowan being Rowan, doesn't give up. She grips my chin between her thumb and fore-finger and lifts my gaze to hers.

"Talk to me, Saint. Please."

"He was never supposed to touch you. That was our deal and he fucking broke it."

A tear slides down her cheek, but she bats it away.

"I'm sorry," she mumbles.

"Don't you dare apologize for him. This isn't on you." Shaking my head, I swipe my face aggressively before I walk away, leaving the one woman I never thought I'd walk away from alone because with how angry I am right now, I don't want to take it out on her.

"Are you drunk during the day?" Reign questions as he takes a seat beside me in the common room.

Everyone's been too afraid to approach me, but of course my brother doesn't care. Raising the tequila bottle toward him in a silent cheers, I confirm his question before I lift the bottle to my lips.

Opening my mouth, I take a huge gulp of the clear liquor before letting it slip back into my lap.

"Talk to me, bro," he says, patting my leg. I look down at his hand and use the bottle to shove it away.

Staring ahead, I continue to ignore my brother and drink my tequila. Finally taking the hint, Reign stands up but before he leaves, he pats my shoulder. Without another word, he leaves me alone with my tequila and my murderous rage.

My phone vibrates, pulling it out, I see *his* name on the screen. I don't bother even looking at what he wrote, I just type out my own message.

SAINT

Go fuck yourself, asshole.

My phone vibrates again but again, I don't read his reply.

Right now, I don't care about him or anything. I just want to be left alone to drink my tequila and wallow in self-pity because, at the end of the day, Rowan needed me and I failed her.

I couldn't save her, fuck, I couldn't even safe myself.

My last thought before I pass out is that maybe she's better off without me because, no doubt, I will just let her down… again.

Someone is shaking me, and I wake with a jolt. Blinking a couple of times, the room comes back into focus and I see Hendrix glaring down at me.

"Fucks offd," I mumble and stand up, shoving him aside. I do my best to storm away but my feet are a little unstable so it takes me a few tries before I get my feet to cooperate.

"Fucking hell, Saint." Hendrix growls my name like I'm five and I took his G.I. Joe action figure. He grabs for me, but I pull away from his grasp and stumble. Gaining my footing again, I start to walk—stagger—away from him. The room is slightly spinning, and my stomach is churning.

"Saint," he growls again and the sound of his voice grates through my tequila fuzzy brain.

"Just leaves me alones," I snap. "Nothing goods comesd from beingd neard mes." My words cause Hendrix to stop in front of me. Somehow, I manage to side step him without banging into him and continue on to my room.

With each step, I try my best not to bring the tequila back up.

My stomach stirs and I'm almost certain it's about to make its debut, but I manage to swallow it back down. My vision is really blurry now and that slight spin has increased to a F5 tornado kind of spin.

When I look up again, I'm standing at my door, "Howds I getz hered?" I mumble to myself.

Rummaging in my pocket, I find my keys and with a concentrated effort, I slide the key into the barrel and unlock the door. Pushing it open, I come face-to-face with Thatcher. Even in my drunken fog, I can see his furious glare staring daggers at me. It's enough for me to halt my steps.

"Whatsch yous wantsd?"

He shakes his head and hisses, "Whatever the fuck is going on with you, drop it. Pull your head out of your ass and talk to us. Don't fucking push us away."

Ignoring his ass, I step around him and head for my bathroom. Stripping my clothes off as I go.

"Saint," he shouts.

Looking at him over my shoulder, I slur, "Unlessed yous wantsd see'd my cock, fuckd offs."

He just stands there and shakes his head. Flipping him the bird, I slam the bathroom door shut in his glowering face.

Fuck them all. I'll deal with shit my own way.

ROWAN

I'VE BEEN CRYING all day over Saint. He was so cold toward me earlier. He's never been like that with me before, hell, he's even being an asshole to his brothers. If they can't get through to him, no one can.

Knocking softly on his door, I wait but begin to think that he's most likely passed out and won't hear me, no matter how hard I knock. Thatcher caught me up on everything that went down, but I can't leave him alone. It's my fault he's been drinking since yesterday, therefore, I should be the one to help him, like he's helped me so many times over the years.

After knocking for the tenth time, still with no answer, I slip the note I wrote under the door.

A letter is so fifth grade, but I need him to know how grateful for him I am. How grateful I am for what he's done for me. I need him to know that I just need him. That we are better together.

Brushing my hand across my tear-stricken face, I head back toward the stairs and make my way down to my room.

I'm almost at my room when I make a decision, and this time, I'm going to stick to it. I need to turn him in. My father, Matthew Ashford, deserves to be punished for what he's done to me. To Saint. And Mom.

It's time.

I'm finally going to stand up for myself.

I'm a nervous wreck but at the same time, a sense of euphoria washes over me at making my decision. I'm almost to my room so I dig my key out. I need to grab my things so I can head to the station, but before I get to my room, a firm hand grips me from behind.

Without turning around, I know it's *him*.

"Rowan." My father growls my name, and from the timbre of the one word, I know he's not in a good mood.

"Dad," I choke on the word as he spins me to face him. He huffs at me like he's disappointed. *Surely, he doesn't know what I just decided?*

"I thought better of you, my precious girl." With my wrist still in his grasp, I'm trapped. He brushes his thumb over the apple of my cheek. If any other father did it to their daughter, it would be a lovely gesture filled with love and admiration, but coming from my dad, it's anything but.

He snatches my keys from my hand and uses them to open my door. The sound of the barrel unlocking echoes in the corridor and a feeling of forboding washes over me as he swings the door open.

Pushing me into my room, he slams the door behind him and flicks the lock. He turns some music on before he turns to face me. With my room half in darkness, it makes him look like the menacing monster he is. He steps over to me and swings his hand back, hitting the side of my face.

My head snaps to the side and my cheek stings from the contact.

Gripping my upper arms, he pushes me down onto my bed. Digging his fingers into my shoulders, I whimper in pain.

"You thought you could turn me in?" he snarls.

How does he know? No one knows, I literally just made up my mind.

"What?" I play dumb. "Turn you in to who?"

"Don't you play dumb with me, you ungrateful little bitch." Standing above me, he pulls me up to my feet, digging his nails into my upper arms and pulling me toward him. He leans in, his heated breath hitting my face. "After everything I've done for you, this is how you repay me?" He lets go of my arms, but before I can move, he wraps his fingers around my throat and squeezes.

My eyes widen and I scratch at his hands. His grip becomes tighter and tighter by the second, and just when I feel like I'm going to pass out, he lets go and throws me to the bed.

Inhaling deeply, air filters into my lungs but it burns. Dad climbs onto the bed and straddles my chest. His palms rain down in my face.

Slap after slap comes, he's not letting up.

My vision begins to blur but I'm powerless to stop him.

A soft whimper escapes me as my father continues to beat me. He climbs off and stares down at me. Through my hazy vision, I see nothing but anger on his face and I know he's not done yet.

Reaching out, he grabs me by my ankle and throws me to the carpet. Pulling his leg back, he kicks me in the stomach. I cry out in agony, but it only fuels him on. He continues to beat on me, using his fists and feet.

Rolling into a ball, I try to protect myself but it's no use. He's a pro at this and knows exactly where to aim.

Finally, he stops beating me. He's huffing and puffing, sweat beading on his forehead. Hovering above me, he lower himself down and stares into my eyes. "You thought I wouldn't know what you've been up to?"

Grabbing me by my hair, he pulls me up into a sitting position and slaps me hard across the cheek again. Gripping me by my shirt, his eyes turn black and he rears his fist back.

"Please, Daddy, no," I beg, closing my eyes. I wait for the punch but surprising me, he drops his fist and shoves me to the floor.

Standing up, he scoffs before he grabs my bath towel to wipe my blood off his hands.

When he's done, he drops the towel and glares down at me. "You will not go to the authorities, Rowan. You hear me? You're mine. You always will be. I'm your father and I'll do with you as I please. No one, not even that fucking Vanderbelt will stop me."

Turning around, he exits my room, leaving me bloody and broken on the floor in my room, the one place that was my safe place from him.

Tears streak down my face and I lie here, wondering how he knew I'd planned to finally come clean. Sobbing, I lie in a heap deciding to give up. Everything goes blurry and I let the darkness take me because no matter what I do, he'll always win.

SAINT

"SHHHH I GOT YOU, DOVE," I whisper into Rowan's ear as she cries into my shoulder.

Remy came barreling into my room moments ago, tears pouring down her face, mumbling about Rowan and blood and something I couldn't decipher. Thatcher appeared behind her and translated Remy's tearful mumblings.

Pushing past them both, I raced to her room and when I saw my dove, my heart shattered in my chest.

Dropping to my knees, I pull her into my arms, and now as I hold her against my chest, I vow that he's touched her for the last time because I'm going to fucking kill him.

She hiccups into my chest, and I hold her tightly. She whimpers in my arms and when she lifts her gaze to mine, I get a good look at her. Shaking my head, I gently place a kiss on her temple. He's beaten her so badly her face is covered in marks and bruises and from the flinches, I'm guessing the rest of her body is marked too.

Pulling her into my lap, I lean against her bed and hold her while she cries. With each rub of my hand on her back, I force my anger down, she doesn't need that right now.

Once she's stopped crying, Remy and I tend to the wounds.

Rowan and Remy slip into the bathroom and when I hear Rowan break down again, I can't contain my rage. I see this as my chance to slip away and fix this. I'm prepared to do whatever it takes to keep her safe, even if it means she has to be without me for that to happen.

Slipping out the door, I'm on one mission and one mission only, make *him suffer*.

Seeking him out, it doesn't take long and as soon as I see him, I become *Rocky Balboa* and inflict my rage on him.

My fist flies into his face before he has a chance to see me and react. It's gutless attacking someone without letting them defend themselves but pot, kettle, fuck him.

Gripping his shirt, I force him into the wall, pressing my arm over his throat, cutting off his airway. "You ever lay a fucking hand on my girl again, I'll chop your fucking dick off and feed it to you." My voice echoes around us. I don't care if anyone hears, I'm done.

Raising my fist, I slam it into his face, a resounding crack echoes in the corridor and it forces him back into the wall. His head flies back cracking against the brick and I smile at the sound. Anger is coursing through my veins as my fist lands on his nose.

Again.

Again

And again.

"You're done abusing her and me," I sneer in his face.

"And I told you to mind your fucking business, Vanderbelt. She's my fucking daughter, and I will do what I please ... I can always punish you as well, and we both know, I'm much harder on you." I begin to shake at his words, but force it all down with one hard thud. My fist lands on his nose again and this time blood sprays between us. I throw a bleeding Ashford to the floor and stand over him. Bending down, I fist his shirt in my hand and pull him up by the material. Bringing him to my face, I give him a look that says you're done motherfucker and headbutt him.

Throwing him to the floor, he lies there semi-conscious, blinking up at me. The fucker is lucky I don't end him right now.

Towering over him, I look down at him and realize he isn't worth jail time. My dove and I will do this the right way.

The legal way.

"You're done abusing her and me," I growl again before shoving him back to the ground. "It's fucking done and it ends now. No more abuse," I shout through clenched teeth and then storm away.

HENDRIX

I'M on cloud fucking nine right now. I'm going to be a dad. Quinn and I have moved in together, and not five minutes ago, did I get the best fucking blow job from Quinn. I mean, they're all good, she seriously is the best giver and I'm not just talking about head. This baby has the best mom, I just hope my DNA doesn't fuck her up.

Rounding the corner, I'm happily humming to myself, but my smile immediately drops the moment I hear my brother growl, "I told you to not fucking touch her again."

Saint's voice echoes around me, and I'm confused by his words. *Touch who?* I'm ready to go to bat and assist him if he needs me. Peeking around the corner, the first thing I notice is my brother's fist is raised, his other arm is holding Mr. Ashford against the wall. *Rowan's dad? What the fuck, Saint?*

Mr. Ashford smirks at Saint and sneers, "And I told you to mind your fucking business, Vanderbelt. She's my fucking daughter, and I will do what I please … I can always punish you as well, and we both know, I'm much harder on you."

I'm ready to step in and help Saint, but I stop when I see him quiver in his boots. Saint is the toughest mofo I know—don't tell Thatch that—and even though Mr. Ashford is the one pinned to the wall, it's Saint who is shaking, but he shakes that off and in the blink of an eye, his fist flies into Mr. Ashford's face.

From where I'm hiding, I hear the crack of his nose, and I see the spray of blood clearly fly from his nose as it spurts out, covering them both.

Fuck, I should stop this from happening, but I'm enjoying the way Saint's giving Mr. Ashford a workup. I'll wait a few more moments and see how this plays out. My money is on Saint hitting him again and I'm all for it. Mr. Ashford is a cunt, not Thornton Vanderbelt cunt level but a cunt, nonetheless.

Saint throws a bleeding Ashford to the floor and stands over him. Bending down, he fists Ashford's shirt, he's in full-on angry Saint mode now and Ashford is fucked.

You don't want to mess with Saint when it gets to this point.

He pulls Ashford up by his shirt, so he's right in his face and headbutts him. I feel the headbutt from where I'm standing, and I scrunch my face up. I've been on the receiving end of one of his headbutts and his head is as hard as fucking rock. He throws Ashford to the floor, and he lies there semi-conscious, blinking up at Saint.

Saint towers over him. "You ever lay a fucking hand on my girl again, I'll chop your fucking dick off and feed it to you." He reaches down and pulls him up so they are once again eye to eye. "You're done abusing her and me," Saint sneers in his face before shoving him back to the floor. "It's fucking done and it ends now. No more abuse."

What the fuck? Abuse?

Saint stalks off, leaving Ashford where he is on the ground. My brother is so angry and lost in his head that he passes by without seeing me. Slinking out, I look back at Ashford who is still lying there, and it takes everything I have to not beat the fuck out of him for what I just heard, but right now, my brother needs me.

Turning around, I chase after him and catch up in no time. My fingers grip his upper arm. He spins to face me, fist raised, ready to fight. But when he sees it's me, he drops his arm and nonchalantly says, "Hey, bro."

What the fuck? He just went from wanting to kill me to 'hey bro,' yeah, not on my watch. "Don't 'Hey, bro' me. What the fuck was that back there?"

SAINT

"... What the fuck was that back there?"

"Nothing," I snap at my brother and turn away from him and head outside. The afternoon sunlight hits my skin, and I soak up the rays.

"Nothing my ass," he shouts and once again, he catches up to me. "Bro, what the fuck did I just witness?"

He grabs my arm tighter this time. "Just leave it, Hendrix," I growl.

"Leave it? Just leave it?" he sneers, and I know this time I won't be so lucky. My secret is about to come out to one of my brothers. "You just all out accused Mr. Ashford of abuse and you're telling me to leave it." He shakes his head incredulously. He steps into me, lowers his voice, and hisses, "Did he fucking touch you?" From the look in his eyes, I can tell he's two seconds away from going back inside and giving the fucker another round. His entire body is shaking, but I need to handle Ashford myself. My thought is confirmed when he spins around.

"Wait," I call out. He spins back around, and without me even having to say anything, he knows his assumptions are correct.

"Motherfucker," he growls and before I can stop him, he sprints back inside to where Mr. Ashford was. He's now surrounded by a crowd, but Hendrix doesn't care. He only stops when I rip him back, shoving him into the wall before he can make a scene.

"I have it handled," I hiss at him.

"Handled, you call that handled?" He points his finger to where Mr. Ashford is being helped up.

Turning my head, I watch as Fuckface Ashford is carried through the hall like a fucking victim. Students and teachers stare after him, all wondering what the hell happened.

Looking back at my brother, I don't say anything, words elude me, but my brother, my triplet, knows what I need. He grips my face in his palms and rests his forehead against mine. He stares into my eyes. "You, me, Thatcher, Reign, we're in this together. One in, all in. Nothing else matters."

His words hit home, and I can't control it, tears slide down my face.

Without a word, Hendrix pulls me into his arms. Once I've composed myself, I tell him I need to get to Rowan. I need to speak with her before I speak with my brothers.

It's not just my secret, it's hers too, and she has more invested in this than I do.

Before I head back to my dove, I beg Hendrix not to say anything to anyone. Not our brothers and definitely not to Quinn. Quinn is Rowan's best friend, but she doesn't even know what's been happening and this late in her pregnancy, she doesn't need this added stress.

"Fine," Hendrix relents. "I won't say anything, but later, you and I will be chatting. You may not want to talk to the others yet, but after that..." He flicks his thumb in the direction of what just went down. "...you will talk to me."

Nodding, I slap my brother on the back and without another word head back to Rowan's room to check on her.

When I step into her room, her gaze falls to my bloody fists. Her eyes widen and she comes straight for me. "Saint." She grabs my hand looking it over before pulling me toward the bed. Even in her injured state, she's worried about me. She leaves me for a brief moment to grab the first aid kit. She begins to clean my hand, in a less than gentle manner, but I probably deserve it. "Please tell me you didn't do anything stupid?" she whispers.

When I don't answer, she looks away and sighs before continuing to clean my hand. I wince again when she rubs the antiseptic wipe over my broken skin, cleaning the blood away.

"Dove," I murmur her name, and when she looks at me, I add, "Hendrix ..." She nods and understands what I'm trying to say without me actually having to articulate it, my brother knows our secret.

She drops her gaze back to my hand and focuses on that before flicking her gaze to mine. "You ... you should tell him everything," she says.

I scoff, running my other hand over my face. "I don't think I can." She drops my hand and lets out a strangled breath. My fingers brush over her cheek before I tip her chin up. "But for you, I will."

"Thank you," she murmurs softly.

Rowan finishes tending to my hand and then ushers me out the door again. I know she's right, I need to talk to someone, but so does she.

"Fucking hell, Saint." Hendrix growls my name as he falls back onto his bed. "He touched you, fuck." His gaze lands on mine, and I don't see disgust or pity, I see anger and rage. "I should have known," he growls, shocking me. "I'm so sorry. Fuck."

"I did it for her. I'll always sacrifice myself for her," I tell my brother.

"So today, what was that?"

"Ashford broke his promise. I found out today he's still been touching Rowan this entire time."

Hendrix growls, "That motherfucker."

"Promise me you'll keep this to yourself?" Hendrix groans, but nods accepting my wish. "I'll tell them eventually," I reassure him, but before I get a chance to confess all to the rest of my brothers, shit hits the fan in a spectacular way and Crestwood will never be the same again.

SAINT

TODAY HAS BEEN A CLUSTERFUCK, but at the same time it was filled with joy, so much joy.

Quinn gave birth to my nephew, officially making me an uncle. Seeing that lil' boy wrapped in her arms for the first time caused something inside of me to snap, and I spilled my guts to everyone. I shared a secret that wasn't mine, and I just hope she will understand and forgive me.

As I watched Quinn and Hendrix with little Ellis, I just knew it was time. The thought of anyone touching that little boy, the way *he* touched Rowan and I was the straw that broke the camel's back, but now I worry Rowan will hate me for outing us once all the emotions of today have settled.

I'm pacing back and forth in Rowan's room. Our emotions are both high and when the adrenaline wears off, we're going to crash, but I need to be strong, for her. For us. We are in this mess now because I opened my big fat mouth.

We've both given our statements to the police and the school board. Fuckface has been arrested and he can never hurt us again. The angst I feel about it finally being over is nothing compared to what I feel knowing that it's no longer our secret, everyone knows.

Fuck, everyone knows.

Me and my big fat stupid mouth revealed it all, but I don't regret it. That lil' baby made me confess to it all, and I will do anything to prevent something like this happening to him.

"Saint," Rowan whispers, garnering my attention.

"I'm right here, Dove," I state, smiling over at her. She's curled in a ball on her bed, her fingers fidgeting with a thread on her quilt. "He … he …"

"He's where he should be," I say, knowing what she's thinking.

She sniffs and nods in agreement, but she doesn't say anything else. I hate not knowing what she's feeling or thinking. I know I need to give her time but it sucks, it sucks big hairy donkey dicks.

"I'm sorry," I voice as I climb onto her bed and shuffle behind her.

Wrapping my arms around her, I repeat my apology over and over. She shakes her head and rolls over to face me. She places her hand on my cheek in that reassuring way. Covering her hand with mine, I stare at the strongest woman, next to my mom, that I know.

"It's okay, Saint," she murmurs. "You've always protected me, and I know you did what you did today to protect Ellis." She pauses. "You're always protecting me. Protecting everyone—"

"And I always will," I tell her honestly. "You're my dove. I'd do anything for you." And I mean it. The day she first confessed to me what her father was doing after I broke into her room, I wanted to kill Mr. Ashford. How he could do that to the sweetest person in the world is unforgivable. She's his daughter for fuck's sake. That was the lowest day of my life, but she'd made me promise to keep it to myself. She didn't want anyone to know, so instead, I vowed to protect her and keep her secret, which became our secret when I found a way for him to use me as his punching bag.

The only good thing was she didn't have to do it alone anymore. She had me then. She has me now and she always will.

My scars are only physical, but Rowan's, fuck, hers are physical and emotional. They are deep and I will be here for her every step of the way.

Taking a deep breath, I let out a sigh. I know we have to eventually face everyone, but for now, I like our little bubble.

We've kept to ourselves since I dropped the 'Mr. Ashford is a predator' bomb yesterday, choosing to hide away, but the need to see my brothers and new nephew is strong.

Fuck, I have a nephew and I haven't even held him yet.

Thatcher and Hendrix were beside themselves, being triplets and not knowing what was going on with me must be killing them. They feel like they've betrayed me some-how, that they broke some secret triplet vow, but they didn't. My brothers *have* tried to talk to me, but I wasn't ready to share.

The moment we step outside these walls, everything will change.

Everything will be different.

The moment I spilled our secret, Rowan and I became the talk of the school. Everyone forgot Arlen killed our father or that Hudson, Reign, and Alani came out as a throuple. Hell, the news of Hendrix and Quinn having their baby at school didn't even make the news because this is so much more. This is the juiciest thing to hit Crest-wood; ever, and right now because of me, my dove has to face the music. I want nothing more than to hide Rowan away so she doesn't have to face our peers. Face the looks and the questions and most of all the whispers. I don't want Rowan to face that because she's been through enough, and now, I have no clue if she's truly going to be okay.

My phone vibrates on the side table. Reaching over to grab it, I know it's bound to be one of my brothers checking in.

HENDRIX

Come meet your nephew, we're in my old
room.

"You had to go there," I mumble and now I feel like a horrible brother.

Hendrix is a new dad. He has a son and I'm an uncle, yet I'm hiding away in fear of what other people will think.

"I want to hold him," Rowan says, reading the text Hendrix sent me.

"You're sure?" I ask, trying my best to sense if she truly wants this.

"Quinn is my best friend. She just had a baby, and I haven't even seen him yet. As much as I'd love to stay in here forever with you, Saint, we need to face them all eventually." She pauses and then adds, "We can't hide forever."

I scoff, "Try me, baby." And I smirk, earning myself a smile.

She reaches up and cups my cheek. "Together," she tells me.

"Together," I whisper back.

Texting Hendrix back, I tell him we'll be there in ten.

Pulling her up, I hug her tightly and then we get ready to go meet my nephew. Hand in hand, we walk the short distance to my brother's room.

Lifting my hand to knock, I look down at Rowan and smile just as the door flies open revealing Hendrix.

As soon as he sees us, a relieved expression appears on his face. He reaches out and pulls Rowan and me into his embrace.

Rowan slips out of his arms and then he tugs me back in for another hug. He murmurs into my ear, "I'm here," and hugs me tightly. Squeezing him in return, I clap his back, giving him a silent thank you.

Pulling back, I slap my hands together. "Now let me see this nephew of mine, because the cool uncle has arrived."

ROWAN

"HE'S BEAUTIFUL," I coo. "You guys must be so happy."

"We are," Quinn answers for the two of them. She gazes lovingly over at Hendrix, but when she turns her attention back to me, I hate the look in her gaze.

"Don't," I tell her, shaking my head. "I … I don't want to spoil this happy occasion."

"Fine," she relents, "but Rowan Vivian Ashford, we will be talking about this, and you will be yelled at."

"Calm your tits, babe," Hendrix says to Quinn,

squeezing her shoulder and staring adoringly at her. "She's fine."

"Fine is a relative term, Hendrix Clarence Benedict Vanderbelt—"

"Dude, she just middle named you," Saint teases him, slapping him on the back.

"Don't make me middle name you too, Saint—" I can't help but giggle when she stops mid middle name rant and glowers at me.

"You think you're immune, Quinlan Stacey Ellis."

"Ummm, it's just Quinn," she hisses, causing Ellis to stir in my arms, but I shush and rock him back to sleep.

"Whatever," she sasses, using her hands to make a 'W' *Clueless* style. "You went through something horrible, and it was happening right under our noses, and no one knew. I should have been there for you. I ..." She starts to cry and I feel like a bitch.

"Quinn, no," I cry.

Handing Ellis to Saint, I slide to the floor and shuffle over to Quinn. I take her hands in mine and look up at her. "No one is to blame except for *him*. I should have said something the first time it happened, but I'd just lost Mom and I thought he was grieving—"

"Yeah, that's how you grieve," Saint growls.

Looking over at him, I give him the evil eye and mouth "Not helping" before turning back to Quinn. "Don't blame yourself, please?"

"But—"

"Nope, no buts. This is not on you. One of these days, over tequila, lots and lots of fucking tequila, I will tell you everything, but for now, let's dote on this little guy and celebrate the miracle of life."

Reluctantly, she agrees and for the rest of the afternoon Saint and I share cuddles with little Ellis. I know we'll have to face everyone else at some point, but this has been a nice easy way to immerse ourselves back into society. Yes, I'm aware I'm being dramatic, with it only being less than twenty-four hours, but there's no rule book for when the secret you've been hiding since you were fifteen is exposed.

A few hours later, we say our goodbyes and Saint and I head back to his room. He tugs me to his side and kisses the top of my head. "Come on, let's get you tucked in." I smile, knowing he means let's watch something and cuddle in bed … and maybe fool around too.

We're nearly at his room when we run into Grayson, Remy's brother. For a guy who doesn't attend Crestwood, he sure is here a lot, but then again, the Hearsts have been through a lot too. I still can't believe what Arlen did. I never pictured him as a killer … or a kidnapper but I guess, love, even if he did love his ex's father, makes you do crazy things.

"Hey," he says, smiling at both of us.

"Hey," Saint replies, eyeing him cautiously.

"Look—" Grayson starts, but Saint holds his hand up stopping him.

"Don't, please. We just want a normal life now." Saint looks down at me and smiles, and like always when that lip lifts, I feel safe and protected.

Grayson nods then with another smile he walks away, leaving us alone again.

Ushering me into the room before we run into anyone else, Saint locks the door behind him before going to his drawers to pull something out for me to wear to bed. I practically live in Saint's T-shirts now. I can't remember the last time I wore something of my own to bed. Nighties remind me too much of the nights my father would come into my room. I thought when he allowed me to board here, his nightly visits would stop, but I wasn't so lucky. On the odd occasion, my dad would break into my room and abuse me. At least with me boarding at school, it wasn't every night like when I was at home. Plus, thanks to my sneaky sleepovers with Saint in his room, I was safe from *him*.

"Hey." Saint grips my face between his hands, running the pad of his thumb over my lip and pulling it free from my teeth. I hadn't even realized I was biting it.

"Don't you dare let him in, baby. Don't you dare. I'm right fucking here, I got you," he says, pulling me into his arms.

Nodding, I sniff against his chest and once the memories are gone, I let him undress me. Saint glides his shirt over my head, covering me, but not before having a grope of my boobs.

Placing a kiss on my lips, he smiles down at me before lifting me and placing me in the middle of the bed, pulling the blankets up, and tucking me in like he's rolling up a burrito.

"I'm going to shower, watch something and get the bed warm for me." He winks at me before he starts to strip off his clothes on the way to the bathroom—luxury of being a Lord, they get their own bathrooms.

Clicking the television on, I put on something random, knowing I'll probably fall asleep by the time Saint is done. Rolling to my side, I stare at the screen and listen as the water turns on. A single tear slides down my cheek. "Thank you, Momma, for sending Saint to me," I say.

My eyes begin to grow heavy. The last few days have been exhausting. The last thing I remember before falling asleep is feeling Saint's lips against my head, and his body pressed against mine as he snuggles into me.

ROWAN

I CAN'T BELIEVE it's over.

It's all over.

Finally.

Everything I've kept hidden is out now, there are no more secrets.

It's funny, I thought I'd feel relieved, but to be honest, I don't know how I feel right now. All I know is I'm numb but also lighter.

My stomach twists as I stare at the closed door. Saint left a few moments ago to speak to his brothers. I don't have anyone to speak to, but that changes when there's a knock and the door swings open. In walks Remy, followed by Alani and Quinn, who's carrying Ellis in her arms.

Pushing myself up into a sitting position, they all hug me hello. Quinn sits beside me, and I glance down at Ellis in her arms. He's so tiny, he has his whole life before him and as I stare at him sleeping, I vow to protect him and those I love with everything I have.

Tears begin to flow down my cheeks, and once again, I'm a sobbing mess.

"Oh, babe," Quinn cries, pulling me one-armed into her side, somehow not disturbing Ellis. Already, she's a brilliant mom and that makes me sob harder 'cause I miss my brilliant mom.

Remy climbs onto the bed on my other side, hugging me, and Alani shuffles around her to my back. She wraps her arms around my waist, resting her chin on my shoulder. The four of us, well, five if you include Ellis, sit here hugging as I cry.

With my friends, my family surrounding me, I cry over everything I've lost.

Collecting myself, I take a deep breath and wipe my hand across my cheek, wiping away the tears. Then I run my finger across Ellis's soft cheek and before they ask *that* question, I start talking. "My father is a monster. I didn't want to believe it, but I knew he was. It was just hard to admit that my dad wasn't who I thought he was," I confess. Closing my eyes, I draw on all my inner strength and I continue. "The first time he … he assaulted me physically wasn't long after my mom died," I admit out loud, and somehow, it's easy to share now. The girls listen as I tell them everything, flipping back and forth between when Mom was alive, when it was me in my own hell, and finally I get to the part when Saint made his deal.

"So, Saint made a deal to protect you?" Remy asks, her cheeks stained from her own tears as I confessed everything to them.

Nodding, I reach out and grab a tissue, blowing my nose. "He made my father promise if he had urges, he was to go to him. That he would take whatever he was going to do to me." Lowering my head, I cry harder because this next part is hard to admit. "Even though he promised Saint he'd stop, he didn't. Saint never knew my father broke their deal; he was still abusing me. He manipulated me into not saying anything and like the meek puppet I was when I came to him, I didn't say a word." Lifting my head, I dart my gaze between the three of them and a smile appears on my face. "But Saint was always there. He took care of me, even without knowing what was still going on. He always made sure I felt loved," I whisper those last few words and then I fall silent.

It feels so dirty saying it out loud. My skin feels like it's on fire with a thousand fire ants biting at me, but one thing is abundantly clear, my father never loved me. I'm pretty sure, he didn't even care about me.

Quinn is the first to speak, "Well, I'm really glad you had Saint. That you had someone there with you." She playfully bumps my shoulder and adds, "Since you never talked to us about it."

Guilt slams into me that I didn't share with them, especially her, my best friend, what was going on. Looking to her, I go to apologize but she gives me that 'don't even think about it' look and I close my mouth.

"I'm sorry he did that to you, Ro," Alani says.

"Yeah, me too," I agree with her. "I just wish I'd stopped it sooner. That I was stronger. That Saint and I didn't have to hide it all, but I can't change the past, all I can do is look to the future."

The room falls silent.

"It's why Saint was always so angry, isn't it?" Remy asks, breaking the silence.

Staring at her, I process her words and then I nod.

Quinn sighs before she wipes her face and sniffles. She places Ellis in my arms and stands up and begins to pace. She has that determined look on her face, and I smile because before she even begins to speak again, I know she has a plan. "It was truly horrible what your father did, and if I had known, I never would have let him near my hoo-ha to deliver Ellis, but at the same time, I'm thankful he was there to safely deliver him. But he's locked away now, and I hope he becomes someone's bitch in there and he suffers like you and Saint did, but let's forget about him. Now we focus on you and Saint. We focus on helping you heal. Saint too." She drops to her knees before me and places her hand on my knee. "I want you to come to me. To any of us if you ever need to talk, Ro. I mean it, night or day, you come to us." She's using that mom voice she's already seemed to pick up and I laugh.

"I promise," I reply with a nod.

"Okay, good, because I will be mad at you if you try to deal with this by yourself. Even though I know you have Saint, you always have us. We're family, Rowan, no matter what," Quinn tells me.

"What she said," Alani says from behind me, placing a kiss on my cheek. She shuffles around and takes the spot next to me where Quinn was, and then we all hug again.

Remy asks Quinn how her vagina is after pushing Ellis out with no drugs, and I take the moment to stare down at the tiny baby in my arms. He doesn't even know it yet, but he saved me. His birth was my rebirth, and from this moment forward I know I'll be fine.

With Saint and my friends on Team Rowan, I know I can do it. I'm Rowan-fucking-Ashford, I lived with the devil and won. Nothing will ever tear me down again, nothing.

SAINT

"FUCK, dude, I can't believe you kept this from us," Reign growls, sitting down on the floor. He leans back against the wall, stretches one leg out and bends the other, resting his elbow on his knee.

"It wasn't my secret to tell, it was Rowan's," I tell him.

He nods, understanding where I'm coming from, but then it's Hendrix's turn to weigh in, "But you, fuck, you should have come to us."

Looking at him I nod, a part of me knows he's right. I should have come to them, but I just wanted to protect

Rowan and the more people who knew, the less I could protect her.

Thatcher is silent in the corner and a silent Thatcher is never a good thing. His arms are crossed and he's clenching his jaw, no doubt grinding his molars. He notices me eyeing him and shifts his gaze to the floor. He's ashamed of me, well that's what it feels like. "Thatch," I say, "talk to me, man." Licking my lips, I nervously wait for him to respond.

"I knew something was wrong. I knew you were dealing with something, but fuck, I never imagined this," he growls, shaking his head and I realize he's not ashamed, he's pissed off that he didn't follow his instinct. That he didn't step in and try to help.

"None of us could have ever imagined that was what he was dealing with. Fuck, it was way worse than any of us imagined," Reign says, trying to keep the peace in the room.

Swallowing, I sigh. "Look, I'm sorry I didn't talk to you guys. I just didn't know how to explain it, and after the first time, I … I just I don't know, I kept it all in. Hell, I didn't even tell Rowan what was going on. I took the beatings for her. I did it to keep her safe," I admit.

"Did he ever …?" Thatcher asks without actually asking.

Shaking my head, I see relief wash over his face. "No, he mostly just watched me jerk off, and while I was jerking, he would too." Pausing, I take another deep breath, something I've been doing a lot of the last few days. "But, umm, occasionally he'd, umm, help get me off by covering my hand with his … he never actually touched my dick."

"So, you took the beatings so Rowan wouldn't have to?" Hendrix asks. I nod and even now, I'd make the same choices. I'd do it a thousand times over for the rest of eternity, just so she wouldn't have to.

Silence falls around us, but Hendrix breaks it, "I can't believe Mr. Ashford—"

"Fuckface Ashford," I correct Hendrix, cutting him off. They all chuckle at my name for him.

"Name's fitting," Thatcher says, agreeing with the nickname I gave him when I was fifteen. "Just promise us, if anything ever happens like that again, you'll come to us. We're your fucking brothers, Saint, and we've got your back. No matter what," Thatcher growls.

"I will," I honestly tell them, and I mean it. It's been so fucking hard keeping this from them, but it wasn't just my secret. It was also my dove's. Her safety and her secrets will always come first. "It was just a lot, you know." I pause. "Plus, it wasn't just my secret, and to be honest, I didn't even fucking know how to say it out loud. I tried so many times, but the words just never formed."

They all nod and I see understanding on their faces. As much as I've hurt them, they understand and that's because they love me. No matter what, we're brothers and we will always have each other's backs.

"As Thatch said, we've got your back, always," Reign says. I smile at him using the words I just said in my head. He holds his fist out for me to bump. Bumping them we chuckle, being a Lord isn't a choice, it's our life.

My brothers.

This school.

Everything we do is a huge part of who I am. Who we are, but in a few short weeks, it's all going to be over. I don't know what's to come after Crestwood Prep, but it's gotta be better than what I've been through. The world is my oyster and now, I can be anything I want to be.

The sky's the limit.

Fuckface Ashford doesn't control us anymore, and together, Rowan and I will overcome anything thrown our way because we have each other. I'll always have her back, no matter what.

SAINT

… two weeks later

EVERY SET of eyes is on Rowan and me as we walk through the halls of Crestwood toward the cafeteria for lunch. The last few weeks have been crazy, so Rowan and I decided to get away. And by get away, I mean that we've been away staying—hiding—with Hendrix and Quinn at their place.

As much as I'd love to jet off to the Bahamas and spend a few weeks on the beach with Rowan, naked, we have finals coming up and need to be here to study. Each of us needs to ace our exams and get the grades needed to get the fuck out of this town. Nothing will stop the two of us from doing that. I refuse to let *him* and the stares and whispers prevent Rowan and me from getting out of this fucked-up town. Will I miss my family? Yes, but there's this thing called stalkbook and FaceTime and there are even these inventions called cars and planes that can bring us back here.

The change of scenery has been nice, and even though we knew we'd have to get back eventually, I hate bringing Rowan back here. As much as there are good memories here, there are many shit ones too.

"They're all staring," she whispers, snuggling closer into my side. There's a slight quiver in her body, and when I look down, my heart breaks for her. It's gone from one kind of fear to another. Now she's fearing the gossip from her fellow students.

Looking around the corridor, I glare at each fucker who can't keep their nose out of our business. I'm about to lose it when Thatcher whistles, gaining everyone's attention, including mine and Rowan's.

We turn to face him and the first thing I notice is the 'I'm a Lord, listen up, fuckers' look on his face. "All right, fuckers," he bellows. "Anyone still here in the next five minutes will feel my wrath and if I catch anyone, and I mean any-fucking-one, looking or saying anything about the events of the last few weeks, you will not like the consequences. Now, get to class and learn some shit."

Everyone falls into line. Thatcher's warning lighting a fuse in their asses and everyone disperses.

"Hey, man," Lennon says, slapping his hand in mine and pulling me in for a half hug.

"Hey," I greet my best friend with a smile. "What's

doing?" But before he can reply, Thatcher comes over to us.

"You good?" he says, eyeing the last of the students hovering around us.

"Yeah, we're good. Just weird to be back, you know?" He nods, knowing what I mean without me having to go into detail.

"Rowan," Remy squeals, running up and pulling her in for a hug.

"Hey, girl," Rowan says, hugging her back.

Reign comes up behind me, clasping my shoulder. "Hey, man."

"Hey." I turn to give my brother a smile and see Hudson and Alani come up behind him, each of them giving me a wave.

"Let's eat, I'm fucking starving," Rian says, coming up behind us and throwing his arms over my shoulder. All of us burst into laughter, trust my cousin to lighten the mood, but when I look at Rowan and see her smile with her friends, it eases my worries. Slightly, ever so slightly.

Every few minutes, my gaze gravitates toward Rowan, making sure she's okay. She's sitting in between Remy and Alani and they're talking girl shit. I'm pretty sure I just heard them say something about Jensen Ackles, that guy from the television show, *Supernatural.*

"Dude, she's fine," Reign whispers in my ear.

"I know," I grunt out, shoving my elbow into his stomach. "I just …"

"I get it, but she's at school, she'll be safe."

"You do realize that ninety-nine-percent of the shit that went down with Fuckface Ashford happened here, at school? Well, for me it did." My dove had to put up with him here and at home until I struck our deal. A deal I don't regret making because it got her away from him.

Rowan catches me staring at her. She gives me a small smile and blows me a kiss before she goes back to talking to the girls. I know my girl has demons to fight, so do I, but I'll be there every step of the way. I'll hold her hand when she needs strength. I'll give her a shoulder to cry on when she needs to let it all out. Whatever she needs, I'm there. I'm willing to sacrifice everything for her, no matter what.

She's my dove.

My everything.

ROWAN

THE CONSTANT STARES and whispers in the halls and cafeteria are unnerving. I've tried to ignore them, but it's just too much.

"Are you okay?" Remy asks as we sit down at our table. She places her tray next to mine and leans into me wrapping her arm around my side. How she knew I was struggling, I'll never know, but I'm thankful she's in tune with my emotions. "It'll die down, they just don't have anything better to do," she whispers before turning her gaze to the table of girls across from us, who keep looking over and murmuring amongst themselves.

"I know it will, but it just feels like they're laughing at me. That I'm the butt of all the jokes." I glance down at my tray and pick up a fry. Biting into it, I still feel like shit. Not even the fried salty delicious morsel I'm chewing on can ease my woes right now.

Looking up, I see the boys head in our direction, and before Saint even gets to the table he frowns, sensing something is wrong. He picks up his pace and all but throws his tray on the table and drops to his knees next to me. Reaching up, he cups my cheek. "Baby, what's wrong?"

"Everyone is staring," I mutter, leaning into his hand.

He pulls away and I mourn the loss, but he has his 'Lord' scowl on his face and I know he's about to defend my honor. As much as I love him going to bat for me, I also hate it because it means that once again, everyone will be murmuring about poor Rowan and her sleazy father.

"Every fucker still looking this way in the next two second will have my foot up their ass," Saint bellows, causing the entire cafeteria to fall silent, well, for a few moments anyway. A soft chatter starts up again and when I look around, no one is paying us any attention.

"Nosy fucking fuckers," Hudson says, taking the seat across from me. He looks over and grins. "You want me to strip naked and dance the Macarena to take the attention off you?" He wiggles in his seat and begins the dance with his arms before offering me a wink. I give him a soft smile and chuckle. I love that he's trying to lighten the mood.

"You'll do no such thing," Alani chastises him, smacking her hand across his chest.

"Yeah, the only people who get to see your cock are me and Red," Reign growls from the other side of Hudson. Hudson lifts his head to look up at Reign. Reign reaches out and takes Hudson's head in his palms. Gripping his cheeks, he kisses him.

When they come up for air, the two of them are breathless, "Fine, spoilsport." Hudson chuckles before chucking a fry into his mouth.

"You and Rem could streak, Thatch, show 'em something good," Hudson suggests with a laugh. Remy's eyes go wide and Thatcher glares at Hudson, ready to jump across the table at him.

"No one is taking any clothes off, especially not my woman," Thatcher growls at Hudson.

"Like I said, you guys are no fun."

A giggle slips out and Hudson winks at me, making me giggle louder, but my laughter dies when a group of girls walk past, staring and causing me to once again fold into myself.

Saint rubs my back with one hand and with the other, he pulls his phone out, dials a number, and waits. My brows furrow and then I hear him bark into the phone, "Can Rowan and I still stay with you guys? People are being assholes." He raises his voice on the last word and stares daggers at the latest group. "Awesome, thanks, man, you're the best. I owe you." He hangs up and drops his phone onto the table. "All sorted, Dove. You and I are getting out of here." He smiles at me and pulls me to his side. He places a kiss to my temple and with our call and a kiss, I already feel lighter.

Once again, Saint comes to my rescue and saves me.

By the time we finish unpacking again and sorting our stuff at Hendrix and Quinn's place, it's nearly time for me to visit my father in prison. Saint insisted he didn't deserve to see me, but I want to see him one last time. I want to face him and tell him everything I've ever wanted to say but have been too scared to voice due to fear.

The drive to the prison is quiet. Saint and I don't utter a word to one another. I told Saint I needed to do this on my own. After pleading with him, he relented, but I had to let him drive me, and I was okay with that because, truth be told, I think I would have chickened out and turned around halfway here.

Taking a deep breath, I put my hand on the door to exit the car, but before I do, he reaches out and squeezes my hand. "Don't let him get in your head, Dove. He's where he belongs and even though I don't think he deserves to see you, I understand why you need to do this. I'll be here waiting for you. I love you, Dove."

"I love you too, and thank you."

"Why are you thanking me?"

"'Cause you are always here for me. You love me despite the things my father has done. You love me for me."

"Too fucking right I do. You, Rowan Vivian Last Name I Will Never Utter Again, are fucking amazing, and I wouldn't change anything I've done. You deserve all the happiness in the world and I'm going to do my fucking best to shower you with love and laughter and happiness. Now go see that cocksucker so we can get on with our lives."

Climbing out of the car, I make my way into the prison. My heart races and my palms become sweaty. I go through the check-in process and then I'm escorted into the visitors' room. It's gray, dreary, and cold. The chairs are bolted to the floor and the glass partition separating us is so clear and shiny that I can see my reflection.

Taking a seat, I wait and a few moments later, he arrives. Seeing my father in orange sets a wave of emotions over me I never expected, and suddenly, I don't want to be here anymore.

My father smiles and picks up the phone.

With a shaking hand, I pick mine up and bring it to my ear.

"My precious girl," he says, and I shudder at the nickname.

"Hi," I murmur softly, not sure what I want to say.

"I knew you'd come. I knew you'd see the error of your ways."

"I'm sorry, I ..." I drift off when I see a look cross his face. His gaze flickers across my body, lingering on my breasts until it finally lands back on my face. He smiles that sinister smile of his, and I know this was a waste of time. Nothing I say to him will change anything. Nothing I say to him will make him apologize for taking my innocence.

He's a monster, through and through. That thought is confirmed when he says, "I know that cunt pushed you into turning me in, but it's okay, Daddy won't be in here long and then we can be together again. I'm working on getting out of here."

My eyes widen at his words and panic shoots through me. Would they really let him out?

"You'll always be mine." He snickers, lickings his lips. "Always."

Closing my eyes, a vision of Saint appears before me and a surge of adrenaline pumps through my system, giving me the courage to say what I came for. "It's over, Daddy. You can't hurt me anymore. You're my father and in some fucked-up way, that matters. I still love you but I want you to know, I hate you for how you made me feel. I hate you for stealing my innocence. I hate you for manipulating Saint and me. I fucking hate you and after today, I never want to see you again." With that said, I place the receiver back onto the phone cradle. Standing up, I turn and take a step but before I walk away, I glance back at my father one last time. There's no need to stay and hash things out, I said what I came to say and whatever he wants to say doesn't mean anything to me.

With what I need to say off my chest, it's like a weight has lifted. I feel free, voicing my hatred toward the man who was supposed to love and protect me was cathartic in a way I can't explain.

He did what he did.

Nothing can change the past, but I have a future, a future to look forward to, and I'm going to grab onto it with both hands and I'm going to soar.

Exiting the prison, I find Saint leaning against his car. His arms are resting on the hood and his legs are outstretched and crossed at the ankle. Stopping before him, I smile.

"You doing okay, Dove?"

Nodding, I take the final steps toward him. Placing my feet either side of his legs, I drape my arms over his shoulders. He rests his hands on my hips, and we silently stare at one another. "It was exactly what I needed. I said what I said, and he can no longer hurt me. I never have to see him again, well, not until the trial but I'm okay with that."

"You are fucking amazing, Rowan. Now let's get the fuck out of here."

"Deal, but first, kiss me."

"As if you even need to ask." He covers my mouth with his and just like always, I lose myself and feel safe in his arms. Saint Vanderbelt really is a saint, and I'm so glad he's mine. With him by my side, I know I'll be fine.

We make our way back to Hendrix and Quinn's place. I'm exhausted, but I put on a brave face and sit out back with Quinn. She can tell I'm struggling—must be mothers' instinct—and she tells me to go lie down and she'll let Saint know I'm resting. He's gone out with his brothers, reluctantly, but I assured him I was fine. As much as he hated leaving me, he knew I was safe since my father is locked up and can never touch me again.

I'm pretty sure I'm asleep before my head hits the pillow, but I'm woken a few hours later by a presence hovering.

"Daddy's home," a voice I will never forget whispers into my ear.

My eyes fly open and fear courses through me as I stare up into the evil eyes of my father. Before I can scream, a hand with a cloth covers my mouth. As I suck in deep breaths, my vision becomes spotty. The last thing I hear is my father whisper, "You're mine, Precious Girl, and we're going to be together forever."

SAINT

LAUGHTER BUBBLES out of me as Reign tells us about the first time he realized Hudson was hot. Thatcher just shakes his head and then sips his beer while Hendrix chuckles like I did.

"You know," I say, interrupting the laughter, "this is the first time in forever we have just sat around drinking beer and talking shit. I've missed it." And I mean it, I missed just hanging with my brothers. Life has been crazy for all of us in the last few years, what with Dad and Arlen and wee lil' Ellis. It's been one fucking crazy rollercoaster ride, that's for sure.

"I just realized," Thatcher says out of the blue, "you two fuckers..." he points at Hendrix and me "...were never hauled into the station and questioned over Dad's murder."

"That's 'cause we're angels," Hendrix replies, placing his hands under his chin, nodding and smiling sweetly while fluttering his eyes. He looks like he's having a fit if you ask me, not very angelic looking at all.

"And I live up to my name, in that I am a Saint," I nonchalantly reply, taking a swig of my beer.

"Saint Fuckhead," Reign adds, earning himself a kick in the shins from me.

"But seriously, why?" Thatcher questions again.

Hendrix and I share a look and then I look to my brother. "We, ummm, well the night he was murdered, wewereonadoubledate," I string the words out in one breath.

Thatch sits up straight and slams his bottle of beer down, causing it to froth up. "Did you just say that you were on a double date?"

We both nod but before he can berate me, my phone begins to vibrate and ring in my pocket. Lifting my finger in a hold movement, I pull it out and furrow my brows when I see Quinn's name. I'm confused that she's calling me instead of Hendrix.

Wanting to fuck with my brother, I answer and make sure to emphasize her name. "Hey, Quinn. What's up?"

Hendrix growls when he realizes I'm talking to his woman and normally I'd revel in taunting my brother, but my face falls as I listen to Quinn.

"Hurry please," her voice trembles. "Mr. Ashford is at our place. Saint. He ... he has Rowan."

Instantly, I regret leaving Rowan and jump up and out

of my seat, her words playing on a loop in my mind jerk me into gear. "I'm on my way," I shout into the phone and like a bat out of hell, I race out of Thatch's room.

Without knowing what's going on, my brothers all jump up and follow. We run toward the parking lot and our cars. *Fuck*, I shouldn't have left her. Why the fuck is he at Quinn's? The fucking cunt is supposed to be in jail.

We all pile into Hendrix's new G-wagon, and he drives like a mad man toward his place. "What the fuck is going on?" Hendrix asks as he takes a corner too quickly.

"Fuckface Ashford is at your place. He has Rowan."

"I thought he was locked up?" Hendrix asks, his tone laced with confusion.

"So did I," I hiss.

Thankfully, we pull up a few minutes later and I'm out of the wagon before it's come to a full stop. Quinn meets me outside holding Ellis tightly to her chest. Her face is etched with fear, and I pull her and Ellis into my arms.

She's snatched out of my arms and pulled into Hendrix's chest. He holds on to her tightly. "He has her," she cries into his chest.

"Where?" I growl, I don't recognize my own voice.

"Living room," she blubbers and without any thought to my safety, I storm inside, not waiting for my brothers.

Busting through the front door, it bounces off the wall and I come to a stop when I see Rowan sitting on the couch. Tears are streaming down her face, Fuckface Ashford sits beside her, a knife to her throat.

Taking a step, he waves his finger at me. "Ahh ah," he sneers, pushing the knife into her throat.

Rowan lets out a strangled whimper and the sound cuts deep into my bones. Clenching my fists by my side, I growl. Watching, he licks the side of her face before whispering something into her ear.

Rowan's eyes widen and panic becomes clear over her face. She's struggling to keep still as he pushes the knife into her skin.

"You fucker," I growl just as Thatcher and Reign come up behind me.

"You should have just stayed away, Saint," he says, tsking me.

"Let her go," I shout at him.

He chuckles like what I'd said was crazy. "I don't take orders from you, Vanderbelt," he snaps. "Never have and never fucking will. You know," he taunts, "I was still fucking my beautiful girl while we had our deal."

Grinding my molars, I glare at the fucker.

"So was I," I throw back at him. "Difference between you and me, I made love to her, and she made love back. With you, she was just a hole to stick it." Rowan flinches at my words and I hope she knows I'm only saying this to fuck with him, to bide time to get her away from him.

Taking a deep breath, I look into Rowan's eyes. "I love you, Dove, and I'm going to save you."

"Not this time, you little cunt bag," he sneers. Pressing the blade deeper into her skin, I see a trail of blood slide down her neck, and I see red.

Before I can strike and make things worse, Thatcher places his hand on my shoulder, holding me back. Looking back at him, he nods and lets me know that he has my back. Thatch, Reign, and I will do whatever we need to save her.

Reaching up, I squeeze his hand and he steps back, giving me space but still being here if I need him.

Holding my hands up, I take a step forward.

Ashford pushes the knife deeper into Rowan's neck and I watch as the blood trail thickens and trickles down her throat.

"Take me instead," I tell him.

He scoffs and shakes his head. "This is between my daughter and me."

"She's not your daughter," I snarl at him.

"She is my fucking daughter and she betrayed me. She needs to suffer like I've suffered. I've missed her. I need her."

"I know you care about her, Matthew. I know that deep down, you don't really want to hurt her. So I'm offering me. Hurt me instead. Hurt me and let her go."

"Saint, no," she cries. "You've sacrificed enough."

"And I always will, Ro."

My brothers take a step forward behind me, reminding him that he's out numbered.

He glares at them over my shoulder before he leans forward and starts kissing the side of Rowan's face.

"Move," he growls, using the knife to usher me into the middle of the room.

Nodding at him, I move where he pointed. He roughly pulls Rowan to her feet and pushes her until she's standing in front of me.

"Saint," she cries but when she goes to wrap her arms around my neck, Fuckface pulls her back again.

Growling at him, I reach out and cup her cheek in my palm. "Shh, it's okay, Dove. I'm here and I've got you. I've always got you."

Leaning forward, I press my lips to hers and before she has a chance to kiss me back, I move my hand to her waist and push her aside and into Reign's waiting arms. He catches her and wraps them around her waist, holding her back as she tries to reach for me.

"I'm all yours, Ashford," I hiss through clenched teeth as I stare into the eyes of a monster. He places the knife under my throat, and steps to the side. "Let's go, Saintly." He forces me through the living room, into the kitchen and out the back.

Rowan's cries can be heard as we walk away. I don't struggle, I want to lull him into a false sense of security. He maneuvers me through the back gate into the alleyway and over to his car. Going to the passenger side of his car, he shoves me inside and then forces me to climb over and into the driver's seat.

"Drive," he orders, pressing the knife to my throat once again.

Kicking the engine over, I start the car but before we drive off, my brothers and Rowan come into view.

"I said drive," he yells. Pushing the blade deeper into my flesh. Slowly I reach forward and adjust the gearshift. Lifting my foot off the clutch and giving it some gas, we pull away. "I'm done with you fucking Vanderbelts." Fuckface Ashford growls.

Lifting my eyes to the rearview mirror, I catch sight of Rowan falling to her knees, sobbing as I drive away with her deranged father holding a knife to my throat.

Reign drops to his knees and pulls her into his arms. Holding her. Comforting her.

The last thing I think of before I turn onto the main road and lose sight of them is that she's safe. I'm so fucking glad she's safe, but me, I'm far from safe.

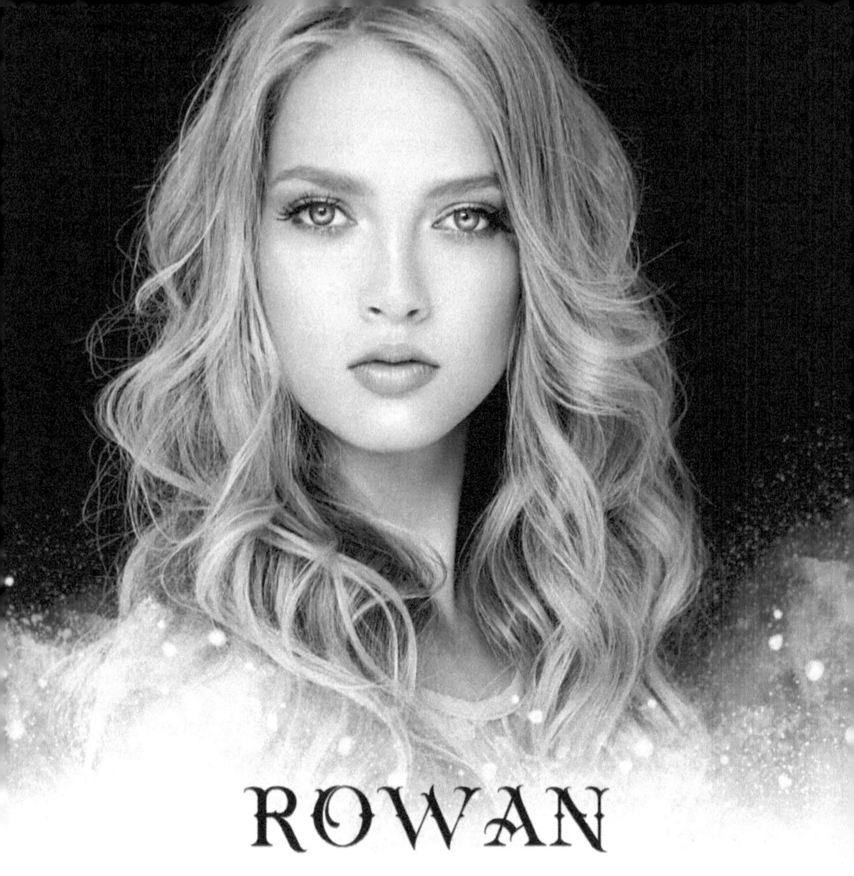

ROWAN

REIGN PULLS me into his arms, and I break down. I cry because, once again, my father has ruined everything, and once again, Saint has stepped in to save me.

Wiping my nose, I pull away from Reign and sit on my heels. Staring at the pavement below me, I make a decision.

This time I'm going to save Saint.

This time, I'm going to stand up to my father. No longer will I quake in fear because of that man.

Thinking on where he would take Saint, I rack my

brain and then the light bulb goes off and I know exactly where my father will head.

Pushing myself to my feet, I race through the yard toward Saint's car. Climbing in, I press the ignition button and start his car. Silently, I thank Saint and his 'I'm a Lord, no one will steal my car' attitude for leaving the key in the center console.

Reign is yelling at me to come back and to stop, but I ignore him and like Steve McQueen on the racetrack, I hightail it out of there.

Gripping the steering wheel, I speed down the street. I'm on a mission. I'm going to save Saint, and nothing is going to stop me.

Pulling up to the spot my father always said was my mom's special place, I glance around and when I see his car, I let out a grateful sigh. Climbing out of the car, I take a few steps, but I can't see any movement.

Walking over to Dad's car, I peer through the window, hoping to see Saint but it's empty. "Shit," I hiss, slamming my palm on the window. Turning around, I lean against the side and lift my head to the sky. "Please, Mom, help me save Saint."

Just as I finish my prayer, a raised voice catches my attention and I duck down out of sight.

Creeping around the side of the car, I move between several parked cars in the direction of the raised voices. When I see Dad and Saint, I come to a stop and watch. My father has his back to me so I'm safe for now.

Crouching down lower, I listen as the heated argument between him and Saint continues.

Peeking over the hood, Saint eyes me and gives me a brief shake of his head. My father continues his tirade, telling Saint he's going to find joy in destroying him and his brothers. Saving him for last, he will make me watch as he takes Saint's life before he does the same to me.

I've never seen Dad this unhinged before and as I watch from my hiding spot, I fear for Saint and myself.

"I'll be worshipped as a fucking god once you Vanderbelt fuckers are gone. You and your family have done enough to warrant your family's demise, and I will be the hero around here," my father sneers. He steps toward Saint with the knife outstretched.

Saint just stares blankly at my father, his face shows no expression.

"Cat got your tongue?" Dad taunts Saint, thrashing his hand with the knife out.

Saint just stands here, blinking at him.

"Say something, you cunt," Dad growls.

Saint's inaction is pissing him off, and I can see Dad becoming more unhinged as the seconds tick by. Dad charges for him and a gasp slips out when it looks like Dad is about to stab Saint, but at the last minute, Saint moves to the side, causing Dad to fall to the ground.

He wails like a pissed-off bear and jumps back to his feet.

From where I'm crouched, it looks like Dad is staring right at me, but it seems his gaze is locked on Saint. Saint shuffles around so once again, Dad has his back to me.

My foot is going numb so I shake it out and when I put it back down, I stand on a shard of glass. It pierces through my flip-flop, and I let out a painful yelp. Saint coughs to try to drown out the sound, but my father hears. I manage to duck down and out of sight just before he turns around.

Dropping to my butt, I lean against the tire of the car and assess my foot, thankful for the streetlight above. Apart from a little blood, I'm in no danger. It doesn't seem to be too bad, but the shining glass from the broken bottle garners my attention.

Reaching out, I pick the largest shard up and grip it in my hand, oddly loving the feel of it between my fingers. Running my finger along the sharp edge, I focus on its sharpness. It's like a razor. A weapon forged just for me.

Taking a few deep breaths, I push myself up into a standing position, gripping the glass tightly in my fist. Without thinking, I push off the car and walk toward Dad and Saint.

Crunching over the rest of the broken glass, the sound garners their attention, but I don't cower under the scowl directed at me from my father. He stares at me over his shoulder and for the first time ever, I'm not afraid of him. Adrenaline is coursing through my veins with each step I take toward him.

"Argh, my precious girl, you're just in time. You've come to watch me slaughter this Vanderbelt cunt."

"I won't let you hurt Saint," I growl. "I'm done and this is over."

He laughs, turning around to face me. "You won't hurt me, Rowan. You never could. You're too weak, just like your mother was. God rest her fucking soul." I see red when he mentions Mom, and before I know what's happening, my body is moving.

Putting one foot in front of the other, I race toward him raising my hand as I get closer. When I'm in front of him, I launch myself through the air, but fate is a bitch and when my body collides with his, he doesn't budge an inch. My father reaches out and grips my upper arms, digging his fingers in, and roughly pulls me into him. With my arms confined to my sides, I still try to strike at him, but he has a tight hold on me and my efforts are futile.

Wriggling, I try to slip free but his grip on me is tight. He slides his hand down my arm, and I know he's trying to get the glass but I refuse to let go. Holding on tighter, it digs into my palms, splitting my skin open. I feel it cut into my skin, blood pouring out of the wound.

One minute I'm in my dad's grasp and the next, Saint is there. He grabs my father's shoulder and pulls him away from me. His grip is enough for Dad to let go of me and when he turns to face Saint, I act.

Lifting my hand, I pull it back and with all the force I can muster, I slam the shard of glass into his side over and over.

My father grunts and turns from Saint to face me. He tries to reach for me, but I just keep stabbing him. He steps back from me and clutches at his abdomen. Holding his side, blood spills from him. His shirt is soaked and he stumbles from the blood loss.

Dropping to his knees, I watch as my father struggles for air. Red liquid spills from the side of his mouth. He lifts his gaze to mine, and I see nothing reflecting back at me.

Saint moves beside me and, together, we watch my father fall to the grass below and take his final breath.

Saint and I stand side by side and we look at my father's dead body.

"I killed him," I mumble. Tears track down my cheeks and I fall to my knees. "I killed him," I repeat as Saint pulls me into his chest and holds on to me as I crumble over taking another person's life.

"We need to clean you up and burn your clothes," Saint says once my tears have subsided.

"What?" I question, confused by his statement.

"I'll take the fall, Dove. Not you, I ... I killed him."

"N-no," I cry, my eyes once again filling with tears. "It was me, not you."

"Not asking, Rowan," he growls.

Sitting here, I stare at Saint and process his words. He pulls me into his chest and places a hard kiss against my lips.

"I fucking love you, Dove," he declares against my lips.

"I love you too," I reply before I wrap my arms around him. I kiss him again, trying to figure out how to fix this because Saint will not go down for this. This was me and I will not let him take the fall for me.

MATTHEW

"YOU WON'T HURT ME, Rowan. You never could. You're too weak, just like your mother was. God rest her fucking soul." As soon as those words pass my lips, I regret them. My Vivian was everything to me, just like my precious girl and precious boy are.

Everything I have ever done has been for them. Every lash, every hug, everything has been out of love for them.

One minute I'm holding my precious girl, and the next, there's a sharp pain in my side and when I look down, I see what's happening.

She's stabbing me.

My precious girl is stabbing me.

Repeatedly, she slices into me with the shard of glass in her hand.

Looking at her, I'm stunned. Why is she doing this to me?

Dropping to my knees, I hold my side and gaze up at my precious girl. I have never seen anger on her face like this before, something must have happened.

Why is she stabbing me?

I'm her dad.

I love her, everything I have ever done has been for her.

For us.

Blood bubbles at my lips, and with each breath I feel my life ebbing away. With each breath I realize this is it; I will no longer be here to protect my precious girl.

Who will love her now?

My vision begins to fade.

A coldness seeps into my bones.

Everything is fuzzy.

Falling forward, my body crashes into the grass, and the last thing I see before my eyes close for the last time is my beautiful daughter.

My Rowan.

My precious girl.

She has tears in her eyes, but she's never looked more beautiful. I can happily die knowing my precious girl is sad that I will no longer be here to protect her. To love her. *"I'll be waiting on the other side for you,"* I think as I take my last breath.

SAINT

"THAT'S the story you're going with, kid?" The detective sighs, again, looking across at me.

Like the other eleventy billion times he's asked, I simply nod and give a curt, "Yep."

Standing up, he shoves his chair back and rests his knuckles on the table, eyeing me suspiciously. Raising his eyebrow, he frowns before looking over his shoulder at his partner, who just shrugs. He turns his attention back to me. "Look, kid. Why don't you just tell us the truth?"

"That is the truth," I snap, getting pissed that he doesn't believe me.

"You expect us to believe you stabbed Mr. Ashford—" He pauses and picks up the file glancing at it as if he doesn't know the number of times. "Thirteen times in his side until he started to bleed out."

"I did," I nonchalantly reply.

"Kid, you're barely covered in blood. You have no scratches on your hand to even indicate you were holding the glass. Now his daughter, on the other hand ..." he drifts off, not finishing his statement.

"It. Was. Me," I bark through clenched teeth. I'm getting frustrated with them not believing my story.

Sharing a look, the detectives give each other the side-eye before they face me again.

"If that's the story you want to go with, kid, we can't stop you. But remember, if this wasn't self-defense and you planned this, you could go to jail for a very, very long time. The last name Vanderbelt won't save you when it comes to murder."

"He touched me for years," I seethe. "Then the cunt breaks out of jail and went to touch me again, so I killed him. End. Of. Fucking. Story," I tell them. It's not a lie, it's just half a truth.

"Look, kid," the other detective says, finally speaking up. "We get it, you're protecting your girl, but we want you to understand—"

"I understand," I growl, "that you two are fucking incompetent." I don't need them to fucking tell me what happens if I get convicted because I don't give a flying fuck. I'll do whatever it takes to protect Rowan, no matter what.

"I guess you can sit here and wait while we speak to Miss Ashford, again." They both glance at me before they open the door and step out, shutting it behind them.

They've left me alone in the room with nothing but my thoughts and worry about Rowan and her safety.

ROWAN

"YOU REALLY WANT your boyfriend to go to jail for something he didn't do?" the detective says, eyeing me across the table. He doesn't believe our story, and I don't blame them. We didn't have time to clean up before the authorities arrived. Seems a prisoner on the loose has the whole force out looking, and they happened to stumble upon Saint and me at the scene just after I killed Dad. I was still covered in his blood, and the murder weapon was in the grass at my feet.

"You know, Miss Ashford," the second officer says, breaking the silence in the room. "If he's convicted of murder, he could spend up to fifteen years in prison, if not more. But let's say it's that, he'll be thirty-three by the time he gets out." He pauses and raises his eyebrows and each time he does that, I want to stab him in the side too. "Do you really think you can wait that long for him?"

My palms begin to sweat, and my throat feels clammy, I swallow looking down at my lap before glancing back at them. My eyes fill with tears. "I did it," I sniff. "I stabbed him, and I'd do it a-fucking-gain if it means the world is rid of that molesting monster."

They look between each other with wide eyes and then back at me. "Are you admitting that it was you who killed your father and not Saint Vanderbelt?"

Swallowing, I nod. "Yes," I hiccup. Tears flow down my face as I confess out loud that I killed my father and not Saint. "It was me and not Saint. I—"

"Miss Ashford—" he interrupts but I interrupt him, needing to get all of this out.

"He raped me for years. He deserved each and every stab," I say through clenched teeth. "And then some." The look the detective gives me makes me think he doesn't believe me so I try again. "My father was a respected man, no one would have believed me. He threatened me so I stayed quiet until I just couldn't anymore. He abused me and my mom and Saint for years. For years." Tears streak down my face as I break down, I let it all out and I have a feeling I've just dug my own grave, but as long as Saint is safe, I don't care what happens to me. The days of hiding behind him and letting him protect me are over.

"Miss Ashford, do you expect us to believe you didn't plan this? That you and Mr. Vanderbelt didn't conspire on how to murder your father? That it was a spur of the moment decision?"

"I didn't want to hurt him, but my father gave me no choice," I cry. "He broke into my room after he escaped YOUR custody and threatened me."

"I see," he sighs just as the door swings open.

"Don't say another word, Miss Ashford," the Vanderbelt's lawyer, Mr. King grumbles, tossing his briefcase on the table in front of the detectives and glaring at them.

Taking a seat beside me, he turns and winks, then lets the detectives have it. "My client acted in self-defense. Her father was arrested recently and is, was, awaiting trial for abusing my clients. He's awaiting trial for multiple counts of abuse against two minors spanning years. Then under YOUR watchful eye, her father escapes incarceration and you didn't think to warn either of my clients that he was on the loose. You—"

The detective interrupts, "Sir, you will find—"

"I'm not finished," Mr. King interrupts, with a raised hand in a Gloria Gaynor 'Stop' way. The Vanderbelt lawyer is a badass, one lift of his hand and Tweddle-Dum and Tweddle-Dumber are quaking in their boots. "As I was saying, this department did not inform my clients that the man they accused had escaped. They were unaware and tonight, Matthew Ashford broke into Ms. Ashford's room and tried to take her, not before Mr. Vanderbelt offered himself up instead. It's clear to me, and anyone with eyes and a brain, Ms. Ashford had a mental breakdown after she saw her father nearly kill Mr. Vanderbelt tonight. The events that occurred thereafter are clearly self-defense and they only came to light due to the ineffectiveness of this precinct." Without missing a beat, Mr. King tells the detectives what will happen next. "Now, we are going to submit that my client was acting in self-defense and if need be, we will claim insanity and that she was not of clear mind about her actions. There's no jury in this world that will convict an innocent girl for murdering the monster who has taunted and raped her since her mother died when she was fifteen." He pauses and once again, the detectives are quaking in their boots. "And if that fails, we will sue this department, this precinct, and the two of you for harassment and negligence." Another pause. "Shall I continue?"

Staring them down, he waits as the two of them talk quietly between themselves. I have no clue how this is going to play out, all I know is I'm so glad to have Mr. King on my side. He's scary when he gets on a roll and I'm glad he's Team Rowan.

My heart is racing as we wait for them to make a decision. "It's clear that you and Mr. Vanderbelt acted in self-defense. Once we get your official statements, with the truth." He glares at me as he says this. "You will be free to go, Miss Ashford." The lawyer raises his eyebrows. "Mr. Vanderbelt too, once he has done the same."

An hour later, after my and Saint's statements—with me as the killer? Stabber? Perpetrator?—have been signed, we're free to go.

Mr. King closes the lid on his briefcase, the click of the lock echoing through the room. "It was lovely doing business with you both." He stands, grabbing his briefcase. "Shall we?" he adds, eyeing me and nodding toward the door.

Standing, I follow him out into the hallway just as Saint exits the room across the hall.

When I see him, I launch myself across the hall and barrel into his chest. He wraps his arms around me and holds me tightly. "I'm sorry," I whisper, "so, so sorry."

Saint doesn't say anything. He just kisses my head and

clutches me in his arms as I cry into his chest. It's been an emotional few hours.

It doesn't hit me until we're outside that my father is gone. He's really gone and for the first time in years, I don't have to be scared.

I'm free, finally free of Matthew Ashford's clutches.

SAINT

"I'M SO MAD AT YOU," I hiss at Rowan.

We're lying in my bed in my old room at Mom's place. We couldn't go back to Hendrix and Quinn's place, our room there was tainted now.

Rowan is snuggled into my side and I'm running my fingers through her hair when she lifts her gaze up, she pouts and all the anger I feel washes away. I can never stay angry at her, and at the end of the day, she's safe now and due to her bravery, she will never be harmed by that monster again.

"I'm sorry," she murmurs. Pushing away from me, she falls to her back and stares up at the ceiling.

Rolling to my side, I stare down at her. Brushing a tendril of hair behind her ear, I lean down and graze my lips against her forehead before I murmur, "It's my job to save you, Dove. Promise me you will never ever try to save me again."

"Saint, I—" Shutting up her response, I slam my lips to hers before she can finish her sentence. Pushing my tongue into her mouth, I ravish her. She moans into the kiss. Her hands grip my arms, her nails digging in as I half cover her body with mine. Pulling away from her lips, I begin nipping and sucking along her jawbone and down her neck. Sucking on her nipple through her shirt, she writhes in pleasure beneath me. "Please," she mewls, and who am I to deny her?

Yanking her top over her head, I throw it to the floor as I pull down her yoga pants and panties in one motion.

Rowan gasps when I push two fingers inside her, pumping them in and out of her pussy. "Never," *pump* "ever," *pump* "defy" *pump* "me," *pump* "again."

"Never," she pants, lost to the feeling of my fingers thrusting in and out of her cunt.

Covering her mouth with mine, I swallow her moans. Her pussy clenches around my fingers and I can tell she's close. She whimpers when I remove them, watching intently as I lick her juices from my digits.

Once they're clean, I free my cock and shuffle between her thighs. Reaching down, I grip my shaft and run it up and down her slit a few times, earning myself a growl of frustration.

Reaching up, she wraps her hands around my neck and pulls me down for a kiss. As her tongue slips into my mouth, I impale her in one hard thrust, causing us both to groan at the pleasure. Moving my hips, I set the pace, fucking her with so much anger and love, the two emotions blur into one.

She cries out with each thrust. Our skin slaps together as my hips move at a rapid rate. I kiss her with as much anger slash love as I'm giving her with my cock.

I'm so goddamn angry at her for admitting she did it. She was supposed to go with our story, it was supposed to me. I was going to save her not the other way around, but at the same time, I'm so proud of her for battling her monster.

With one final thrust, I empty inside her, grunting as I come. Rowan follows me into the orgasmic abyss, clawing at my back as her pussy clenches around me through her release.

"Fuck, me," I moan, exhaling a deep breath.

"I just did," she cheekily replies. Lifting her hand, she cups my cheek. "I'm sorry, Saint. Sorry I defied you."

Closing my eyes, I rest my forehead against hers. "Don't ever try to save me, Rowan." Opening my eyes, I gaze into hers. "Never save me, it's always you first. I'll always protect you, no matter what."

Nodding, her eyes well with tears as she pulls me down and kisses me. "I love you," she whispers against my lips.

"I'll always love you, Dove. For eternity and beyond," I murmur softly.

Gripping her face between my palms, I slip my tongue between her lips and together they tangle. I know we just fucked, but I need her again, especially when she moans into our kiss. The sound is like a lightning rod to my cock, jolting it back to life.

"Fuck, Dove," I hiss, grinding my still very hard cock back into her pussy. Gently and slowly, I push each inch inside her. Her fingers fist my hair, tugging gently as we rock back and forth. My fingers grasp her face and I devour her mouth as my tongue tangles with hers.

With each thrust, her pussy clenches around my cock. "Saint," she whimpers, pulling me on top of her as she wraps her legs around me.

Holding her to my chest, I thrust in and out of her.

This is what making love feels like. It's heaven on Earth and it's all because of this woman. My woman. My dove.

"You are so beautiful, Rowan," I murmur softly before my lips plunge to hers in an all-consuming kiss.

"Saint," she whimpers, moaning as my hand slips underneath her, holding her ass cheek in my palm as I move.

Rowan's hands tighten around my neck. Her fingernails dig into my skin and together we explode, my cock twitches as I empty into her.

"Fuck, baby," I pant, moving to the mattress beside her. She curls into my side, resting her head on my shoulder as we catch our breaths.

"I love you, Saint," she murmurs softly, moving her fingertips across my chest then around my nipple.

Placing my finger under her chin, I lift her head and I gaze into her eyes. "I love you too, Dove. For eternity and beyond," I tell her again before I take her lips. A warmth filters through me at the knowledge she's finally safe.

ROWAN

AFTER A CRAZY FEW WEEKS, no months, life has settled down.

Finally.

Our exams are behind us, my father is dead, and I can finally breathe. I can focus on me and the night ahead, it's finally time for prom. It's time to close the chapter on school and him. It's time to start a new one ... if only I knew what I wanted to do with my life.

My therapist has told me it's okay not to know what I want to do with the rest of my life. For so long, I was trapped but now, now I'm free. I've finally come to terms with what happened with Dad and I'm moving on with my life.

Matthew Ashford no longer has any control or bearing on my life. I have no father, just a sperm donor as Quinn calls him. I have Saint and my friends, and I'm okay with that.

Saint pulls up outside the hall where I'm about to attend my first abuse support group. Silently, we sit in his car. Turning my head, I look out at the building, but I make no move to get out.

"You okay?" he asks. Reaching across the center console, he takes my hands and squeezes, in only the way he can. It instantly calms me.

"I will be." Turning my head back to him, I smile. "With you by my side, I can face anything."

"Too right you can. You are Rowan-Fucking-As—"

Pressing my finger to his lips, I shake my head. "Don't mention my last name, I'm just Rowan."

"Deal, now go on in and be the amazing woman I know you are. Quinn is picking you up because I have something to take care of," he raises his hand, "and no, I'm not telling you what I'm up to."

"Not even for a blow job?"

"Dove, as much as I love your lips wrapped around my dick and the head choking you as I thrust down your throat, Remy and Alani will kill me if I'm late, and if I stay here talking about your lips wrapped around my dick, I'm gonna be late."

"I'm okay with that," I nonchalantly reply with a shrug.

"I promise you tonight, after prom, I will choke you with my dick till the sun rises."

"I'm going to hold you to that promise, Saint Vanderbelt, because I love choking on your dick. It makes me so wet. Wanna feel how moist I am at the thought of your dick in my mouth?" I spread my legs and begin to lift my skirt to show him the wet spot on my panties, but he reaches out and holds my wrist.

"I know how wet you get, Dove, I can smell it, but this stalling tactic isn't going to work. As much as it pains me, you need to go to your support group, and I need to go see some girls about a thing with a rock-hard dick."

"I can fix that before you go," I sweetly offer, sucking on my index finger. It falls out of my mouth with a pop, causing Saint to groan.

"You will pay for that," he hisses, adjusting himself. "Now get the fuck out of my car."

"Sir, yes, sir." I salute him before leaning over to kiss him, and because I can, I reach out and cup his dick. His hard dick. Giving it a squeeze, I jump out. "Laters, baby." With a sway to my hips, I walk over to the door and let myself in.

An hour later, I walk out of the hall feeling lighter than when I walked in. "See you next week," one of the leaders calls out as I wait for Quinn to get here. My phone pings with a text and I smile when I see Quinn's name.

QUINN

Ellis just shit everywhere ... like
everywhere, everywhere ... be there soon
... if I survive Shitmageddon.

An unladylike snort slips out and then it turns into a belly laugh when Quinn sends a picture. "Holy shit, Batman," I whisper.

ROWAN

How does someone so little produce so
much shit?

And why is it green? All he eats is milk.

QUINN

I don't fucking know but the smell, OMG,
Rowan, the smell.

Another snort slips free.

ROWAN

Look, don't worry about me. I'll call an
Uber and meet you at your place.

QUINN

Are you sure?

ROWAN

Positive ... just have the shit cleaned up
'cause you know I don't do smells.

QUINN

You are the best friend ever.

ROWAN

I know ... we can hit up the park when I
get back before your mom comes to get
Ellis so we can get our prom on.

Twenty minutes later, my Uber drops me off and Quinn and a non-shitty Ellis are waiting on the front steps for me.

"Let's get our swing on," I singsong as I reach them.

"I think you like the swing more than Ellis does," Quinn says, kissing me on the cheek as she reaches me.

"Hell yes, I do. There is nothing freer than being on a swing. The air whooshing by as you go higher and higher."

"That's a good look on you."

"What is?" I ask her, confused 'cause I'm wearing a sundress and flats, nothing special or out of the ordinary for me.

"Happiness," she replies with a smile. "You are radiating genuine happiness and that makes me genuinely happy."

"Are you getting all soft on me, Quinn Ellis?"

"Nope, not me. I'm a hard-ass through and through."

"Let's agree to disagree on that but you are correct, I am happy. I can't remember the last time I was this happy."

"Me neither. Now let's go get our swing on."

We loop arms and make our way toward the park, but before we make it to the park, shit hits the fan and it's worse than Ellis's green explosion from earlier.

SAINT

"YEAH, yeah, Rem, I'll find them," I tell her, rolling my eyes at her and her 'I need them now' rant. "They'll be here somewhere, just calm your tits."

"Did you just tell me to calm my tits?" she hisses through the line, and in the background I hear Thatch yell, "Why you talking about your tits with my brother?" Then I hear shuffling, followed by a giggle … and then a moan. Not wanting to listen to them get it on, I hang up.

Throwing my phone onto Fuckface's desk, I continue to look for the photos that Rem is after.

Searching his desk, I open and close the drawers after

shuffling the files and random shit around. Rowan is going to have to decide what to do with his shit. I vote for a massive bonfire, with him in it, and then I can piss on his burning ashes. It's still surreal that he's dead, I keep expecting him to walk through the door coming back from the grave, but this isn't *The Walking Dead* and he's not going to come back as a zombie cunt.

One after the other, I open and close drawers in search of baby photos of Rowan. Remy was quite vocal that she needs them and I'm really not in the mood for Thatcher to curse me out for not doing as his Peach asked, so here I am, searching in the dark.

Walking over to the shelves, I drop to the floor and open the drawer at the bottom. Lifting up an album, something shiny underneath it catches my eye, the flicker of gold is enough to have me doing a double take. Pushing the folder covering it aside, I lift it up and my eyes widen when I see what it is.

"What the fuck," I whisper as I reach into the drawer and lift it out, it's the exact same medallion Thatcher found at the cliffs and the same medallion that belonged to my father.

Shuffling around, I stretch my leg out and look at the medallion, spinning it round and round between my fingers.

This has to mean something, right?

Looking back into the drawer, I pull out the folder that was covering it and begin to read but the more I read, the more confused I become.

Fuckface Ashford has to have this for a reason. Something doesn't feel right, and my stomach swirls as a thought forms, and then my stomach drops when I come across the one thing I never thought I'd see again.

A file with times, dates, and names all lined up on a sheet with a photo attached to each piece of paper.

"Fuck," I hiss, covering my mouth in complete and utter shock.

Fuckface Ashford was a part of it.

He was just like them.

He was working with my father and Remy's mother on the trafficking ring.

Turning back to the drawer, I pull out all the files and splay them out before me. My eyes dart across everything when a name jumps out at me.

Picking up the papers, I read over them and that shock deepens because surely the name I'm reading isn't involved. "No fucking way," I whisper when I discover that Róisín Doyle aka Crestwood Prep's Dean isn't just involved, she's the mastermind behind it. We all thought my father and Remy's mother were the ringleaders, but we were wrong. Dean Doyle was working alongside them and if I'm deciphering what I'm reading right, she was the one to start all of this.

Pulling my phone out, I call Rowan. I need to ask her if she remembers the Dean being here more than normal or if she's heard something and just repressed it.

A feeling of dread starts to build when her voicemail kicks in. "You've got Rowan, be a normal person and text but if you so desire, leave a message and I'll text you back like a normal person."

A chuckle escapes me at her message. "Dove, it's me. Please be not normal and call me back. I'm fine but I have something to ask you."

Hanging up, I stare at my phone. Something doesn't feel right but I can't put my finger on it.

Trying again, it once again rings out and this time I

know something is wrong and the need to get to her is strong. I have to find Rowan and I have to find her now.

Sprinting from his office I don't stop until I'm at my car.

Before I climb in, I try Rowan again and like the previous times, I have no luck getting hold of her. "Why aren't you answering, baby?"

Jumping into my car, I start the engine and drive to her support group but when I get there, the hall is locked. "Fuck," I growl, running my fingers through my hair.

"Dude, you okay?" Lennon asks, placing his hand over my shoulder. When I look at him, I see a tray of coffees in his hand from the new place that just opened, which has become a popular hangout for us.

"I think Rowan's in trouble," I tell him, spinning in a circle. I stumble, tripping over my own feet. "Quinn's ..." I mumble, and then I turn around and head back to my car.

Lennon wordlessly follows behind me and that's when I notice his car farther down the street. "I'll muster the troops," Lennon shouts, and I nod. Then I climb into the driver's seat and close my door. Reversing out of my spot, I put my foot down and take off. I don't know what's about to happen, but I get the feeling everything we thought was over, isn't, and shit is about to begin, again.

QUINN

ONE MINUTE ROWAN and I are arm in arm walking to the park and the next, we have burlap bags over our heads and are being dragged into a waiting van, no doubt white like in all the movies where the heroines are kidnapped.

All I remember is screaming for Ellis. His little cries echoing down the street as I'm whisked away and then feeling utter relief when I realize they have him in the van with us.

"Give me my baby, you fucking cunt asshole fuckers," I

shout. "You touch a hair on his head and I will fuck you up."

"Shut your mouth, bitch," a deep voice growls before they slap me across the face. The force causes me to slam into the side of the van and I black out. When I wake up again, my hands are zip-tied together and Ellis is asleep in a cradle beside me. "Ellis," I cry. I try to pick him up but with my hands tied, I can't. As if he can sense me, he begins to cry harder, and I do my best to calm him with my tied hands.

"Shut that fucking kid up," my captor shouts, causing Ellis to cry louder and harder.

"Untie me and I will," I demand, thrusting my hands out in front of me.

"Promise you won't do anything stupid?"

"I just want to comfort my son … please."

Surprising me, the man stands up and walks over. Flipping open a pocket knife, he slices through my restraints and before he's even taken a step back, I pick Ellis up and hold him tightly to my chest.

Tears streak down my cheeks as I clutch on to my little boy. Rocking him gently in my arms, I kiss his head and whisper, "Shhhh" over and over but nothing I do works.

Softly, I begin to sing "Hush Little Baby" but it does nothing to hush or soothe him.

The man just sits in the corner glaring at me. The gun in his hand points toward us and I'm filled with fear. "Shh, it's okay, buddy," I gently whisper to Ellis and when he starts to suck on my chest, I realize why he's crying—he's hungry.

Turning my back to my kidnapper, I lower my top and begin to feed him. He latches on to my breast and suckles.

The only sound now is that of my lil' man slurping down his milk.

Walking over to the wall, I slide down to my butt so it's more comfortable to feed Ellis. The guard eyes me and I notice his hungry gaze is focused on my tit. *Typical man.* He licks his lips and I turn my shoulder to block him and focus on feeding Ellis. Watching him drink, I worry my lip between my teeth wondering where Rowan is. Vaguely, I remember there being two assailants. One grabbed me and the other grabbed her, but after losing consciousness in the van, I lost her, and I have no clue where they've taken her.

Ellis now has a full tummy and has finally settled. My boob pops out of his mouth and he's sound asleep.

Leaning against the wall, I hold on to my baby and stare at him. My eyes well with tears but I swipe them away, crying won't fix this, and I refuse to be a victim again. I survived an attack once and I will survive again. I will not just sit here and wait for whatever is about to happen, to happen.

In this moment, I vow to protect my son and my friend. I'm no damsel in distress, I'm a mother-fucking-Queen.

The man's eyes rake over my body and I realize that my tit is still out. Putting it away, I cover my chest from the leering eyes of my captor. Since having Ellis, Hendrix has become obsessed with my boobs. I don't blame him, pregnancy has agreed with the girls, and right now, they are currently busting from my top slightly. Seeing the look of desire in my captor's eyes, I know how to get out of here. I will use my tits to my advantage.

Placing Ellis back into the crib, he stays asleep. He's in a milk coma and I smile down at my sleeping little boy and say a silent prayer that I can pull this off. I've watched enough *Alias* episodes and bringing out my inner Sydney

Bristow, I turn around to face the man who is going to wish he'd skipped work today.

Shuffling away from Ellis, I be sure to give him an eyeful of my chest.

"Don't fucking move," the guy barks, but I ignore him and push myself up onto my knees.

"I was going to offer you a drink," I flirt with him. "It must be hard work just standing in one spot like that," I say, pressing my boobs together and like a moth to a flame, his gaze falls down eyeing them. His tongue darts out, wetting his lips and I know he's a goner.

"You can offer me something else," he suggests, smiling sheepishly.

"Ohh, yeah?" I lean forward. "And what might that be?"

"This," he declares and he cups his junk. I notice his large hand covers more than just his junk, and it's hard not to laugh at the thought of his mini dick.

Unzipping his trousers, he begins to pull his cock out, and I have to bite the inside of my cheek to hold back my laugh. My eyes widen and he mistakes it for fear. Stroking his dick, he smiles at me and nods down to his cock, if you can call it a cock.

"Go on, little girl." He chuckles. "Suck it. Let me fuck your face."

Those words cause me to flash back to that time when Brennan took me, and I shudder. Memories of that event play on a loop in my mind and I whimper.

"No need to whimper," my new captor says, and the sound of his voice snaps me back to the present. "I'll be gentle, I'm not a monster."

Blinking rapidly, I stare at him. His cock is now hard, and I shit you not, my pinkie is bigger than his dick and, for some reason, that gives me the courage I need to take him on.

Swallowing, I nod and taking my time, I slowly make my way over to him. Stopping before him, I stare up through my lashes and with my eyes locked on his, I lean forward. His head dips watching my mouth open and my tongue dart out. He's so focused on what's about to not happen that he doesn't see me grip the lamp beside the table. With all my might, I lift my arm and swing. Smashing it into the side of his head, the lamp shatters against his skull, breaking in to hundreds of pieces. His eyes are wide open in shock as he falls to the floor with a thump. Just to be sure he's out, I slam my fist into his face, shaking my hand at the pain lancing through it. They never tell you in the movies how much it hurts to slam your fist into someone's face.

Ellis makes a sound and hearing him gets me moving.

Standing up, I run back, grab Ellis, and pick him up. Poking my head out into the hallway, I look around and listen. I think it's just us. "Rowan," I whisper-shout as I tiptoe down the hallway.

Stepping into the main room, I run across it to the front door. With my hand on the handle, I look back into the house, but I know Rowan isn't here. They've split us up, probably for the best.

Opening the door, I step outside and squint at the brightness of the sun.

Looking back into the empty house, a feeling of defeat hits me. I know I should wait and find Rowan, but Ellis coos in my arms and I know she'd want me to get him to safety.

"I'm so sorry, Ro," I murmur, holding Ellis to my chest. "I'll get the guys and save you, I promise."

Putting one foot in front of the other, I race down the stairs and head for the dirt driveway. The house is in the middle of a field, and I have no clue how far the main road is, but I need to get my son to safety so I run. I run like *Forest Gump* and hightail it out of there. I really don't want to leave my friend behind, wherever she may be, but I can't risk my son.

I know Rowan will understand.

I hope.

Making it to the main road, I look left. Then I look right. "Which way?" I cry and then make a choice and turn left and start running again. I keep running, doing whatever it takes to get Ellis to safety.

Coming to a crest, I stop and hunch over. Breathing deeply, I take big gulps, filling my chest, but before I can catch my breath, the sound of an engine garners my attention and when I look up, I cry with relief.

It's Saint.

His car comes to a screeching halt in front of me and in seconds, he's out and pulling me into his arms. I breakdown with relief and sob into his chest.

"Where is she?" he demands, pulling away from me. He grips my upper arms and stares intently at me. "Quinn," he barks. "Where is she?"

"I-I-I—" I stutter, and my legs give way, but Saint catches me before I hit the pavement. The only sound I can hear is my cries as he holds me in the middle of the deserted road while I break down.

ROWAN

MY ENTIRE BODY begins to shake as they grab me, forcing me to follow them down a set of stairs and away from Quinn and Ellis. Quinn was still unconscious and Ellis, the good little boy that he is, was sleeping soundly next to her. Our asshole captors have provided a cradle for him and in a weird way, I'm thankful for the gesture, but then again, you can't sell a baby that's distressed so it's for their benefit and not his.

They drag me through a long, narrow, and dark hallway and eventually, we reach a door. It's shoved open and I'm pushed through. I fall onto the ground with a thud.

Lifting my head, I squint at the bright light from the shining sun. A hand grips my upper arm, and I'm once again thrown into a waiting van. The door slams shut behind me, cloaking me in darkness once more. Curling into myself, I cry into my knees as the van drives away. I wonder what fresh hell will be waiting for me at my next destination.

The van comes to a stop, and the hairs on the back of my neck stand on end. This is it, this is where I have to make my move or I'll be sold to some rich fucker, and who fucking knows what will happen then.

I've lived with a monster before and I will not do that again. I wanna live with Saint and get the happily ever after I deserve.

Through the wall of the van, I can hear voices and they make my stomach churn. During the trip, my hands were bound in front of me. I may be tied up but with them in front, I can still fight and I'm going to fight till the end. I don't care what it takes, no one will touch me against my will ever again. I refuse to let them touch me and I will happily die before that happens.

The back doors swing open and the face of an unknown man stares back at me. He's dressed in a three-piece suit but it does nothing to hide his evil side. What with the oily slicked-back hair and a sadistic smile across his face, I know a monster when I see a monster.

"Hello, pet, welcome to your new home." He smirks. "Well, your home until you're sold and make us millions."

He nods at a man beside him and his lackey leans into the van, wraps his hand around my ankle, and drags me toward him. I begin to kick at him, smiling in delight when my foot collides with his nose, causing blood to burst free.

"Fuck," he growls, but it doesn't stop him. He digs his fingers in, his nails piercing my skin.

"No, let go of me," I scream as he throws me over his shoulder and slaps me on the ass.

He doesn't flinch when I begin thrashing my legs and slamming my fists into his back. "Let me fucking go, you cocksucking asshole cunt," I scream.

Reaching out, I grab on to a doorframe as he walks through, causing him to stumble. He's three times the size of me, and with a gentle tug, he pries my hands off the frame and not so graciously tosses me to the floor in front of him.

Stepping over me, he leans down and wraps his hand around my throat and squeezes. Breathing through his clenched teeth, he stares at me as the grip on my neck tightens.

A woman in a figure-hugging sparkly silver dress comes up beside him, and looks down at me with a scowl on her makeup-filled face. In any other place, she'd looks stunning, but here, she looks like the devil.

"Behave and he won't strangle you to death." She looks to the man and with a nod, he lets go of my neck and I fall to the floor holding my neck and gasping for breath.

"Fuck you both," I sneer through my teeth.

"Now now," a familiar voice says and when I look up, my eyes widen I shock. "Surprise," she sing songs. She's dressed just as elegantly as the other woman and when she sashays into the room, all the air is sucked from my lungs. "You belong to me now, dear, and it'd be in your best interest to not piss me the fuck off," she growls. "Thanks to your cunt of a father, we're behind, but you being here makes up for everything. I've wanted my hands on you for years, but your father never let us touch you." Squatting down, she runs her finger along my hairline. "And with him gone now, thanks by the way, all bets are off and well, here you are." She stands up and looks to the guy who just strangled me. "Take her to the room," she commands.

With a nod, he bends down and once again, throws me over his shoulder. Without uttering a word, he makes his way down a corridor, through an open room, and up a set of stairs. Opening the third door, he throws me from his shoulder, and I land on a bed.

Bending down, he grips my ankle and from the floor picks up a lock attached to a chain, which he clips it into place.

Sitting on the bed, chained up, I watch him walk away from me. He closes the door behind him and then the lock clicks loudly into place, leaving me with my confused thoughts a to why Dean Doyle is here and a racing heart.

Even from beyond the grave, my father is still messing with me. I shouldn't be surprised that he would be a part of something like this. Fucking with people's lives was his favorite pastime.

As I sit here chained to the bed, I wonder what's going to happen next. Maybe I was wrong before and this is the worst kind of hell, only time will tell what happens next, but I know one thing, I will not go down without a fight.

SAINT

"WHO THE FUCK ARE YOU?" I growl at the newcomers who walk into Quinn and Hendrix's living room behind Grayson Hearst. *Why the fuck is he here?* Ever since Arlen returned from the dead, he's been hanging around more and more. The guy's all right, for a Hearst, but fuck, give your sister some space, man.

"This is Agent Cox and this is Agent Cruz," Grayson introduces them.

"We're with the FBI," Cruz, I think, says. "We have been following this ring for a few years now, and when

Grayson called us with new details, we jumped on a plane and here we are."

"Why did you stop?" I ask.

"With the deaths of Thornton Vanderbelt and Rochelle Hearst, we thought it was over, but Grayson thought it was wrapped up too easily and kept digging. Turns out, he was right."

"You're FBI?" Remy asks her brother.

"Surprise," Grayson says with a shrug.

"You and I will be talking about this later," she growls at her brother. "But for now, what do we do to get Rowan back?"

"We need to speak with Ms. Ellis—"

"Like fuck," Hendrix bellows. "She's been through enough. She doesn't need to rehash what she went through." As much as I want to punch my brother for his comment, I understand his need to protect Quinn.

"And she," Quinn states, walking in the room in sweats and a LOCP hoodie with her hair wrapped in one of her hideous orange towels, "will do whatever it takes to get Rowan back."

"Babe," Hendrix says, walking over to her. "Are you sure?"

"Positive," she turns to the agents, "what do you want to know?"

"Everything from the moment you and Ms. Ashford—"

"Rowan," I growl, "her name is Rowan."

"Okay, I need to know everything from the moment you and Rowan were taken. Smells. Sounds. Names. Anything that you can remember? The smallest of details will help."

Nodding, Quinn drops onto the sofa, and she fills the agents and us in on what she remembers. They nod and jot notes, asking questions at times, and Quinn tells them everything she can.

When there's a pause, she looks to me. "I'm sorry I didn't find her, Saint. I'm so sorry." She begins to cry again, and Hendrix pulls her into his arms and glares at me.

"You have nothing to be sorry for, Quinn. Ro would have wanted you and Ellis safe, plus, she's tough. She survived her father. She can survive one crazy Dean and a trafficking ring."

"Róisín Doyle is not to be underestimated," Agent Cruz informs us. "She has been doing this for near on twenty years. We were so close to bringing them down last year, and we thought it was all over when Rochelle Hearst was arrested and subsequently killed in prison."

"My mom committed suicide," Remy states. "Right, Gray?" She looks to her brother and all eyes move to him.

"Umm, Rem," Grayson says, squeezing his neck and looking uncomfortable. "Mom was actually murdered. It was staged to look like a suicide."

"Why didn't you tell me?" she hisses at her brother.

"Because it's part of an ongoing investigation and we needed the rest of the players to think we were done investigating. So, to the public, it's a suicide and to them, it looks like we gave up and closed the investigation."

"But why kill Mom?"

"We think that Róisín had her killed so she wouldn't spill the beans on the rest of the operation. Illegal fight clubs and underhanded adoptions are just the tip of the iceberg when it comes to Róisín Doyle."

"Let me guess, she's involved in the Irish mafia?" I voice with a laugh, but when I see the look on all three of their faces, I realize I'm on to something. "Are you shitting me? Doyle is linked to the mafia?"

Cruz nods, opens a file, and throws a photos of the Dean and another man onto the coffee table. "Róisín Doyle is the daughter of Liam Doyle, head of the Irish Mob out of Dublin. She's head of the U.S. family."

"Fuck me," I whisper, shaking my head. "Well, that's a great story and doesn't really concern us, but what are we going to do to get Rowan back?"

"It's not that simple."

"Yeah, it is 'cause I don't give a flying fuck about the mafia shit. I just want my girl back."

"We do too," Agent Cruz declares. "And we will do everything we can to safely bring Ms. Ashford—"

"Her name's Rowan. Don't refer to her by that fucking name again."

"Okay, Rowan it is. We will do what we can to safely get her back, but we really think this is our chance to take down the whole operation, and from what you've all told us about Ms. Ash, I mean Rowan, I think she'd want that too."

Staring over at the fucker, I realize he's right. Shaking my head, I sit back on the sofa. Lacing my fingers, I place my hands behind my head. "You're right, but if anything happens to her, I will kill any fucker who gets in my way."

"Did you just threaten a federal agent?"

"No, I threatened anyone who gets in the way of saving my future wife."

ROWAN

AND THE SURPRISES just keep coming. When will they end? Turns out our Dean, Róisín Doyle, is the mastermind behind all of this. We all thought it was Rem's mom and Mr. Vanderfuck. How wrong we were. There's a new person at the top of my shit list, Róisín Doyle, and I cannot wait to see the smirk wiped off her face when I take her down. I refuse to let her sell me off to the highest bidder.

She's messed with the wrong person.

I'm not the shy timid girl I once was. I'm Rowan No-fucking-last name, and I will survive this.

Dean Doyle is furious as they tell her Quinn and Ellis

escaped. She slaps the guy so hard across the face that even my cheek tingles. Then before the asshole knows what's happening, she pulls a gun from the waistband of her pants and shoots him point-blank.

The tears on my face are in relief at knowing both Quinn and Ellis are safe, but they turn to fear when I see the rage on her face. The look in her eyes reminds me so much of my father when he was angry.

She's a delusional bitch and knowing what she has planned for us, well me, now, I'm so fucking glad they escaped. I always knew Quinn was tough, and I'm so fucking proud of her right now.

Sitting here, I listen to the Dean rant and rave over it being hard to find good help, and when she steps over the goon she shot point-blank, I vow to end the bitch. I did not survive all the shit my dad put me through to go out this way. No fucker will ever lay a hand on me again without my permission, and this bitch will not sell me to the highest bidder.

Then my thoughts turn to Saint and my lip begins to tremble. I have a gut feeling I will never see Saint again. My hero, my everything.

"Why are you crying now? I'm not going to shoot you."

"No, you're just going to sell me to some monster, who is going to rape me for the rest of my life."

"Yes, yes, I am and you are going to make me a fortune. Thank you for taking out your father. As much as he was a great partner, he was also a cunt." She pauses and stares at me. "Maybe I'll buy you myself and make you work for me. Your father would roll in his grave if I put you to work in my whorehouse."

My eyes widen at her revelation. "Ohh, don't be frightened, dear. It's all fun and games when it comes to selling women and children, well, children if my men don't fucking lose them."

"I am going to fucking end you. When Saint rescues me —" She cuts me off cackling like a witch.

"That pussy won't save you. Hell, he couldn't even save you from your father. He made a deal with the devil and the devil pissed all over that deal. Matthew and I used to laugh about it. He'd have his way with you and before the cum had even dried, there he was, back at it with your precious Saint. Maybe I should sell him too. A pretty boy like him would cause a bidding war. Maybe I should wait and sell you as a pair, but I'm no fool, you two will never be together again."

"He will find me and when he does, you're a dead woman."

"Yeah, I don't think so. Look around, sweetheart. I'm the last woman standing. I've won, and watching you being sold tonight is going to be the highlight of my year. Now shut the fuck up and get ready, it's nearly showtime."

Without another word, she turns on her heel and walks out of my room, leaving me alone with my thoughts and a racing heart. I have a feeling this is the end for me. After all I've been through, this is what it all comes down to.

I'm going to be sold to a monster, but what Dean Doyle doesn't know is that I'm a fighter and I will fight to the fucking end.

"I was right," Dean Doyle coos, walking back into my room. Her sinister gaze runs over me. I've been washed, waxed, and dressed up like a fucking Barbie doll. I'm wearing a skimpy red dress that leaves nothing to the imagination, not that I'm wearing anything underneath. "You are going to fetch me a pretty penny tonight."

"Fuck you," I seethe at her.

"That mouth on you is filthy. A lady doesn't speak like that."

"And a lady wouldn't fucking sell women and children to the highest bidder."

She storms over to me and slaps me, my head flies to the side. "Watch your fucking tongue or I'll shoot you where you stand."

"Can't sell me if I'm dead," I throw back at her.

"Please," she scoffs, "I could sell ice to a fucking Eskimo. Dead or alive, I will sell you tonight. Now, let's go. The auction is almost over, but I've saved the best till last. Everyone out there knows you are Matthew Ashford's precious daughter. Your daddy has quite a few enemies in the crowd tonight and those people will want to get their revenge. Buying and fucking you will be the ultimate fuck you to dear old daddy. God rest his fucking soul."

"Fuck you," I hiss.

"Your words wound me," she says, covering her chest and pretending to wipe a tear from her eyes. "Now, fucking move, it's time for you to shine."

She roughly grabs my arm and drags me down the hallway and into another room. She parades me down the aisle and up onto the stage. She spins me around to face the audience, but I can't see a thing.

Standing next to the Dean, I stare out at the room. It's dark and I can't make out any faces. The only light is from the one shining down on me and the dull glow from the bar.

"Gentlemen and lady." She nods to the silhouette of a woman. "I give you our pièce de résistance and our final lot tonight. I give you my late business partner's, may he rest in peace, daughter, Rowan. Isn't she a doll?"

Murmurs echo from the darkness and the hairs on my neck prickle.

"Give us a spin," she says. "Show the good people what's on offer." She pauses and glares at me when I don't move. "Spin," she demands, and her tone has me quaking in my stilettos. Swallowing deeply, I do as I'm told and shuffle around in a circle. "You've all heard Matthew boast about his daughter and with him gone, now it's your turn to taste what was his." She looks to a man off to the side. "Over to you, Walter."

Without another word, she walks back down the stairs and takes a seat in the front row.

"Shall we start the bidding at one hundred?" Walter says and before he's even finished, the bids are coming in.

Two hundred.

Three hundred.

Four.

Five.

Tears coat my cheeks as my life flashes before my eyes.

Someone bids one million and I gasp. One-fucking-million dollars but it doesn't stop there.

One point one.

One point five.

The bids keep coming, up and up the numbers go.

I zone out as the auction continues around me.

Inside my head I'm screaming, demanding they let me

go. I want to run, but my legs are frozen, and I stand here on the stage as people bid on me.

This is what true hell looks like.

They bid on me like I'm a priceless artifact and not a human.

My mind thinks about all the women and children before me who have been sold and I shake my head, bile sits in the back of my throat.

How many kids have they sold?

How many lives have they destroyed?

The gavel bangs down loudly and the auctioneer yells, "Sold to Mr. and Mrs. Brandy for ten million dollars."

My bidders stand and wave to the crowd. I can't see their faces, but I can tell they're grinning. Before they can take a step up onto the stage and claim me, the doors at the back crash open and all hell breaks loose.

SAINT

SOMEHOW, I managed to convince Agents Cruz and Cox to take me with them. They didn't give me a gun, which is probably for the best because I can't guarantee I wouldn't kill Dean Doyle on sight ... or possibly shoot myself since I've never held or fired a gun before.

I'm ready to fight, my entire body is running on pure adrenaline as we wait. On the other side of these doors, Rowan is in there and some sick bastard is bidding on her. He wants to fucking own her like she's a goddamn cow or something, but she's mine and I will not let the highest bidder win.

"Relax, kid," Agent Cruz murmurs, reaching out and squeezing my shoulder.

"I can't, my girl is in there and I—"

"Want her back. Yeah, yeah, I get it." I give him a look that says, 'you don't know fucking shit' and the asshole just chuckles. "Trust me, I've been there. My wife was kidnapped when she was heavily pregnant, and like you, I was on the other side of a door waiting."

"Did you save her in time?"

"You doubt my skills as an agent?" he throws at me, but before I can answer, he continues. "When it's the one you love in peril, you will go above and beyond to save them. I don't know your girl, but I promise you, we will rescue her. The bad guys will not win."

"How can you be so sure?" I ask him.

"Because you have three of the best agents on the case. Cox and I always win, and with Hearst on the case too, this time will be no different.

Agent Cox moves behind me. "They won't be walking out of here with your girl, we will. Trust us."

For only meeting these guys a few hours ago, I believe them. I feel like I've known them all my life, and I know they have my back. I also know, they will do whatever it takes to save Rowan and anyone else we find inside.

Cruz holds his earpiece and listens intently, then nods and replies, "Good to go." He looks to me. "Stick behind us and do as we say. I know your girl is in there, but one wrong move and it'll all be over." I nod, but we both know that I'll do whatever it takes to get to Rowan, my safety be damned.

In the movies these things happen really fast, but in real life, it's slow, really fucking slow, but as soon as the doors open, everything speeds up.

The doors splinter from the force of being kicked open and that's when all hell breaks loose.

Agents descend on the room and people scatter in all directions, pushing and shoving one another so as not to get caught, but these people don't stand a chance.

"Nobody move," Agent Cruz shouts, but his words have little effect.

My gaze flits around the room, trying to find Rowan amid the chaos. A smile appears when all around me people are handcuffed and arrested. Some are tackled to the ground while others just sit there with not a care in the world.

"Where are you?" I mumble to myself and then, in amongst all the chaos, I hear her. Rowan's scream echoes around me.

Following the sound, I see Dean Doyle trying to drag my dove off the stage.

Without a second thought, I take off toward them. Taking the stairs two at a time until I'm on the stage, I race toward them.

Before my mind has a chance to think, I leap. My body flies through the air and I tackle both of them to the ground. My body lands on top of the Dean, knocking the wind from her as I do.

Rolling off her, I stare up at the ceiling, breathing deeply.

Turning my head, I see the Dean pushing herself up and I reach for the knife I stashed in my pants and pull it out. Shuffling over to her, I reach around her body and pull her into my chest as I hold the blade to her throat.

My hand shakes as I press it in deeper, but before I can slice, a hand covers mine. My gaze tracks along the hand and up an arm. Then I'm staring into the bluest of blue eyes. Everything around me fades away as I gaze up at the woman who owns me, heart and soul.

She squeezes my hand. "Don't, Saint. She's not worth it."

Silently I blink up at her, my grip on the blade wavers and before I do something stupid, I pull my hand away from the Dean's neck.

"You're right, bitch isn't worth it," I hiss through clenched teeth.

"Give me that," Agent Cox growls, snatching the knife from my hand.

Two agents pull Dean Doyle to her feet. They read her her rights and cuff her before they drag her away.

"Glad we didn't need to arrest you too, kid," Agent Cox says, spinning my knife in his hand.

"That tackle was something," Agent Cruz says with a smile as he joins us.

"Thanks," I reply with a shrug. "Felt good to take the bitch down."

"Ever thought of being an agent for the FBI?" Agent Cruz asks.

His question shocks me. "Never really gave it any thought," I tell him honestly. I have no clue what I want to do after school. Surviving was at the forefront of my mind, and now that I don't need to worry about Rowan or myself anymore, I guess it's time for me to think about the future.

"Well, kid, I'm impressed. I think you'd make a fine agent." Agent Cox says.

"Are you offering me a job?" I ask, confused.

They both chuckle then Agent Cox slaps his hand over my shoulder. "Yeah, kid. That's exactly what I'm doing."

"Oh, okay," I reply, confused as fuck right now.

"I think I like the sound of that," Rowan says. She slides her arm around my waist and snuggles into my side.

"Yeah?" I smile down at her. "Agent Vanderbelt." I try out the title and I have to say, I don't mind it.

"Agent Vanderbelt does have a nice ring to it," she says, then she lowers her voice and adds, "And you get handcuffs." She waggles her eyebrows at me. The thought of Rowan naked and cuffed to the bed flashes before my eyes and my dick begins to throb.

She leans up and kisses my cheek. "Thank you for rescuing me, again."

"And I always will, Dove. You are it for me."

"I like the sound of that."

She smiles at me, and I feel her smile deep in my soul. "You know what else has a nice ring to it?"

"What?"

"Rowan Vanderbelt." I smirk at her.

She laughs and slaps my arm, not answering, but I notice she didn't say no. I know it'll happen, soon. I'm sure of it because Rowan is mine. Always has been, always will be.

The room is in complete chaos as agents drag people out, hurling them into vans. People are pleading with them to let them go and that it's all one big mistake. These fuckers actually want mercy to befall them. They can all rot in hell as far as I'm concerned.

Agents Cruz and Cox escort Rowan and me out of the auction hall and while the paramedics look over Rowan, she fills the agents and me in on what went down.

A shudder runs through my body at the thought of what could have happened had we not arrived when we did. Rowan could have ended up with that sick fucking couple, and who knows what would have happened.

They sure as fuck didn't buy her to have as a daughter. They no doubt bought her to do sick and twisted sexual things with her.

I can't believe this shit has been happening in Crestwood and that the Dean of Crestwood Prep was the mastermind behind it all. It sickens me that people actually buy other people, but thankfully, after today, it'll be over.

Dean Doyle and her operation are finished and now we are all safe. I can enjoy my dove and together we can move on, without the threat of her father or a psycho Dean coming after us.

Lacing my fingers with my dove, we walk toward Cruz's car, and I know that together we can overcome anything.

Rowan is my other half. She's the light in my world, the meaning to everything and nothing can stop us now. The future is ours.

ROWAN

TONIGHT WILL BE our last game of 'Ready or Not' held at Crestwood Prep because last night, we finally got our prom after a slight delay, and by this time tomorrow, we will have graduated and be set forth into the world.

Like always, The Lords pull their pompous macho shit but between you and me, I love it.

We girls, including Lauren and Risa who came out for graduation, are all lined up against the building and the guys are giving their spiel about the rules and what is accepted and not accepted. Since this is the last one for the year, an invitation is given to the juniors who will officially be allowed to participate.

The guys are sticklers for the rules, but we all know that if you wanna play 'Ready or Not' you play and follow the rules.

"Right, for all you newbies here, listen the fuck up. I'll only say this once." Thatcher's voice booms across the grounds and even though the air is filled with excitement for the night ahead, I swear I see sweat starting to pour off them, and I can't help but chuckle. "You'll each have a pick, choose any girl you want, except for the ones who will be branded. By branded I mean they'll be wearing a colored bracelet. They have already been assigned. Under no circumstances, I fucking repeat, NO FUCKING CIRCUMSTANCES, are you to pursue any of these girls. If you do, you won't like the outcome.

"Remember, you can do whatever you want for twenty-four hours, but she has to say yes. If we find out anyone was forced against their will, you will suffer the consequences, and trust me, a fuck ain't worth what will become of you if you force anyone.

"You can keep your identity a secret if you wish." The sound of Saint's voice echoes through the night air. The tone of his voice vibrates through me, and I cannot wait to play. "Don't be a dick and remember if she says no, she means no," Saint growls that last part and everyone nods.

The 'no means no' rule, has been a part of the games for as long as I can remember, and as far as I'm aware, it's only been broken once. Consequences were served by The Lords, and no one has dared to break the rules again.

"Now, go forth and have fun," Thatcher shouts. The air

fills with excitement and the girls around us all squeal in delight as the guys don their neon masks and they begin to light up.

One by one they flick on and like usual, I keep my focus on Saint. Even from this distance, I know which one he is. From the moment I laid eyes on him, he was imprinted on my soul.

Together he and I endured the worst of the worst, and I know without a doubt, I only survived my father because of him. I would have ended my life because living and dealing with the devil himself would have been too much for me to handle, but my Saint, my literal saint, swooped in and saved me. I will never be able to repay him for what he did for me. He made the ultimate sacrifice, and I will forever be grateful. Had he not made that deal with him, I don't think I would be standing here about to graduate and about to move away. Sure, it didn't quite go as Saint had planned, what with my dad still manipulating me, but Saint got me out of that house. I will forever be grateful to him for what he did for me.

Ohh yeah, Saint accepted Agent Cruz's suggestion and he applied to Quantico—yes, suggestion. He didn't just offer Saint a position, this is real life, not the movies. Stuff like that doesn't happen, but with Cox and Cruz's recom-mendation, his application was fast-tracked and approved. We have yet to tell the family but that's Saint's problem, I'm just along for the ride and I cannot wait to see what the future brings for us.

Thatcher shouts, "Let the games begin!"

The girls around us all take off, lambs running to the slaughter. Alani, Quinn, Remy, Lauren, Risa, and I all hang back, as do our guys.

"Run," Grayson growls and before I can ask who he's

referring to, Risa and Lauren both take off across the quad into the darkness. Holding hands and squealing like girls.

"That's an intriguing development," I say as I look to Rem. "Did you know your brother was fucking them?"

"No," she hisses, "but Lauren did tell me she thought Gray was a hottie."

Then we hear from across the way. "Are you fucking my sister?" from Rian and a "What the fuck, Hearst?" from Hudson.

"Ohhh, this is gonna be good," Alani says, rubbing her hands together and settling in for the fireworks.

While they bicker over who's fucking who, I slink away from the group. Walking backward, my eyes are locked on Saint. He hasn't moved a muscle, but I can tell his eyes are on me.

Just before I step out of the light, I lift my hand and beckon him to me with my index finger. He pushes off and begins running toward me, spinning on my heel, I race away from him.

Like always on game night, Saint and I have plans to hide out in our place and with tonight being our last one, it feels poetic to run and have him chase me.

My short legs are no match for his, and before long, he catches me. He slides his hands around my waist and pulls me back into him.

"Got you," he pants into my ear. I shudder as his breath passes over my neck.

"Ohhh no," I play, "what will you ever do to me?"

Spinning me in his arms, he grips my cheeks and leans in. His lips hover over mine and then he whispers, "I'm going to do everything to you, Dove, every-fucking-thing."

Raising my eyes to his, I breathlessly stare at the neon mask of the man who owns me heart and soul. "Then do it," I challenge. "Do everything to me, Saint."

SAINT

"THEN DO IT. *Do everything to me, Saint.*"

Her words are like gasoline on a fire. Bending down, I throw her over my shoulder and for good measure, I slap her on the ass—causing her to squeal—and the sound heads straight to my dick.

Switching my mask off, I make my way inside, then sneak through the hidden door and make my way to 'our' place.

Unfortunately, I have to lower Rowan down because with her over my shoulder, we won't fit through the secret passageways. Once she's on her feet, I slip around her and turn to face her. "Do you trust me?"

"With my life," she replies, and I know she means that.

"Close your eyes," I demand.

Without any hesitation, she closes her eyes and holds out her hand. Lacing our fingers together, I turn back around and guide us farther behind the walls of the school.

Before we reach our spot, I dig into my pocket and press the button on the remote in my hand. Ahead of us lights up and I continue guiding Rowan.

Stepping into the room, I stop and she bumps into my back and stumbles. "Shit, Dove, I'm so sorry."

"It's fine, just warn a girl when she has her eyes closed that you're gonna stop."

"Noted for next time." I step behind her and cover her eyes. "You ready?" I whisper into her ear.

"Yes," she breathlessly pants.

Lifting my hands from her eyes, I wait for her to take in the scene before us. Scattered around the room are several battery-operated lights, bathing the room in a soft yellow glow. The blanket on the mattress has been replaced with a hideous orange duvet and several just as hideous orange and black pillows are scattered around, giving away that Quinn helped set this up.

"Saint," Rowan coos, "this is perfect."

"You're perfect," I tell her, nuzzling her neck.

She spins around and drapes her arms around my neck. "You don't need to sweet-talk me, I'm a sure thing."

"It's not sweet-talking when it's the truth." I stare intently at her, and warmth fills my entire being. "You are the sweetest of them all. Now, lose the clothes and let me feast on your sweetness."

"You have such a way with words, Saint Vanderbelt. But I've been wet since you slapped my ass and since I'm not wearing any panties, my arousal is dripping down my leg right now—"

"Fuck, seriously?" I ask, and she just nods. "Show me?"

She kicks off her ballet flats, reaches behind her neck, and undoes the button on her flowy halter top. The shimmery pale purple material falls down her chest, exposing her naked tits to me.

"Fuck, no bra either." She just shakes her head and lifts the material over her head, dropping it to the floor below. Then she hooks her fingers in the waistband of her jeans and shimmies the denim over her hips and kicks them to the side, leaving her gloriously naked before me.

"You are exquisite and I need a taste," I tell her as I drop to my knees before her. Proving to me that she's *the* woman for me, she lifts her left leg and drapes it over my shoulder. Opening her pussy to me and in the dim light of the room, I can see her lips glistening.

Licking my lips, I lean forward and lick her from taint to clit.

"Saaaaaaaint," she moans, adding seven extra a's to my name as I lick and lap at her pussy. Her sweet juices coat my face and chin and I dine on her cunt.

Her thighs squeeze my head and I know she's close. When I bite down on her clit, she explodes, drenching my face, but I suck up every last drop of her release.

"Saint," she pants. "I need you."

"You have me, Dove. From the first moment I laid eyes on you when we were fifteen, you were mine."

"I agree but not that, I need your dick."

"You can have that too, baby."

Quickly, I strip off my clothes and drop down to the orange-covered mattress. Rowan straddles me and I wrap my arms around her. She grips my cheeks in her palms and kisses me. Swiveling her hips on my rock-hard cock, she lifts up and slides down my shaft.

When she's fully seated, she pulls away from my lips and looks between us, watching my dick slide into her. Dropping my gaze too, we watch as my dick slips in and out of her.

Her hips rock back and forth, and we languidly make love to one another. She lifts her head and when our gazes connect, something between us shifts.

We become one.

"I love you," I murmur.

She swallows and nods. "I love you too, Saint. So, so much. I never want to be without you."

"And you never will."

She rests her forehead against mine, our breaths mingle as we continue to make love. Closing her eyes, her body stiffens and she lets out a guttural moan as she comes. That sexy as hell sound sets me off and I release deep inside of her.

Collapsing back to the mattress, I bring her with me. Her body covers mine and we lie here, breathlessly panting.

We spend the rest of the night, lying naked in each other's arms, plotting out our life in Quantico.

A few hours later, my phone pings with a text. Reaching over to my pants, I dig it out and slide open my messages.

THATCH

Put your dick back in your pants and get
to my room.

Now.

Replying with a thumbs-up, Ro and I dress and make
our way back through the passageway and into Thatch's
room. The rest of the gang are already here. As we drink
coffee and eat muffins from the cafeteria, they regale us
with stories of the night that we missed out on.

Apparently, the party was epic and it ended with
orgasms, lots of orgasms. Sounds like my night too. And
like them, I was with the woman who makes me the
happiest man in the world. I cannot wait to see what the
future holds for us … but first, we need to graduate.

SAINT

FUCKING FINALLY.

We're done.

We're graduates.

A few short hours ago, I walked across that stage and collected my certificate from the interim Dean and then threw my cap into the air and let out a whooping "fuck yeah" with the rest of my classmates.

Our mother insisted on cooking—well, Lisette will be cooking—a spectacular meal to celebrate our graduation today, so we are all at Mom's and this is a dinner I want to be here for.

Mom's been cooing over Ellis since the moment Hendrix and Quinn walked in, but I don't mind. It's great to see her smiling and laughing. I missed hearing her laugh.

We're all here at the dinner table, my family, and I could not be happier. It's been a long road to get to this point. There's been plenty of ups and a fuckton of downs, but we got through it, together.

Pulling Rowan into me, I kiss the side of her head and smile down at my girl while we wait for everyone to shuffle into the dining room.

"Looks like your next, Thatch," Reign jokes as he drops into his seat across from me.

"What?" Thatcher goes ghostly pale at his words. His gaze flicks from Rem's face to her belly and back again.

"Dude, relax, I was just kidding." Reign chuckles and picks up his dinner roll, taking a bite and chewing loudly.

Thatcher visibly relaxes, but when he glances over at Remy and they both share a smile, a secret kind of smile, I have a feeling our brother may have some news to share with us.

"I mean, I don't know, Alani has more of a chance of getting knocked up, especially since she's getting dicked twice." I smirk, throwing a wink Thatcher's way.

"Saint, language," Mom scolds. "There are little ears."

"Mom, E's dad is Hendrix, his first word will definitely be fuck … and Thatch's kid's is gonna be cunt."

Mom just shakes her head and goes back to cooing over her grandson.

"And Reign's kid's will be dick," Thatch adds.

I snort at that, for some reason dick as a first word is funnier than fuck or cunt.

"Wait, what?" Hudson pipes up, his face pales causing us all to burst into laughter.

"Fuck, guys, I mean Ellis needs some cousins. One of you three can surely slip one past the goalie," Hendrix says, earning himself a smack from Quinn at his stellar way of articulating how to get pregnant.

"I mean, yeah, one day." Hudson's face is one of panic and I silently chuckle at his unease.

"Relax, Hudson, I'm not pregnant," Alani reassures him, and he visibly relaxes, "… yet. I'd ideally like to wait till I've finished college and left my mark on the world."

"Sounds like a plan to me," Hudson says. "But in the meantime, we can practice, I'm happy to practice anytime."

"Deal." She places a quick kiss on his lips and from the heated look in their gazes, soon they will be excusing themselves and practicing in Reign's old room.

"Like, fuck, Red," Reign states. "I plan to knock you up as soon as possible. I want our kids to be close in age so they can rule over Crestwood together." Reign kisses the side of her head while Alani shoves him gently away, shaking her head. Seems those three are on different pages when it comes to having kids.

"I most definitely won't say no to more grandbabies," Mom says, smiling down at Ellis.

"To the future and what it holds," Hendrix says, raising his glass in the air. Following his lead, we all raise our glasses in a toast. "No matter what happens, our future is going to be pretty fucking awesome." His words hit home because once again, I'm keeping something from my family.

"We need to tell them," Rowan whispers, laying her

head on my shoulder, but my brother has supersonic hearing.

"Tell us what?" Reign asks, eyeing Rowan and me.

Fuck.

"I, um—" Taking a deep breath, I stand up and look down at Rowan. With a smile on her face, she nods encouraging me to keep going. "I accepted a job offer to work for the FBI. Rowan and I are moving to Virginia at the end of the month."

"What?" Thatcher shouts.

"You're leaving?" Hendrix states.

"The fuck, man?" Reign hisses.

All three of my brothers look at me like I've lost my damn mind, but I've never been more sure of anything in my life. Crestwood will always be my home, but I want to start a new life with Rowan. I want a fresh start in a place that has no memories.

"It's a fresh start for us," I tell them. "No memories. No secrets. We're just two people starting a new chapter of our lives."

Silence befalls the room and my gaze darts around to each of them. I stop when I reach Mom, she has tears falling down her cheeks and I feel like a cunt of a son.

"I'm proud of you, baby," Mom blubbers.

"Mom," I murmur as I stand up and move toward her. Taking Ellis from her arms, I hand him to Quinn and then pull Mom up and wrap her in my arms. Hugging my mother tight, she squeezes me back just as hard, her arms barely fitting around me.

Suddenly arms wrap around me from behind and when I turn my head, I see that my brothers have joined us.

"I'm so proud of you, boys," Mom says. "And Saint, baby, I'm going to miss you and Rowan so much."

"What Mom said," Reign says. "We're going to miss your ugly mug around here."

"We don't want you to go," Hendrix adds, "but we want you to be happy and I know this will make you happy."

"I am happy," I tell him honestly. "And I'm excited for this adventure. It kinda fell into my lap and ever since Cruz offered it to me, I haven't been able to stop thinking about it. This is my chance to right the wrongs in the world. If I can stop one person being trafficked or abused, then it'll be worth it."

Over the top of my brothers' heads, I see Rowan with the girls and I know, with her by my side, I can do this. After meeting her that first day, I never imagined I'd fall so quickly, but from that first glance, she stole my heart.

True love does exist. Even after pain, you can find something beautiful.

ROWAN

EPILOGUE

QUINN and I have just finished setting up for my and Saint's going away party. This time next week, Saint will have started at Quantico, and we will be living in Virginia.

Ellis is down for a nap and we're taking a breather—that's code for having a sneaky margarita before the chaos of the party begins. Estelle will be here to pick Ellis up soon. The lil' dude is having his first sleepover at Grandma's so Quinn and Hendrix get a night off.

"Doesn't sleeping with Saint bring back memories of …

you know who?" Quinn asks me as we sit on the porch swing with our margs in hand.

Shaking my head, I bite my lip. "It's weird, but having sex with Saint is cleansing as such. It's like being with him removes *his* touch. Saint makes me feel whole and special because with *him* it was just sex and an abuse of power, but with Saint, it's more than just sex. What—"

"You and he share as a couple is everything sex is meant to be," she interrupts, finishing my sentence for me.

"Yes, exactly. How did you know?"

"Because I've been in your shoes, remember?" I nod, remembering the moment I found Quinn in her room. As soon as I saw her, I knew. She had that broken look in her eyes, but unlike me, she had someone to break down to. Someone to share her innermost thoughts and feelings with about what happened. "I really wish you'd told me what was going on …"

"I wish I had too, but I didn't want anyone to know. I was ashamed my own dad would do that to me."

"You never have to be ashamed of anything, Rowan Ashford." She scrunches her face up. "We need to change your last name 'cause every time I say it, I think of your dad and I want to vomit."

"What should I change it to?"

"Vanderbelt," a deep voice says from the doorway.

My head snaps in his direction. "What did you say?"

"Change it to Vanderbelt."

"I can't just change it to your last name."

"You can if you marry me."

"Saint, I'm eighteen, I can't get married."

"You're almost nineteen," he says while Quinn adds, "If I can, you can." And for emphasis, she wriggles her ring finger at me.

"I … umm, I can't."

"Why the fuck not?" Saint hisses.

"Because I'm—"

"If you say eighteen, I'm going to shove my dick down your throat."

"That's not a punishment," Quinn says. Then she covers her mouth in shock that she said that out loud. "Ohh, umm, I think I hear Ellis." Before Saint or I can say anything, she hightails it back inside.

"Well, that's something I never needed to know about your brother and my best friend."

"Are you surprised?"

"Well, no. I always knew they were kinky fuckers, but I didn't actually NEED to know. You know?"

"A good throat fucking isn't kinky, Dove." He pauses. "If Hendrix was wearing a red bondage suit and Quinn was naked and tied to the bed, that would make the throat fucking kinky."

"Wow, you've really thought about this, haven't you?"

"No," he quickly replies. "I'm just making conversation."

"About your brother wearing a bondage suit while he fucks a tied-up Quinn?"

"Shut up." He sniggers, and I can't help but laugh.

"FYI, that was mighty specific, Mr. Vanderbelt. I'm beginning to wonder about you and your kinks," I tease, and as soon as I say his last name, his eyes widen and I realize my mistake.

"Now getting back to my question. What do you say about becoming a Vanderbelt?"

Before I can answer, his mom arrives to pick up Ellis, saving me from having to let the man down. Don't get me wrong, I love Saint with all my heart, and one day, yes, I would love to marry him, but I'm only eighteen and I've just finished school. Planning a wedding is not something I want to do right now. Besides, he's about to start at Quantico and me, well, I have no clue what I want to do.

Estelle and Ellis pull out of the driveway, and I swear Quinn is about to run down the street after them, but Hendrix slides his arms around her waist and she turns to a pile of goo, but before they can start making out, the first of our guests arrive.

"Don't think I didn't notice that you didn't answer me earlier," Saint whispers into my ear as I stand in the kitchen mixing myself and Rem and Alani another pitcher of margaritas. Quinn is not drinking hard tonight since she's still breastfeeding, but I make her a virgin one so she doesn't feel left out.

"I knew you wouldn't let it go," I tell him as I replace the lid on the tequila.

"You should know by now that when I want something, I go after it."

"I know, it seems to be a Vanderbelt trait, taking what you want, when you want."

"You love it when I take you." He slides his arm around my waist and nuzzles into my neck.

Leaning back into him, I slide my hands up into his hair and gently tug. "I do love it when you take me." To emphasize this, I swivel my hips and feel his cock harden.

"So why don't you take my name and then I can take care of you forever?"

Spinning in his arms, I take a step back and stare at him. "Saint, I don't need you to take care of me anymore. My monsters have been fought and we won. And if that's why you want me to take your name, you can shove your lack-luster proposal up your ass sideways. I want you to want me to take your name so we can carve out a future together. So we can become one and leave our mark on the world. Now, if you excuse me, I need to get back to my girls."

Picking up the pitcher and Quinn's drink, I head outside to where my girls are waiting for me.

"Uh-oh, who pissed in your Cheerios?" Quinn asks as I hand her her drink ,and then I top off the other girls' glasses before doing the same to mine. Lifting my glass, I chug it back and top my glass up again.

"Okay, babe, spill?" Rem asks but before I can answer, Saint walks out onto the deck and without me even having to say anything, Rem nods. "Okay, so, Saint did something stupid and now you're pissed. Do we need to kick his ass? Or just get drunk?"

"Both … maybe … I don't know."

"Well, tell us what the dickhead," Alani shouts the word 'dickhead' loudly, "did so we can fix it. When you hurt, we all hurt."

"He told me I should change my last name to Vanderbelt, and in a non-romantic way suggested we become one."

"And you don't want to marry him?"

"Well, yes, but not like this. I don't want him to ask me just so my last name is no longer Ashford. I want him to ask me because the thought of not being with me is too unbearable to live with."

"And you don't think that he loves you unconditionally?"

"I know he does … I just—"

"Want to be swept off your feet and feel like without you saying yes he'll die, and his life will never be the same again."

"Yes, is that too much to ask for?"

"Well, I was proposed to while I was naked in the bathtub. Does the how or where really matter? Isn't it how you feel about one another and all that jazz?"

"Well, dammit, Ellis, you're supposed to be on my side."

"Hey, I've always got your back, but right now, Ro, that man looks like his puppy just died."

"Well, I can't say yes now, it's going to look like a pity yes."

"Well, go give him a blow job. Give him something else to focus on and then next Tuesday at 11:54 a.m. you propose to him."

"That's oddly specific, Alani."

"Just telling it as I see it."

Looking over my shoulder, I stare at Saint. I mouth, "I love you" and his lip lifts in that sexy lil' smirk of his. I also realize the girls are wrong. Just because we love each other, doesn't mean we should get married.

"Be right back," I say and then I'm on my feet walking over to Saint.

"Come with me," I growl and before he can say anything, I grab his hand and I'm dragging him inside.

The guys all hoot and holler and Rian sing ongs, "Boom-chicca-wow-wow."

Walking into what was our room, I drop down onto the bed and look up at Saint. He stands in the doorway, his hands shoved into his pockets.

"Please don't be mad at me," I whisper.

"I'm not mad, Dove, I'm just …"

"Just what?"

"Pissed at myself for doing this all wrong. You deserve

the world and me demanding you take my last name isn't that. Can you forgive me?"

Looking over at him, I just sit here and quietly stare at him standing there. Tapping the mattress, he walks into the room and drops down next to me, staring at his feet.

Reaching out, I take his hand and squeeze. "Look at me, Saint." He turns his head and with my other hand, I cup his cheek. "I love you, Saint. I have since I was fifteen. It's going to take more than you demanding we get married so I can take your name to push me away. You and I have been to hell and back. We survived the devil, and we have the rest of our lives to live. I cannot promise the next time you ask I'll say yes because who knows what life will throw at us. Just know, I love you with everything I have. For now, I will just be Rowan. I can be cool like Madonna and Beyoncé, just the one name thing, but until I become Rowan Vanderbelt, love me for me. Please?"

He leans into my hand and presses a kiss to my palm. "You really are an extraordinary woman, just Rowan. I'm never going to give you up and I promise the next time I ask, you won't be able to resist saying yes. You are going to be proposed to like no one ever has been proposed to before."

"I'll hold you to that, Vanderbelt. Now gimme a kiss and then let's get out there and party with our friends."

"I'd much rather just stay in here and party with you naked."

"Of course you would but, Saint, I promise that once we get to Quantico, we can party naked whenever the hell you want."

Saint pulls me into his lap, and I straddle him. "I love you, Dove."

"And I love you, Saint. Now hurry up and kiss me." And kiss me he does.

We don't get naked, but we do have a quick P in the V party that has me smiling like Ronald-freaking-McDonald when we rejoin the party.

This will be one of the last times we're all together like this and I don't want to miss a thing. I will never take life or my friends for granted again.

Sitting here on the deck of Hendrix and Quinn's place, I look around at everyone and I find myself smiling.

My heart is full.

These people are my family, my chosen family, and I know with them on my team and Saint by my side, we can face anything that comes our fucking way. We are The Lords and Ladies of Crestwood, and no one can tear us down.

THE END!!!!

… And in case you're wondering, later that night I caved and I asked Saint to marry me. My name will soon be Rowan Vanderbelt because, right now, Saint and I are in his car on our way to Vegas to get hitched before our move to Virginia.

SPOTIFY PLAYLIST

Sick - Evanescence
When Im Gone - Alesso feat Katy Perry
Mixed Signals - Ruth B
Too Young - Sabrina Carpenter
Purpose - Justin Bieber
One Day - Tate McRae
The Feeling - Travis Atreo
Truthfully - DNCE
Consequences - Camila Cabello
I Fall Apart - Cimorelli
Sorry - Halsey
Closure - Hayley Warner
Barricade - Paxton Ingram
STFU and Hold M e- Liz Huett
I Only Miss You When I Breathe - Christina Grimmie
Shadows - Sabrina Carpenter
Run To You - Camila Cabello
Anchor - Cailee Rae
Survive - Madilyn
I Can't Breathe - Bea Miller
Made In The USA - Demi Lovato
Bruises - Lewis Capaldi
Because Of You - Kelly Clarkson
Hold On - Chord Overstreet
You Are The Reason - Callum Scott
Praying - Kesha
Say Something - A Great Big World
When I Look At You - Miley Cyrus
When Someone Loves You - Tim Be Told

Head Above Water - Avril Lavigne
Love Is War - RUNAROUND

This playlist can be found on Spotify.

ABOUT TARA LEE

Tara Lee is an Australian author who writes spicy romance, and men to swoon over. She comes from Hobart, Tasmania where she lives with her husband and two children.

When she's not a stay at home mum wrangling her two small children or fighting the voices in her head to be quiet she's getting up before the sun rises as a qualified baker.

Tara is a Pisces who survives on energy drinks, chocolate frappes and busting moves at Jazzicise for some me time.

ALSO BY TARA LEE

PLEASANT GROVE SERIES

Taking chances

Second chances

New beginnings

THE BEAUTIFUL SERIES

Beautifully Broken

Beautifully Mine

Beautifully Damaged

STANDALONES

Chance Encounter

HARLING HILL DUET

We All Fall Down

We End With Us

All of these books are available on Amazon.

ABOUT DL GALLIE

DL Gallie is from Queensland, Australia, but she's lived in many different places all over the world, including the UK and Canada. She currently resides in Central Queensland with her husband and two munchkins. She and her husband have been together since she was sixteen, and although they drive each other crazy at times, she couldn't imagine her life without him.

Shortly after her son was born, DL began reading again. With encouragement from her husband, she picked up the pen and started writing, and now the voices in her head won't shut up.

DL enjoys listening to music, drinking white wine in the summer, red wine in the winter, and beer all year round. She's also never been known to turn down a cocktail, especially a margarita.

ALSO BY DL GALLIE

STAND ALONES

Antecedent

Doc Steel

Oops

Off the Books

Fractured:A driven world novel

Deck…the Balls

Secrets and Sunrises

Always in the Cards

Out of Nowhere

The Jerk in 7C

Faking it with the Billionaire

Making it with the Billionaire

Love Me Like You Do

Never Let Me Go

Seven Nights

Seven Kisses

Before the Ashes

After the Ashes

PUCKING NOVELS

I Pucking Hate That I Love You

A Pucking Good Christmas

I Pucking Hate That You Love Me

It's Pucking Fake

…and a few pucking more

FALLING NOVELS

These men make it hard not to fall for them

Falling for Dr. Kelly

Falling for Dr. Knight

Falling for Agent Cox

Falling for Agent Cruz

Falling: The Complete Collection

THE UNEXPECTED SERIES

When it comes to love, expect the unexpected

The Unexpected Gift

The Unexpected Letter

The Unexpected Package

The Unexpected Connection

The Unexpected series: The Complete Collection

THE CASTAWAY GROVE COLLECTION

Love has arrived in the Grove

Oasis

Unequivocal Love

Five Words

Broken Rules

…and a few more to come.

The Castaway Grove Collection, Vol 1

THE LIQUOR CABINET SERIES

Liquor has never been so disturbingly saucy

Malt Me (Book 1)

Tequila Healing (Book 2)

Wine Not (Book 3)

The Final Shot (Book 4)

The Liquor Cabinet: Series boxset

All of these books are available on Amazon.

www.ingramcontent.com/pod-product-compliance
Lightning Source LLC
Chambersburg PA
CBHW030525120726
47904CB00005B/1629